PAINT OUT

PAINT OUT

by

Robert Wallace

LONDON
VICTOR GOLLANCZ LTD
1990

First published in Great Britain 1990
by Victor Gollancz Ltd,
14 Henrietta Street, London WC2E 8QJ

© Robin Wallace-Crabbe 1990

British Library Cataloguing in Publication Data
Wallace, Robert, *1938–*
    Paint out.
    Rn: Robin Wallace-Crabbe   I. Title
    823 [F]

ISBN 0–575–04587–6

Typeset at The Spartan Press Ltd,
Lymington, Hants
Printed in Great Britain by St Edmundsbury Press Ltd
Bury St Edmunds, Suffolk

for Julia Wisdom

'Love of art makes the loss of real love.'
Jean Richepin

(As quoted in a letter written by Vincent
van Gogh to his brother Theo in the
summer of 1887.)

Chapter 1

I was thrown by the force of the explosion. My head hit the pavement. And after that, with consciousness returning, I spent some time crawling about like an abandoned infant, on hands and knees, shocked, moaning.

About me there were the noises of panic, and of rescue; the cries and groans of others equally disoriented. Then I remember thinking, with a sudden curious clarity, of how it had been a good thing that I'd decided, at the very last moment, to leave Desdemona at the apartment. I was in the midst of death and mayhem, while in my imagination peering into the face of the Great Dane, Desdemona! And she beseeching me: 'Come on Essington, take me along, don't leave a dog cooped up inside here.' Me shaking my head at her great sad eyes. Just as I was shaking my head at the begrimed pavement when somebody, a *pompier* — your French fireman and general crisis hero — was grasping me by the shoulders and muttering sweet nothings into my little pink shell: deep, reverberative syllables.

The sound, the thud of the explosion, it was like all sound and no sound. Part of me will forever inhabit its infinite space.

Destruction, horrible beyond description. A boy blasted away. Totally. People all over the place, clasping heads between bloodied hands, wailing, screaming. The window of the restaurant where we had agreed to meet, it was blown to pieces just as the boy had been.

Robert Carbentus, he'd disintegrated. Bits of automobile and of human flesh were everywhere. One God-awful mess. Gore smeared over the stone wall of a building. The cries of horror spiralling into my deafened ears, like electric corkscrews, and above all that, the sirens as emergency vehicles sped towards us.

Me being sat down in a gutter. People reaching inside my jacket to find papers. Who was this? Needing to know, needing

9

to understand that I was the big Australian who'd come up from where he lived out in the Villa du Phare on enchanted Cap Ferrat.

Because I couldn't find voice to explain a thing for myself. There was no way I could tell of how I'd been walking to meet one of the dead.

I only managed sobs.

Maybe sobs for myself, for my own dear skin, that it had survived.

In the ambulance I started worrying about Desdemona. I began to repeat her name, to mutter it low. That was the way I reapproached what faculties I possess, through the name of a big, lovable dog that is so evenly black and white I can never be sure which is background, which the spots.

And then I was pronouncing names out of the past, my personal dead: lost friends. They were flying through my mind — supermen, superwomen, each one passing with a whoosh, like jet planes on reconnaissance flights. But first the 'boom' as they broke the sound barrier.

Were they rushing to meet me? And by cheating death had I let them down again, failed them somehow?

Cheating my father as well. He was there in the space that I'd entered on the far side of the bomb blast.

I guess that the ambulance was pelting through the Paris streets, mounting footpaths, heading the wrong way round corners, with two wheels lifted off the pavement. That was one kind of travel. Trapped in that speeding wailing shell another me was zooming through time down the tunnel, past the lost friends who'd have to wait around a little longer before the reunion. I was reaching out for the man who had died at the moment that his eyes had met mine: reaching for Robert Carbentus.

Robert Carbentus, who was standing outside the restaurant, watching for me, waiting.

And I'd been late, just late enough to stay alive.

In Paris that day I had been killing time, having arrived too early for the meeting we'd arranged. A week before I'd had a call from Amsterdam: Robert Carbentus, more than thirty years on and suddenly feeling it urgent that we should make contact, face to face. It was his call that brought me north out of the sunshine of the Côte d'Azur.

10

Paris had been Robert's suggestion, it was approximately halfway between Amsterdam and Cap Ferrat. In fact he'd insisted on Paris as though fascinated by the symmetry of the arrangement.

Since I'd seen him . . .? I guess it would be 1956 or '57. He'd have known, Robert, he had the tidy mind—I'd thought of it as a Dutch mind. But there were all sorts of other properties tucked away inside the man as well. I had the distinct feeling that to him we of the antipodes were simply another bunch of bumpkins. People who'd devolved.

Being too early for our meeting, and disinclined to wait on the spot, I traipsed off aimlessly around the block. I even found a Marais guide explaining to her group that Mozart had played in the house at which they were all gawking. It was a cashmere-and-Burberry set she had in tow, but French, or at least that was the language in which she was delivering the spiel. They were peering in through a narrow arched entrance at where something had once happened. I joined the group.

There wasn't too much time to dwell on history's magic, the English language version of the same tour was pressing hard on our heels. And so we all bid the Hôtel de Beauvais goodbye — myself, the freeloader, included.

But not before I read an unauthorized inscription on the building's outer wall: 'Women need men like fish need bicycles'.

Sprayed on through a stencil.

Curious the way small things like a piece of graffiti will stick in your mind. I wouldn't have a clue if the sun was shining on that tragic day but I can still describe the face of the small boy riding his bicycle past me and then on around the corner into the rue des Ecouffes. I'd already gone around there once myself while killing time: unwittingly saving my skin, the Essington Holt skin.

I'd been looking forward to seeing Robert Carbentus again. Time makes you like that, makes you curious to see the way it's treated your contemporaries — Robert was older than me, true, but after thirty years we'd become creations of the same era.

We were planning to eat in a restaurant near the rue des Rosiers — solid Jewish territory, wall-to-wall synagogues, three within a football kick of each other. And a great place to wonder at the culinary inventiveness of mankind. It was a part of Paris I liked,

11

the old part; the meeting in that *quartier* had been my fatal suggestion.

Initially I'd lingered outside the restaurant, hoping, but not expecting, that Robert might have come to suffer from the same tendency to arrive early. You never could tell.

I've always been the same, we don't change: too eager for what's around the next turn. Me being the big blundering Essington, looking forward to things as a child does. So unchic. But the same mind, my mind, quick on the aggro. How was it again? The Bard: 'One not easily wrought but perplexed in the extreme . . .' — something like that. Little wonder I called the dog Desdemona. I'd been stuck in an Othello groove since they'd cast me as the Moor for the school play.

None of which counts for anything against the total force of a bomb.

My mind, when I try to put the shattered street together again, it's a college. I get the proclamation about women needing men like fish need bicycles . . . and I see that boy on the bicycle going past me and on around the corner. I remember the Marais guide too. She's very clear, wearing a cotton gaberdine coat with the belt knotted, nonchalant. A silk scarf loosely tied around her neck. A Nefertiti profile and the good judgement to head off in the other direction, towards the Hotel de Ville.

I seem to recall that I took a long look in the window of an artisan's shop which was devoted to marbled paper — in sheets; formed into envelopes; as rolls, I guess for wallpaper; there were elegantly bound address books and diaries as well.

The blast knocks me off my feet.

That moment doesn't exist as the past, it's part of a perpetual present. I don't say to myself: 'The bomb blew up.' But: 'The bomb blows up.' And I carry about with me, inside my head, a number of snapshots, black-and-white prints of the action. No, not action. The shots are of non-action, of people frozen on an instant. The boy is there, leaning on his bicycle, gazing at nothing through large brown eyes. He's standing beside a dustbin which doesn't have a lid, his hands and arms are limply wound around the handlebars.

Another shot shows a man waiting in the street, he's facing away from the restaurant window, hands clasped behind his back, chin high with eyes gazing down along his nose. The mane of blond hair is turning grey-white, the skin of his face is smooth, youthful still. He sees me, past his nose, but has not yet changed expression: Robert has not registered that it is, in fact, me, that Essington has arrived on the scene. He's a tall man with a moustache turned up at the ends like that of some dandy from the *belle époque*. There remains a hint of the old corruption about him. Does this surprise me?

Other shots as well. Details of a car standing across the road. It's missing a wheel. That one is a close-up. There's a view along the rue des Hospitalières-St-Gervais to where it forms a T-junction with the rue des Francs-Bourgeois. The street's empty. A curious thing for that time of day. Empty — but I've never been able to find an explanation for that shot. I also have the image of a waiter peering out through the glass window, staring directly, it would seem, at the back of Robert Carbentus.

Later, much later I'm afraid, I discover another shot, one of a motorbike with pillion passenger. Actually, a series of images like the printed frames of a strip of movie film. The pillion passenger's arm is stretched out, then there is the hand, just at the instant when it lets go of a large package so that it falls into the rubbish bin. I see the driver's head as he comes towards me. He has a thick blond moustache, but one of quite a different character to that adorning the face of my Dutch friend. This is a soft moustache that would grow on the upper lip of a young man, of a man in his early twenties. It grows down past the corners of the mouth. I can make out nothing else of his face because he's wearing a crash helmet with a perspex visor. The pillion passenger, mostly hidden from my mind camera, he seems to have a scarf wound about his head. But, as I said, it was some time before those last few images came up clear. Almost as though I was resisting, as though I didn't want to know who threw the bomb, or what they looked like. I think that sequence emerged only as a response to the reports in the press, particularly in *Le Figaro*, which made a great thing of a bombing timed so close to the first round of the French presidential elections.

An Arab bomb in the Jewish quarter!

Yet another one!

That was the gist of their message. And it added fuel to the fire already lit by those demanding the deportation of a million and a half immigrants from North Africa and beyond.

13

The moustache that I see in my snapshot is too blond by far for any North African to grow. The skin around it had that full blotchy whiteness of the northern French.

Four dead, thirteen injured.

The dead: Robert and the little boy with the bicycle and big brown eyes. The waiter too; it took a day — the wonders of modern medicine, even keeping him going that long! I saw what they had to work with, what was left of him, saw it through the gaping hole that had been the front of a medium-priced restaurant recently opened and written up in the press as quality for money. That was why I'd chosen the place.

You see, I chose it! Robert was dead as a result of my judgement. Because of this mean streak I have.

There's no way you can remake yourself: money doesn't turn a miser generous.

My wife Karen kept on at me about that, my parsimony; she even attempted retraining. Karen railed against my being unable to let go, being incapable of living up to the wealth I'd inherited.

A pregnant woman standing in a doorway across the street, three buildings up, she'd been killed by a piece of metal which flew from somewhere and slotted itself right into her skull. Direct, like an arrow. If the fates have that sort of aim, what chance for us poor mortals?

They said it was the work of a right-wing group. That was without me managing to deliver the information about the motorbike, the blond moustache. Then they got the culprits' identities by tracing a call claiming responsibility. A message purporting to come from an Arab group. It seemed that Mr Le Pen, the white messiah of the far Right, had attracted some pretty inept, if enthusiastic, supporters to his cause. After the bombing they'd driven their bike straight off home, up into the Nineteenth Arrondissement, and made their misleading phone call. Hadn't even faked the accents. The police picked them up mid-morning the following day.

Chapter 2

Way back then, in Australia, Robert Carbentus had said: 'My father was a swine.'

He'd explained: 'That's what colonies do. They change people, Essington, transform them.'

I remember the conversations. For me it was the newness of them. I'd felt it then, all those years ago, as though I was coming awake — simply through having met him.

'The white man's dream.' Robert going on all the time about Indonesia.

I'd never known anything of Indonesia. It was nothing more than part of the 'Yellow Peril' we Australians warned ourselves about endlessly. They all wanted to swarm over our northern boundaries. That was the myth. As though the hordes of Asia suddenly coveted the dust, the rabbits, the plagues of flies.

Robert's father had been sent to Indonesia as a young man. Part of the family business was there, they grew peanuts. Not that he initially went to the colony to farm. He was to serve his country, that was the first responsibility.

I remember the moment quite clearly. Robert standing there, breaking a stick in his long white fingers — it was a habit of his, snapping sticks or shelling off the bark by using the edge of his thumbnail as a tool.

Us, out in the bush, an unlikely couple. The idea of growing peanuts, of the family's wealth accruing from such a source, it had seemed to amuse him.

He was smiling, a bitter edge to it: 'Peanuts . . . oh and other things of course, Essington. There was a farm for instance, with cows.'

Cows in Java! That was news for me too. I could have told you Raleigh's bowls score when the Armada came into sight, or re-enacted the Battle of the Boyne, that was the kind of education

15

I'd suffered. Cows in Java were . . . well, I wouldn't have known what they had in Java.

Pigs probably.

He'd told me: 'If there was a Moslem coming to visit, to eat with the family, the pork must not be in contact with any of the other food. That is very important.'

I think Robert Carbentus was always aware of his role: the instructor, the superior being introducing a simple hick to the mores of a wider world.

Even though he was Dutch, and a foreigner in my homeland.

The car had been enough, imagine turning up in the middle of Australia in a vehicle like that? Driving it right out into what was so close to being desert that it didn't matter. People run stock over that dust bowl but, it has to be faced, it's desert. A couple of dry years and it starts to blow.

'My father was in the Dutch Colonial Army. It was the thing for a young Carbentus of that era. So he was sent to the East Indies in the service of his country. That suited the family, after all they had the business interests out there. I suppose that was why, later, just before the Second World War, he abandoned us . . . because of his Javanese connections. He went out again at that time, thinking he would be safe. But he'd underestimated the Japanese. They would get us out of there.

'For my mother it was a relief . . . well, that is what I believe. For me? I hardly knew him. Not until he was about to desert us in the face of the German threat. He said that no harm would come to a woman and a child. Of course he was right. My mother was to die of natural causes during the occupation, his conscience would be clear.'

Once we were on the top of the southern tip of the Mutwanji Range in far-western New South Wales. The two of us, setting up camp — the horses hobbled, chains clinking with each short step. And he told me: 'It was my father's colonial mind. He applied it to all things. The truth is he was transformed into a monster by it, by the experience. I think that was why he believed he could have as many wives as he wished. Those native ones, with him they didn't count for anything at all.'

Robert's stories were endless. You could sense him watching,

16

alert, as he told them. Gauging the effect. It was as though he was thinking, but wasn't saying: Take this you innocent.

Yet there was no real malice there, that I could detect.

'Before he left Holland, my father told me things about the family, about the business. You see, Essington, he was passing on the mantle. So that one day I could grow up to be like him. I was six I suppose, six or seven at the time, but he was telling me things as though I was an adult. It was thrilling, I can tell you that now. I still remember the excitement. Secrets. He had hidden things away for his return. Hidden them so that they might be safe from discovery when the Nazis came.'

We spent more than two years together, him talking and me listening. I'd just sit, the pupil, while Robert lectured. He was so much older at a stage when it showed. I looked a boy still, he was the man. He wouldn't flush with embarrassment. You sensed that he was already sexually experienced since what interest he displayed in the subject was more ironic than enthusiastic. It bored him, he claimed. Sex bored him to death!

The way he spoke, the way he pronounced the English language, that was engaging in itself. Full, rich, a slight rolling of the 'r' sounds. His accent like that of an American.

'So I have a brother and a sister,' he said. 'Each of us by a different mother. Two of us by *nyais*.'

'*Nyais*?'

'Concubines, Essington. A true Dutch plantation owner had his concubines. But of course. Why do you have colonies?'

It wasn't till later that I looked up 'concubine'. It excited me, the idea. The word was erotic in some way, even though now, on reflection, it sounds more like a salad vegetable than . . .

Who in Australia had concubines?

'So I am the legitimate son.'

'Your brother and sister?'

'My half-sister lives with us in Amsterdam. She came over there directly after the war. That was when the troubles started in Java, the movement for independence. And my father was dead already. There was no protector, not any more. Her mother brought her to Holland so that she could be educated and raised as a Dutch lady. In Indonesia she was an Indo, she was of mixed blood. That means she was in the middle. The natives — now they try to run the country . . . you see the way I speak,

17

Essington? They say "like father like son". It's true. I am the same as my father. I don't want to be. I don't enjoy the idea of becoming like him. In Holland that was what people told me all the time: "Robert, you are so like your father, the same face. Doesn't he look the image of Cornelius?" That was my father, Cornelius Carbentus. Now it is my cousin who carries that name, who is just a small boy. He is the son of my father's brother, my father's younger brother.'

I'd get lost in the details, he went on and on about his family. It was an obsession. It was as though he was trying to talk his way out of it. Yet he never appeared agitated, psychologically or any other way, not Robert. Always the same cool stare out of that definitively blond face. The same slightly uneven smile pulling his mouth up to one side.

We were together day and night for most of that two years, out there working as stockmen for the sisters. It was good, we were the effective management, they hung back inside the homestead worrying about the books. A pair of women dried out by the sun and by life; a widow and a spinster. Brooding over money and over the text of the bible. When, on Sundays, we ate together, the four of us, conversation would hunt around the meaning of biblical passages, on the differences between the accounts given in the four gospels. Robert could do that as well. The Carbentus family, he told me, had, in the nineteenth century, married into a family of ministers of religion.

'A curious combination they were,' he said. 'Preachers and art dealers.'

Robert's family name, it seems, was the same as that of Vincent van Gogh's mother — Carbentus. There had been Carbentuses who enjoyed the title: 'bookbinder to the King'. Anne Carbentus and her sister both married van Goghs. Anne finished up with a minister of religion while the younger sister tied the knot with the successful art dealer, Vincent van Gogh, the artist's uncle.

He told me about the half-brother and the half-sister. He had visited the half-brother in Java on the way out to Australia. All the Carbentus property had been taken over by the new Indonesian government; the farm that he had heard so much about as a child was broken up. They'd been very proud of that farm where everything in the production interconnected, the

18

peanuts yielding not just the nuts themselves but the nutritious leaves and stems for fodder. The cows were milked. That had been for the local market. Then there was another company which had imported agricultural machinery and veterinary products.

'The Boerderij Carbentus, Dutch for Carbentus Agricultural Company. That was quite a concern in its day. Yet when I was in Java nobody remembered. Not even Haryanto . . . How he got that name I would never know. Names were very important in the social structure. If you were a native you had one name only. An Indo, like my half-brother' — Robert always insisted on emphasizing the 'half' — 'would have two names like a true Dutchman. Indos strived to be like us Dutch. For them that was the only way out of their situation. Haryanto, you see, it becomes Yan, so much like Jan. Useful in a European world.'

Robert was particularly obsessed with his father so I heard a lot about the man, not much of it good. It was the feeling the son had of being locked into a kind of life, his father's life, and of not being able to throw off the influence that attached his mind to the subject.

'Essington, it is important to realize exactly what this man was. He could not live a normal life. Never. Not after that first time in Indonesia.'

We were both up on the sisters' place, Yaltaminta, west of the River Darling. The terrain was uninviting despite its moments of pictorial grandeur. The sort of country that looks best in colour photos, taken late in the day, with long shadows and tinted light.

'I remembered how large my father was when I saw Haryanto there with his mother. Both so small. The woman was the size of a child. It is hard to imagine. My father, he drank a lot as well.

'That afternoon, Haryanto stared at me all the time, trying to communicate something with a look. His mother made an effort to make things right between us all. They are very polite people, the Javanese . . . Malays. Malay, that was one of the main languages in our time, when the islands were Dutch. You spoke it between races, between castes. My father, he roared it. Even back in Holland, in our house in Amsterdam, I remember that well. He would go into a drunken fit of temper and scream at us in this foreign language; ranting, as though we were native servants. As though we had no rights at all. None.

'Haryanto's mother was behaving in their traditional fashion. I was a European visitor to her house; it was a great honour for the woman, for me to be there at all. So, we took a meal together. Haryanto, speaking his very good Dutch, made a point of not being polite. Only a boy of twelve, but already advanced in his hates and in his ways. I asked the woman about my father. I wanted to know, to have some detail of how he was, up to his death. It is a natural interest for a son, don't you believe so, Essington?

'She didn't want to tell me very much. "Oh, he was a kind man, he was a good man." She used the same tone, all the time, respectful, as though Indonesia was still a colony. "He was a savage!" That was what Haryanto had to say. "He beat my mother when he was drunk. How often did he beat you?" He asked that of this tiny woman.

'This boy with a strange authority in his voice. A child who believed he was headed somewhere in this world, that he had a destiny. I could sense it. Strange, I could feel the ambition there, and him being my half-brother. My father had left some code even in this Javanese boy. It was an amazing thought for me to have, Essington. For me to look at Haryanto, to know that we were connected by blood. Something of what I am, he is too.

'And today that boy is a part of a different country. There are now few cultural ties, no natural ones, and yet there he is, my brother across the ocean.

'The mother, she shrugged. It appeared she had no desire to talk about what had happened. You see, she didn't want to offend. She was a *nyai* after all, living only to give pleasure to my father.

'Haryanto screamed at her suddenly: "Speak the truth, tell him how his father beat you. Tell him how he treated us both. Tell him also about the way that he begged for you to save him in the end, but never asked to be forgiven. Tell him that." Such anger, so much hate, Essington.'

There was plenty of time for talking out there where the hours stretched with the land to the edge of the world.

Cornelius Carbentus had been an alcoholic. That was the long and the short of it. You tend to refer to it in different ways, depending on how you're set up in life. Robert talked as though it was something strange, terrible and dramatic.

20

Old man Carbentus had been a drunk who got cornered, then caught. Two women, Tina's mother first and then the mother of this bitter twelve-year-old boy, had tried to shield him from the Japanese forces. They hid him, putting themselves at risk in doing so. With the situation reversed that would never have happened: a colonial protecting a native! Unimaginable! Robert saw that as being the unavoidable truth, and it came through as he told the story.

He was open, Robert, the way he talked, that was part of the fascination; he would tell you things straight. Perhaps adding a barb of worldliness as an afterthought: 'Myself, I would never have risked my life for a native.'

They were 'natives', the word cropping up again and again, that was the way he regarded those women, his father's wives. He made no bones about it. You didn't risk your life for one, that wasn't expected, it wasn't in the nature of the relationship to do so.

It had been Haryanto who'd told him, with the mother becoming agitated at this point, butting in, trying to stop the boy. Haryanto had described how a group of Japanese soldiers had come to their village. Of course, he was too young to remember but he had learned the story. Cornelius Carbentus had been in hiding in a small building which was obscured by bushes at the edge of a swamp some distance off from the group of dwellings. He spent his days there and returned to the house only after sunset, when he expected to be fed. He was half mad by that time and there was a problem because he was drinking wood alcohol whenever he could get his hands on it. Haryanto's mother and the baby had been away, visiting relatives in another village. That was what saved them.

The Japanese patrol arrived and went to that hut down by the swamp. Somebody had told them about the Dutchman hiding out there. Cornelius was dragged from his shelter, screaming for mercy. The people of the village gathered around. He pointed at individuals, attempting to have them implicated, to have them killed as well. Or he begged. He wept like a child.

There was a Madurese who lived in the community — Robert explained that these people, from Madura, they were fighters. The Japanese, who were concerned to get the support of the population against the Dutch, asked this man to come forward.

Robert told me: 'Of course, I knew how the story was going to end. I sat there. Haryanto watched me as he told it. His mother fidgeted about with the things, the food dishes she'd arranged for us to eat from. Haryanto dwelt on each detail of the terrible event. How the man had stepped forward, dressed in black — black shirt, black pants, a sharp, thick-bladed knife stuck in his belt. He would kill the Dutchman.

'The Dutchman who was by then grovelling on the ground, incontinent, Essington; yes, he told me of how my father was shitting himself, crying out for mercy.

'His head came off with one blow.'

We've all got our stories. By any standards Robert's wasn't too bad.

At another time, talking of his half-sister, Tina, Robert said that Haryanto hadn't been aware of her existence.

He said: 'I think, once I told him about her, that Haryanto hated the idea of Tina more than he hated me. From that moment on, whenever I mentioned her name he'd go completely out of control.'

Suddenly chilly, distant, cold, Robert said: 'A nasty piece of work.'

He pulled a photograph out of his wallet and showed it to me. 'Tina.'

'That's Tina! She's . . .'

'Beautiful, isn't she, Essington?'

The face of a young girl smiling. She seemed more than beautiful, beyond it. Also she seemed exotic.

Just a photograph.

He said: 'She is the most exquisite girl in the world. She is — how many years? — thirteen years younger than me. I am like the father, she is the daughter.' And there was something quite extraordinary about the way he stared at the photograph.

We worked our butts off out there, the two of us, inseparable, the sun doing what it could to shrivel us up. Then, after two years, suddenly it was over. I'd had enough. And Robert, he said he felt that there was a life to pick up over in Holland.

We cranked the Vauxhall and, still together, headed back in a

22

southerly direction. That was the way Robert put it: 'a southerly direction'.

I let myself get dropped off in Mildura — to mix it with the Italian immigrants picking grapes.

And that was the last I saw of him.

We wrote. One of those things you keep up. Every so often, a letter. Nothing to say. Nothing in common. Maybe a try at wit. Other times using the communication as an excuse to let off steam about something or other. That was the way, over more than thirty years, in which we'd stayed in some sort of contact.

And I never forgot what he said one night. I often told people about it, particularly in my art dealing days, told it to ridicule myself more than anything, because of the low-grade works that passed through my hands. Told it with irony. Said to whoever took the trouble to listen that one night, after we'd been at the sisters' place, Yaltaminta, for more than a year, we were looking at the sky from the ranges to the west. Sleeping out, the horses hobbled. Smoke drifting up against the stars and me going on about how Vincent van Gogh had painted them with auras and great physical movement: swirls like those of the fire rising between our sleeping bags.

And Robert said it was a secret, said that he didn't ever tell a soul. But he owned a van Gogh.

'Stars?' I asked.

I'd believed him. Why shouldn't I? Out there in the semi-desert, why lie? What was in it for him to invent the story? You didn't score with an admission like that. Not out there, and in faraway Australia, for Christ's sake!

'It isn't the stars, Essington,' he replied, 'it is a portrait of the artist himself.'

Chapter 3

The house was on Looiersgracht which runs away from the city centre and out from Prinsengracht, south of the Westerkerk — that's the West Church, Amsterdam's landmark and the burial place of Rembrandt who came an economic cropper there, proud before his fall. Not untypical of artists: they go up and down like yo-yos — living like yesterdays and tomorrows don't set tripwires.

I hadn't rushed north directly after the bomb blast. In fact, for a full week I hadn't done much at all. I just hung around the apartment in the Sixteenth Arrondissement, hugging the dog, avoiding contact with the outside world. Also, the bomb had stuffed up some internal thermostat: I overheated. Mid-spring in those reaches was hardly tropical. Yet I was changing my shirt three times a day. My hair went greasy, my scalp itched. Sweaty palms, I got those too. It was frightening seeing myself get like that, and unable to throw it off. Blow a bomb up in my face and what did you get? A piece of human jelly.

Desdemona seemed to understand. I didn't imagine that anyone else would have. Except, perhaps, Karen. Even though we were going through a low, a lot of which was to do with motherhood and how difficult that was to come by. More people had counted my sperm in the past months than I'd imagined had got into medical school in the first place. With the sperm, I wondered if they did it like sheep in the yards. You know, you open the gate and they're through before you can say 'Jack Robinson'; and then some smart character says out loud: 'Two hundred and thirty-six, how many did you make it?'

Karen wasn't offering me any sympathy because she was somewhere between two points and I couldn't work out which two points they were. She was lost, that was the way I explained it to myself and to Desdemona; lost somewhere in the silk trade. I'd grown to hate silk and everything connected with the stuff. I'd have happily DDT'd the very worms in their cocoons. Initially, when the business first got off the ground, when she'd started the shop in Nice, when we'd gone off looking for places to get designs printed up and they'd let me stay involved, I hadn't minded so much. I even worked up the occasional idea for a print myself. An interesting challenge, not the least of it calculating the repeats, how they joined up. The problem was that what I'd contributed, except the money — for Christ's sake, it was my money they were playing with — hadn't gone all that well. Now I was phased out, redundant! Even the Holt fortune was no longer required. They'd started to rake in what they needed, the business was off and rolling.

'Them' being the key word. 'Them' being Dawn and Karen. Dawn the idealogue, the born-again feminist who might have had a point on some things but who in general had totally buggered up a happy marriage. My perspective.

Of course they said it wasn't like that. They would. It was in their interest to stick together. They said that whatever troubles existed between Karen and me would exist anyway — Dawn or no Dawn. In my softer moments I'd accept that maybe they had a point. The rest of the time I was totally pissed off.

OK, we had problems; me being old and set in my ways not the least of them. Me having got out of line a couple of times, to keep the Holt ego alive, that hadn't helped all that much either. Although infidelity didn't seem to upset Karen and Dawn. They found it funny. I got the impression that it made them pity me.

That's what I felt most of the time as a matter of fact — the two of them being sorry for the old boy, for me being so out of it, part of some lost age.

I was pre-androgyny.

Not 'was', 'am'. It's true.

Standing on the Looiersgracht, knocking on a door.

Behind me a grotty barge, with what looked a lot like mother earth's last hippie doing nothing much for no reason at all on the junk-littered deck. There was sun filtering through a milky sky and trees bursting into leaf. Bits of styrofoam floated on the water's less than immaculate surface. Well, we were in the twentieth century!

Desdemona was cooling her heels at a kennel outside the city.

25

I'd left the car there for company. I had no use for a car in a society given over to water and the bicycle. I couldn't so much as look at the latter without remembering the boy in the Marais. That meant I remembered him everywhere I looked. I was still a wreck.

And starting to believe that the condition was going to be permanent. Sweaty, agoraphobic, subject to splitting headaches. Even my knees were showing signs of giving up the ghost. I walked, they got sore.

Panicky stuff.

The door was so well painted I could see myself in the deep green finish — more like what you'd call a lacquered surface. It is impressive the way they use paint in Amsterdam. Still the house painter as craftsman. It's nice to see these things surviving here and there around our globe.

The door opened. By the time she'd got there I'd worked out the reason for her taking so long. The set-up was the same as in my hotel. Tall, narrow buildings joined by steep, narrow stairs. It took time to get from the top to the bottom of a house. Miss Carbentus, I gathered, had time. So did I, tons of it, waiting wasn't a problem.

'So?' That was what she said when she saw me standing there. She moved straight into English because I'd rung, told her I was coming. Could be she'd rehearsed it, the 'So?'

'Essington Holt,' I said, taking the hand she proffered. Delicate bones, I was cautious not to break such a fragile thing.

'You are a surprise, so . . .'

'What could be surprising about me?' Trying for the light touch. There was a chance that this meeting with the half-sister could get to be emotionally heavy.

It's not every day that a bomb . . .

'Oh, not in yourself.' She had shut the door and we were standing, observing each other. The room was deep. At the front it looked out onto the canal through a large plate-glass window. No curtains in place. It is a Dutch habit to let the outside world look in. Robert had told me about that all those years ago.

'How then?' I asked.

'To be here like this . . . so sudden.'

It had taken some getting used to, this population all speaking near-perfect English. A change after France. Even when I'd dropped off Desdemona, out in the sticks — well, as near to the sticks as Holland could permit itself — very good English. A national achievement.

'You mean that Robert talked about me, about his friend from the other side of the world?' I bit back on that, 'Robert' was clearly a painful word. Agony had travelled across her eyes.

'Distance is nothing in this family. I can assure you of that.'

'Of course,' I said, 'I'd forgotten.'

'You know so much?'

The room reminded me of some of the small seventeenth-century paintings I'd been looking at in the Rijksmuseum that morning. Visiting galleries, that's what you do in a strange city. Particularly if you're on your lonesome.

And given to overheating.

So I'd whiled away time with the pictures of one Pieter de Hooch. He'd painted rooms like that on the Looiersgracht. He liked to put dogs in them — women going about domestic duties, and dogs. Windows opening on to the canal. No curtains, so the passing world could know you weren't up to mischief: witchcraft, or a bit of illicit slap and tickle.

Indicating that I should take my place on a ladder-back chair, Tina pursued the distance theme. We were seated either side of a low oak table.

'I, Mr Holt, was born in Java . . . now Indonesia. For me that part of the world doesn't seem so far away.'

'It takes an age sitting in an aeroplane.'

That was the sort of talk we were into. Pussyfooting around. Neither daring to remention the connection: dead Robert.

'You see, I am only a half-sister.' Like an apology.

'Only?'

'Would you like a drink, some coffee?'

Right from the start I sensed something. Sort of half cottoned on, and then I missed it. Maybe I didn't want to think about much, other than the way she looked. And that was amazing.

Tina was still the girl I'd seen in the photograph, thirty years on, hardly changed. Very elegant, like a butterfly, that was the association I made — score one to Puccini. She was casual, in black slacks hanging loose, and a silk print blouse, white flowers on a black background; that made me think of Karen, of her cursed business.

Then I was on my own. Except when she called down the stairs

27

to tell me that she didn't live there. As though that was something terribly important. She said she had an apartment over near Vondel Park. Now she'd moved in to look after the place, because of . . . Silence, back to the coffee-pot. She let the explanation fade away, avoiding having to say: 'Because of Robert's death.'

So I was surrounded by Robert's taste, was I? Austere, that would have to be the word. Modern in that austerity, yet, at the same time, extremely traditional. The floor surface was of coloured ceramic tiles laid as a geometric pattern and well worn, centuries of wear, perhaps. Back from the window where I sat was the set — the oak table and chairs — grey-black with age. Right across on the far side from the window, at the back of the room, maybe twenty feet away, there was a harpsichord and stool. On the walls, three paintings. Two nondescript seventeenth-century-style landscapes that could have been painted any time in the last three hundred years. The world was stuffed full with that kind of thing. The third painting, totally out of character in the room, was a loud attempt at cubism — colour values all over the place. There were lots that had been done like that everywhere, executed well after the cubist bird had flown. Never as brave as the originals their creators sought to emulate. Not the taste either. In this painting — yes, it had the regulation guitar — the colours were too bright and the abstraction crude. It was like naturalism with angles. The decoration on the tablecloth — it had one of those as well as a guitar — was a key pattern, really celebrating geometry!

I liked the sensation of sitting in that room, in that de Hooch interior. That was more an art feeling than anything I got from the three paintings. To be fully de Hooch there should have been a dog.

As Tina brought in the tray I found myself remembering her half-brother's description of visiting the other one of his father's children. Remembering the description of Haryanto's mother's servility, her excessive politeness serving at table. And of how she had wished for no bad words to be spoken.

Silence while pouring from a polished copper coffee-pot. Her head tilted, shoulder-length black hair hanging vertical away on one side and, on the other, a lock fallen across her subtly sculptured features.

28

She was such a beautiful woman it was embarrassing sitting there. Beauty that was like a force or a charge in the atmosphere of the room. You couldn't avoid it, couldn't go past or through to the consciousness it masked. One of those people in whom the gods have taken things too far.

And she seemed so fragile. It was frightening. Her head under the almost metallic gleam of the hair was like an egg. The skin, oh so smooth. Full and painted lips with tiny half-circular creases at either side. The eyes were large and dark.

The hand that poured the coffee trembled.

'You do not mind if I smoke?'

What could a gentleman say? Even if the smell of cigarettes was something I'd come to dislike. Funny that. It was all right while half the world puffed. As soon as the contra movement started I went off the smell.

She lit up a long, thin cigar.

Wow — that made her exotic indeed.

I breathed in, caught the aroma. Not so bad after all. It mixed with the perfume she wore. 'Perfume', just the word has something . . . mysterious.

'I cannot tell you, Mr Holt . . . what emotions I've been through.' We'd hit the subject.

'I saw it. I was there.'

Then I said: 'Look, wouldn't it be easier if you called me Essington?'

'It is so much longer than Holt.' The wan look of someone who'd caught herself being brave.

'It comes first.'

She smiled, a flutter of the eyelids. 'All right, if you like, I'll try.'

'Tina, I wish you would.'

'I must try in everything. It is that . . . since I learned of Robert's death, I am . . . I don't know how I can tell you.'

'I understand.' Meaninglessly. What did I understand?

As it turned out, nothing.

We sat in silence, sipping the thick, Turkish-style coffee.

Tina drew too often on the panatella while crossing and recrossing her legs. I gazed out the window at the stepped gables across the canal. I liked that about Amsterdam, the seventeenth-century-style architecture, charming.

29

Tina got up, walked to the window, stood with her arms crossed; cigar, half-smoked, gripped loosely between two fingers.

'He will never come again.'

What could I say to that?

So, more silence. This time it was my turn to try. To her back, to the expanse of printed silk, to the black hair that dropped first to one side then to the other as she tilted her head to and fro.

'Robert played the harpsichord?' I asked.

'Robert . . . no.'

'Decoration?' In Australia we'd been known to gut them, turn them into drink cabinets. That was a display of real balls.

'It is my harpsichord.'

'You play it?'

The shoulders shrugged implying: What does it matter? What does anything . . .?

She turned on me abruptly. Intently, she studied my face, as though searching for something, something to fear. The thought shot through my mind: This woman blames me for the death.

Then I thought: So what? People believe what they will.

'You were the reason he went to Paris. You know that? You wrote to him, didn't you? Then he went.'

'Wrong way around.'

'Wrong way around?'

'He wrote to me.'

'I do not believe it.' Why wouldn't she? I made no difference either way.

'You don't have to.'

The cigar had gone out. She pulled a lighter from her pocket, lit the stub, drew in. She tossed her head back, let the smoke drift about inside it for a while, opened her mouth, out it came, curling past scarlet lips.

Now the face was transformed with grief. 'I have been terrible, I know. Please, Essington, do forgive me. It is only that I am so . . .'

'You're upset. That's understandable. You want to go up somebody's nose.'

'What do I want to do?'

'Put the blame somewhere.'

'I expect that is what I want to do.'

30

'And who wouldn't? Except it isn't going to do any good. You'll have to take my word for that.'

She was looking out the window again. Now with smoke swirling about her, being picked up by the gilded light. She looked nice that way.

'You play it?' I asked after another of our silences. There was the ghost of a feeing at the back of my mind that I was being manipulated. Not an altogether unfamiliar sensation either. Yet I couldn't see why or for what, let alone how. Just the feeling. I knew it from long ago. From childhood. My mother operating on my mind in her own sweet fashion.

Not that I was sure. With Tina, as soon as I tried to check it out I got the feeling that I'd been wrong. The truth was she had me confused. The strongest urge I had was to help in some way. That was dangerous. You try and help, as often as not you finish up finding it was yourself you were serving, your own interests.

'Play what?'

The fucking keyboard.

That was the ancient anger of a manipulated child. I left it unsaid.

'The harpsichord.' Mild as anything.

'I did.'

'Till when was that?'

Long silence. She strode half the length of the room, grabbed her hair in two tightly clenched fists, stood like that, head lowered.

'I can go,' I said, standing.

The head came up. 'Please don't. Stay, do stay.' Some wild staring. 'I had expected that we would eat.'

'There's time.' I said. I realized I was reacting to this display of grief, or whatever, in the only way that I knew how. I was locking it out. Defending myself. At the same time I knew that was less than an adequate response. In my own fashion I'd turned out as cold a fish as the Robert Carbentus I'd known out there on the western plains.

Karen had had her emotional downs too. The miscarriage, that was what brought them on. And then the subsequent discovery that we were low on nature's list of the fertile. Well, it wasn't fertility so much. It was something that had gone wrong mechanically, something inside.

And I'd been less than adequate.

31

We'd had our difficulties, yes. And I'd failed at the point where it mattered.

'Better I go. Grief . . . these things . . . Tina, we work them out best on our own.'

'Or we do not.' Frightened now. 'I have been on my own.'

I suggested a compromise. That we walk. Saying I'd like to see around the town.

This didn't seem to be going down too well. Talk about non-communication! 'It'd do you good,' I coaxed.

She gave a shrug. Eventually I learned to read those shrugs as signals for mood changes. Tina could go through a lot in a short time. 'So, we walk.'

I grinned.

'I'll go and get my coat,' she said. 'Amsterdam, at this time of year, in the spring, it can change so quickly.'

So there I was, first day in Holland, trying to bring the Dutch out of themselves. There was some pleasure to be had from stepping along with Tina. Her catching people's attention, turning heads. And I got satisfaction from the way she began to come alive, showing me the city. I'd heard of that: people seeing their own city afresh when displaying it to friends. That way they register the delights around them. If cities can be said to have delights.

Well, Amsterdam certainly does.

We headed in towards the centre, dodging bikes and cars and dog shit. There were so many bikes they put me through a kind of therapy. Not aversion therapy, the reverse; they'd have a name for it somewhere. The Marais kid with the dark eyes went the way of all thought.

I told Tina about him, and about the waiter, as we sat in the sun drinking tea and eating cake. She had another of her panatellas smouldering in an ashtray between our cups.

When she heard about the boy: 'All this time, ever since I have known, I have only thought of Robert. That is not right of me, is it, Essington?'

'We think the things we think.'

'What do you think of?'

'I try not to, and that's the truth.' I looked at her, my head close to her head, close to that unblemished skin which wore for wrinkles only those half-circles waiting for a smile to lift the corners of her mouth. And about the eyes, folds, more like the marks of an Oriental painter's brush, described them as the shape of almonds. I could smell the cigar on her breath. She stayed close, hanging on my banalities.

I said: 'The bomb . . . it's with me, locked up in there. We all keep on living. I don't try to forget it—more to avoid worrying it. I try not to scratch at the scar, get the bloody thing to start itching.'

'And that is what I should do?' she asked. As though it was the million-dollar question.

'If you want my opinion.'

'I do.' Frightening the amount of sincerity in that. I munched on some cake to get away from it. Took a sip at my cup to wash it down.

'Get on with living?' she asked.

'Something like that. The decision's yours. Or maybe it's best to brood, to make a cult out of the dead. When it comes to life I'm only guessing.'

'And on what subjects are you more certain?' There was a full smile this time.'

A long silence.

'Those boats,' I said, pointing to a glass-topped sleek model, half filled with a motley group of people who were snapping shots of the city as they passed. 'They make me feel artificial. To go in one would be like being inside a model of an historical town . . . if you see what I'm trying to say.'

'That's out in Madurodam, the miniature village. It's not here. The boats . . . I do not think about them. Those people they carry, they aren't giants though.'

'Americans, I guess.'

'And Japanese. Australians too.'

'Sure.'

'Why should they worry me? Essington, something about you reminds me so much of Robert.'

'I thought we were trying to change subjects. Thus the walk, the pep talks.'

'No . . . it is not so painful to go over it like this. Robert might say things like you have said. Suddenly he'd come out with an observation that is not expected.'

'Maybe it was being in Australia . . . you get that way out there, see the joke. Well at least you used to.'

33

'Used to? Why . . . has it changed in some way?'

'Not so much changed as got more the same.'

She dragged hard on the cigar, getting it going again full bore. 'Yes,' she pronounced abstractedly, 'I think living out there made him what he was, how he was.'

'How was that exactly?' I asked. There didn't seem much point in trying to steer her off Robert. 'It's a long time since I saw him. You realize that?'

'But you wrote.'

'We wrote.'

'Yes, I know. It was always a pleasure for him when he got a letter from you. I think it made him remember his time when he was a cowboy. It had been an adventure for him. I think he regretted that it could not be an adventure which lasted forever.'

'Who doesn't . . . about a lot of things?'

Suddenly serious again. She stubbed out the cigar, stood up. 'I don't,' she said.

'That's all right . . . The world's made up of different people.'

'I don't want to be different either.' She picked up the bill. 'I'll pay,' she said.

So I let her play the hostess. And play with her moods as well.

Chapter 4

She'd heard my voice as I stood there, at the door, talking. A full booming bark sounded over that chorus of yapping. Like the bass in a dog's opera. In this case the bass was female.

The woman who ran the kennels displayed surprise, but in her book as long as there wasn't a change to the financial arrangements everything would be all right.

'You'll keep it vacant?' I asked. 'In case she has to come back?'

'You have paid for it, the enclosure remains yours for the period. Of course, it will be cleaned.' She was picking hairs off a dark blue smock.

'It's me, you see . . . I'm missing the dog.'

She smiled like a doctor relaxing you after diagnosing a malignant lump.

When I left I had the car as well, my Maserati, long, Italian, athletic. We cruised around a bit with Desdemona's head out the windows, taking it in. Fields of the season's first tulips like some large-scale form of pointillist painting, without the optical mixing. All the coloured dots were of the same value in each block. But what a wonderful thing where they changed from red to yellow or whatever, along a straight line. I would have liked to see the effect from the air.

I think the dog preferred the occasional restored windmill. The great head would pick it up and then follow till the structure disappeared, got sucked into that void behind a speeding car.

Interesting, the tulips — the Dutch painting on the ground. Making pictorial images closely related to those of their great modern artist, Piet Mondrian, with his rectangles of pure colour.

There was another link with more distant ground painting. I had got to discussing it on the phone ten hours earlier, at midnight, when I finally made contact with Karen. We talked for more than an hour. 'The way you Australians spend!' Tina had exclaimed when I worked out the cost. She seemed pleased to take the money, explaining that if it had been her phone it would have been a different matter but, since it was Robert's, it was now the property of the family. She would have to fix it up with the others. That type of thing. A mean streak? It didn't worry me. I got satisfaction from the fact of her apparently improved spirits.

Tina had been horrified at the idea of the dog cooling its heels out in the kennels.

'You cannot do that! This poor creature!'

I explained that there was no way out. You couldn't cart an animal that size into a hotel — they'd notice. And they wouldn't be able to find a place to put it. Or sufficient food.

'Desdemona frightens most people to death.'

'Still, Essington, it is not right. Not if the creature is dear to you.'

Which she is, I have to admit it.

'You must make use of my apartment. While I am here looking after things, it would be absurd for you not to do so.'

I wasn't so hard to convince.

But first I'd made the call to Karen from the house on the Looiersgracht. I promised solemnly not to ring around the world from the apartment. 'Anyhow, it's saving me hotel expenses. You've got to let me contribute to the costs.'

'If you like.' She did one of her shrugs.

Karen had been out in the Australian desert. She had been to Papunya, near Alice Springs, to where the artists work. Mostly people from the Anmatjera and Pintubi tribes. They make big paintings on canvas dealing with Dreamtime stories and containing detail about the landscape. In a way their paintings are maps. The original ones were done directly on a ground of crushed ant bed, using natural materials — ochres, powdered minerals, charcoal, flower seeds, down, blood, even semen (that more for the significance) — big, ephemeral, but beautiful, things; up to a hectare in size. Then certain artists began to work on canvas and they started to sell. They are the great art of contemporary Australia. As well as having meaning they are decorative in a complex kind of fashion. You can respond to them on many levels: read their story (if you find out how), read the details of the tract of country they describe, or just enjoy the interplay of colour in the dense patterns of dots from which they are constructed.

It had been Dawn's idea that Karen commission a few to go on to silk. That was why she'd been out there. Papunya was a long ride — if you made it — from where Robert Carbentus and I had roamed as young men. Of course you wouldn't have made it, not a chance. First you'd have had to cross the Simpson Desert —that's a desert in the middle of a desert; the Simpson's the real thing. Karen went by aeroplane.

So the silk was more on the go than ever and I was put on to a burner even further back, to simmer.

There were limitations in our conversation because, for some unearthly reason, Tina had stayed in the room while we were at it. She'd hung about, stalking up and down, puffing on a cigar, pulling faces at herself. She really was jumpy.

So, with Karen, I couldn't broach those subjects that kept on surfacing in my mind. Things like, why couldn't we stop becoming strangers?

That was what it was all about really, or so it seemed to my dull mind, getting used to each other. There was room for a lot of that even after a couple of years.

Karen wouldn't stop talking about the beauty of the Papunya paintings and the spirituality of the people who made them. As though she was trying to make some point about me, by comparison.

I finished up with a splitting headache and sweat trickling down from my armpits. The hand which cradled the receiver shook.

Tina took to Desdemona: 'But he is beautiful!'

'She.'

'Oh.'

'You're sure beautiful is the word?'

'Oh yes, I am. She is a very beautiful dog.'

'You don't mind my moving her in?'

'I would be glad, Essington. I have told you.'

Tina was wearing a vibrant green headscarf and a light cotton trench coat, washed-out lemon in colour, over basic black.

'Where to?'

'Today . . . the flower markets.'

'You sure we're not overdoing the tourist thing?'

'Not at all. Anyway, what else would you suggest?'

'There's all those van Goghs, we could look at them.'

'But the dog could not, Essington.' She put a slight, perhaps an ironic, edge on the 'Essington'. As though a name like that was the funniest thing in the world. Or in her world.

'You're part van Gogh,' I coaxed.

'Robert told you a lot of things, it seems.'

'We spent so much time together.'

'Our father was exactly the same as Robert. My mother told me that, you know. He was the same face exactly. I didn't really know my father, I was too young. I had Robert instead.'

'As a substitute.'

'As a substitute. Life is so sad.'

'Carbentus . . . he said that was van Gogh's mother's family.'

'It's true.'

'Strange, isn't it?' I observed. 'Families . . . you born in Indonesia and probably related to the great Dutch painter.'

'There were others. You must not forget Rembrandt and Vermeer, just to name two.'

'But in Amsterdam they don't rate museums of their own.'

'They did not produce so many paintings.'

'Always a simple answer,' I said.

'Not always.'

We were heading down Leidsestraat, making for the flower market. The less optimistic predictions about Amsterdam weather were proving to be correct. A fine mist of rain had drifted in. I turned up the collar of my jacket, pushed on. The dog couldn't have given a damn.

The flower market: boxed-in barges that didn't give any indication of being afloat. The blooms . . . well, it wasn't a market in the sense that I'd anticipated. More like a line of flower shops. I'd hoped for a bit of: 'What am I offered for this lovely tulip? Do I hear a hundred?' Something left over from the Dutch bulb market boom that took place hundreds of years ago and which has now become the archetype of speculative insanity.

There were deep purple blooms. Were they what is called black tulips? Tina shrugged as though she hadn't heard the question, as though it had been nothing more than noise, an irritation in her ear. I asked for twelve, belonging as I do to the age of 'the dozen'.

I gave them to Tina. 'In France,' I said for something to say —

Essington trying — 'they give flowers in uneven numbers. They believe it's more elegant that way.'

'With such a number as this it wouldn't matter, surely.' A radiant smile. Thank Christ for that.

I tried a question: 'Have you ever studied art? Music?' We do that, we try. Mothers teach it. It's called being polite. I get the feeling that it's out of fashion now, thank God for that. It's a hard habit to kick, nevertheless.

'Robert told me you are an expert. And a collector.'

'Robert told you what?' I was surprised.

'Before he left for Paris.'

'He was very keen to meet me there. Very insistent. It struck me as strange at the time . . . after thirty years.'

Tina stopped, faced me. 'It was in his character to develop the desire to do a thing on the instant. Then he would have to do it, he couldn't escape that, you see?'

'You haven't answered my question. What have you studied?'

'I have done art history at the university, yes, at Leiden.'

'Then why are we looking at flower markets? Tina, I could be picking your brains in front of masterpieces.'

'That is what I am afraid of.'

'Afraid of!'

We were dropping Desdemona off at Tina's apartment overlooking Vondel Park. The ultra-chic part of town. Hard to imagine why she'd flee it to move into Robert's house. Not that he was living where you shouldn't be caught with your roots down. Not at all.

The Great Dane knew the drill, could sense she was being dumped. The eyes asking: 'Why do you do it to the one that loves you?' I suppose, when you put your mind to it, that's a reasonable question.

Then Tina was tired, she was stretching her arms over her head, one hand gripping the wrist of the other arm. I was suggesting that we wait a while before the art. Would she like a drink?

Yes she would.

Where did she keep the booze?

She kept it in the kitchen, in the cupboard above the work bench.

What would she like?

A tomato juice. I'd find that in the fridge.

I poured myself a whiskey with a lot of ice and a little water. There was just the chance that I'd be needing it. What's the term? Dutch courage.

Before I returned to the spacious, Bauhaus-style living-room — all bent chrome tube and glass, except for the walnut-veneer grand piano — I heard the opening notes of some Debussy piece. An *étude* or a prelude or something. They called it 'The Sunken Cathedral'; maybe it was 'submerged'. Slow, big, searching chords.

Back in the room where she was playing, I recognized it as another interior with which the good de Hooch could have done something. There was the dog he liked to pop into his compositions, the sparse — if modern — furnishings, the Dutch light. Tina, her gaze concentrated on some spot beyond the walls, out there in the middle of the flatness that was Holland. Desdemona crouched at her side, a miniature Sphinx but with the head of a dog: a carving out of the Egyptian desert. The great body lowered to the floor between front and back legs. She might have looked prepared to pounce, about to kill the pianist. But I knew that was one of her relax postures as well as the coiled spring for attack. You could read the difference once you understood the dog. It was limited, the range of positions available to such a bundle of huge bones. Life isn't easy if you are a dog designed for giant leaps. Not if you have to spend sedentary days, day after day after day. The head was pointed at Tina — rapt expression. The flop ears twitched.

The tomato juice was slid on to a glass table-top. I plonked myself into a simplicity-itself chair, sipped the whiskey, and listened. Outside there was blue sky breaking through. Even a shaft of sun.

It was a kind of contentment that the wandering Essington didn't often experience away from home. My metabolic tempo slowed down. I looked around me, at the walls, at the floor — one Persian rug — I gazed at the pianist. Body heat eased back a little.

That beautiful woman, still in the lightweight trench coat. Her torso immobile; the arms, mostly the hands, and the feet working pedals, were the only movement in the room.

I wondered: Is she mad or just terribly clever? Or a mixture of both?

I thought: No questions, Essington. Relax, for Christ's sake, just relax.

You could have thrown a cat from Tina's apartment to the van Gogh museum. If you had done that Desdemona could have beaten you there and caught it, except Desdemona had stayed home and we, the human beings, were going to get an eyeful of some art. Anxiety-ridden art in this case.

There's a problem when an artist suddenly takes off with the capitalists. People stop observing the work and start to see the dollar signs in its place. Next thing, you get reassuring utterances about art as national collateral — something to set off against a deficit.

Apart from anything else that sort of talk is vulgar.

Deficit! Eighties talk.

I've got a vulgar streak. It permitted me to recognize that with a *Sunflowers* going for around fifty million US dollars, a while back, the Dutch could sleep secure behind their curtainless windows. They had the money as paint on canvas, put there by Vincent.

We were surrounded by them, a real slab of his output. And there are other museums as well in Holland, stacked with his paintings.

He was prolific enough. Prolific and ignored. Will they ever learn, the fat cats?

'He would repeat the one painting several times, Essington. You see, he was searching after style.'

We had started at the end, the pictures were arranged chronologically. We were standing in front of one, *Wheat Field with Crows*, painted in Auvers, up near Paris, in July 1890.

'You see, here . . . you see the brush strokes? I should say that this is the one done directly from nature. It was his habit then to make copies of the paintings again in his studio, working on the colours and the rhythms of the brushwork. In that way perhaps he might produce three or four versions of the one composition.'

You could see it, in that one, the urgency, the directness of the marks he'd made. Less a pretty surface than some of the others.

'This would be late?' I asked.

41

'Very, it is likely that he didn't have the time to make more copies, that is true. He killed himself in a wheat field in that same month. It is quite possible that he killed himself in this one that he has painted here.'

She seemed to like the idea of the wheat field, of him standing in it, firing a bullet into his chest.

When Tina talked about paintings the slight stiffness of her English made her sound like a fanatic of some kind, like a person obsessed with detail.

She said: 'There was a girl, her name was Adeline Ravoux; van Gogh made a portrait of her, an innkeeper's daughter. He was staying there, at their establishment. She watched him shoot himself.' Tina's eyes narrowed, as though she was the girl and out in front somewhere the demented artist was pulling the trigger. 'He had painted her only some weeks before, and then she watched as he put the gun to his chest. Yet, by most accounts, it seems she did not tell anything of what she had seen.

'A curious thing. This young girl who kept a secret to herself.'

'Isn't that supposed to be the way they go on, kids?'

'Van Gogh managed to return to his room, he took to his bed. It was only later that he told the girl's mother and father what he had done.'

Then she said: 'We shall start at the start, if that is what you want.'

'It's your territory, Tina.'

'There is more sense to it that way.'

In the early van Gogh paintings, even though the brush already formed the sharp strong strokes developed to the full in the later works, there is no colour. He was working with the palette of Rembrandt: browns and greys and whites. And making use of tonal contrasts. This had an effect on his subjects as well. They were mainly peasants out of the Brabant area in southern Holland. Vincent was interested in showing how they lived, in establishing, through his art, some kind of a connection with these people. They sit around eating their potatoes, painted in dark on dark on dark.

The subjects indicate Vincent wearing his heart on his sleeve, working up a compassion for the poor who, so the story goes, inherit the earth. He was, after all, the preacher's son.

There is one of the brown pictures showing the top section of a skeleton, like they use in art schools — I know, I've been there, trying to learn; that was in my post-rural phase. Van Gogh has put a cigarette in the skull's mouth. The painting has a dashed-off appearance, even though it is a difficult subject — and fiddly too.

There are inconsistencies in the brown paintings, you could see that his style wasn't set. And changes of mind, as well — ridges showing up through the brown-black background of the skull painting, betraying where he'd painted out a form or worked over an earlier version.

The skull with the cigarette between its teeth seemed to be saying something about an aspect of van Gogh's character, something that was more difficult to pick in the rest of his work. It struck me as being a childish touch; with a wrongness to it, as well. But not the expected wrong-footedness of the tormented artist, of the genius spurned. Something altogether different came through in that painting. Something more gauche.

Mind you, there might not be a lot to be gained from reading too much into a painting that is a kind of art-school prank. Not unless you look at the date: painted in Antwerp, 1885. Vincent was thirty-two. It was the year his father died. Tina pointed out the chronology to me. The father died in March. Vincent went to Antwerp in November. There was no particular reason to connect the skull, the image of death, with the loss of his father. Yet he'd painted the cigarette in the skull's mouth! As a schoolboy might. In the year that he'd become head of the family.

I got that feeling later from reading the van Gogh letters — the ones he wrote to his supportive and ever patient brother, Theo. I sensed a quality about the man, a self-obsession: somebody who couldn't see outside his own mindscape. It was in the self-portraits as well. Something dangerous. They showed a man determined to take anyone who dared to love him with him when he went. I'd picked up some of this before I read the letters. I tried to explain it to Tina.

She said he was a genius. The standard line. As though that was an answer. I mean . . . I hadn't said he wasn't!

43

Continuing around the gallery we found that our ideas conflicted on more or less everything. I felt that perhaps we should start again: me put another foot forward, stop getting on her nerves. Maybe I was picking it up from Vincent? We got into arguing nastily about the pictures. Attracting attention to ourselves. I couldn't stop offering downer comments in response to Tina's unguarded admiration for the paintings.

Things got really rugged when we came to a wall of the small paintings that Vincent had done in Paris. They were of plaster casts. I'd never seen anything like them from him, not in reproduction either. There'd been similar work produced in the art school I'd tried for a term. In each one the plaster cast was grey to white, without any reflected colour, and set against a mid-blue background. Banal. To my eye, totally without quality.

We left the museum, tight-lipped. And stayed like that all the way back to Tina's apartment. Not a word spoken.

Intensity.

I got insensitive. I asked myself: Why not come right out with it? Ask the questions, find out what you want to know?

We were standing outside the apartment building, on the street.

I brought up the subject of Robert's van Gogh.

'Robert's what?'

'He told me he'd inherited a painting by van Gogh . . . when we were working cattle together.'

She studied me. It was as though she was playing for time while inventing what to say next.

'There wasn't any reason for him to make it up,' I said. 'He wasn't using the information to score points.'

'Why would he need to do that?'

'I'm not saying he would, I'm saying there wasn't any need.'

'Well,' she said firmly, 'it is not true. He has told you a lie. There is no such picture.'

Later I repeated that to myself, the way she'd said it: 'There is no such picture.' Emphatic. You might have thought the proof of the van Gogh's existence was there, in her tone.

'Shall we go up?' I asked.

She shrugged. We entered the building. When we got to the

44

second floor, to the level of the apartment, we found the door open.

And no dog to greet us.

I felt like a tyre that has blown out.

Chapter 5

I could see the two of us in pictorial terms, as though we were painted images trapped within a frame. I remember being rather impressed with the thought. We could have been a painting by Balthus — something like his *Wuthering Heights*-inspired *Cathy's Toilette*. Except Tina was wearing clothes. It was the drama of the painting that we replicated. Me, bunched with anger, playing Heathcliff, whom Balthus has grasping one of the pieces of timber forming the back rest of his chair, screwing it between both hands.

I was trying to crush the telephone handpiece.

Tina had been cooperative. But only after making a visit to the bathroom. I'd already noticed the pill bottles in there. Being a visitor, a guest, I hadn't paid them much attention. Yet there was no way of avoiding the fact that there were a lot of them, each one containing its magic tablets or capsules, all calculated to put you up a fraction, or take you down; to bring sleep, to wipe it away again.

When she came out of the bathroom she was as cool as a cucumber. She calmly found the phone numbers I was hunting, but couldn't locate in the Dutch language. Calmly, while I was only just nursing irrational anger, and a pulse set up a rhythm of its own somewhere behind my forehead.

There was that terrible feeling: Why hadn't I let well alone? The dog had been fine out at the kennels, not so happy, but not missing either. It was me who'd taken it into my head to interfere with that. Me and my sentimental yearning for company.

Next I was turning my anger on Karen, the wife who wouldn't slip into the role. Then it was Dawn's turn, her stirring all the time, keeping things uneasy between us.

I cursed babies, cursed the silk trade, cursed my dead mother . . . the whole fucking mob got a blast. There would have been a lot of turning in graves, people twitching; and where

46

my mind stuck in the needles, little unexpected spasms of pain. Serve the bastards right — less than they deserved.

Now I was on the phone, working my way through the departments, explaining my problems to people who couldn't give a damn, people who were more interested in the way the door got busted open than in my missing dog.

You can always close a door again.

Anyhow, from the tone I got, it was plain a jemmied door wasn't big news in Amsterdam. You say 'Amsterdam', people don't say 'Rembrandt', they say 'smack' first and then 'bicycles'; there's a certain lawlessness, by Dutch standards at least.

The admission that nothing was stolen, just a missing dog, that put the cap on it. They were busy people down the other end of the line, they had things to do . . . real things.

'My dog!'

'A giant, a Great Dane, black and white. Mr Holt, I do not believe you will have so much trouble finding that in our city.'

I didn't say I hoped she ate the lot of them. Instead I prayed for the Desdemona temper to stay under control. And she had it in her, the aggression, if pushed or pulled by unfamiliar hands. Then that would be that. They haven't done away with capital punishment for dogs.

Me on the telephone, that was the scene. Bashing out the numbers, trying everything I could. Over there, away from the window, the grand piano — waxed, mute. The chrome furniture, glass table, Persian rug in the middle of which Tina now performed a slow, agonized — or was it ecstatic? — dance.

She had stretched her arms into the air, the fingers were intertwined, clenched tight, wrists turned out. Her eyes were hidden behind dropped lids. She was turning slowly to some secret rhythm.

I saw them, but they didn't register at first. Not with me trying to get my anxiety for Desdemona through to that stream of faceless officials down the telephone wires. I must have been staring at Tina but not seeing.

She'd slipped into a kimono decorated with large gold-embroidered birds — piercing eyes, ravenous beaks. The cloth flowed as she turned. Underneath she still wore the black slacks that appeared to be her trademark, together with a black polo neck. Her hair flared out with the movement. Beautiful, yet

47

there was no getting away from the idea that something was very wrong with the dance, as well as with the dancer.

And with me too. I'd lost my dog.

Funny, the fact that the flat had been broken into didn't seem to intrude on Tina's mind.

She was half concerned about Desdemona, maybe. The most important thing seemed to be the performance itself: the dance! She was concentrating on it, developing new steps as she went.

Raised arms and hands with fingers intertwined flashed past as she turned, and I saw them then, those telltale white scars across that tender skin of the inner wrist. Scars of slash marks where the skin had been stitched and healed.

At attempt at suicide!

I have to admit that up till then there had been this hormonally driven interest of mine in Tina. Growing. It happens. But the wrist scars, coupled with the pills, were too much for old Essington — memories of domestic madness from life with my mother. I put the phone down. I forgot the dog for an instant, just for an instant. 'Tina,' I asked, 'have you ever been married?'

She stopped that spinning around the room. It was making me dizzy, not her. I can't say exactly what brought the question to my mind. It came out of nowhere — product of the wrist scars perhaps.

Tina watched me, cold-eyed now. What business was that of mine? Go find your fucking dog. Piss off stranger.

'Robert was never married.' That was her reply.

'I know.'

I'd already written that little fact down to excessive early adventure, fear of the ties. There are men like that who enjoy the illusion of freedom, they like simply being able to get up and go — hunt lions, climb Kilimanjaro.

That self-absorption was madness of a kind, too. But different from Tina's. Or was I wrong? She so beautiful, so perfect, seemingly untouched by forty-five years on this earth; untouched, that was, except by her own hand. Was she not perhaps equally selfish, and thus remote from the rest of us?

I needed to go out of there, to get away: action. That is a kind of cure in itself, for everything, or it can be.

'I'm off, looking for the dog.'

'If they ring back, if they discover it?'

'You can take it, can't you?' I snapped that out. Then I slowed myself down, moderating the tone: 'Tina, I've got to do something. It's in my nature.'

'That is plain to see. Let me come and help you find your Desdemona.' Suddenly she was laughing, it was all some big joke for her. 'We must find the dog,' she pronounced, tucking her chin into her neck, wrinkling her brow, being the comic.

'Yes,' I said, 'but it isn't that funny, Tina.'

'I know, I am sorry. It is just that two people are off hunting a dog. It struck me as . . . no. Essington, I am sorry. Such a lovely dog.'

'I'm jumpy,' I said.

'Tell me,' I asked as we came to street level, 'the break-in . . . nobody seems to care. You don't even comment on it. Is life that rugged in Amsterdam?'

'Last week, it was Robert's house that they searched.'

'Searched? They?' But I didn't pursue the matter because suddenly I saw her. Right over the other side of the park, Desdemona. Loping about, being her own good self.

I ran, shouting.

People turned, watched. I don't know, I'll never get over it, those continentals make me feel so rough around the edges. Not that the people of Amsterdam aren't relaxed. Not that they don't affect a casual style of dress. But there I was, big, loud, sweating, belting across Vondel Park, skirting around the artificial lakes. Every inch the caveman out of the mists of time.

Still I got her, the dog, and was she pleased to see me? Well, yes and no.

You think: My dog. You say: 'My dog'. But a dog is its own creature. The rest is a charade.

A genteel old woman had attached herself to Desdemona without actually taking hold. We had a man-finds-his-errant-dog conversation while I was examined for signs of honesty. Then off I trotted to where Tina, still in kimono, stood by the edge of the lake.

It's terribly frustrating that dogs can't talk. But then, if they could, they wouldn't make such good friends. For surely the basis of the man–dog relationship is man's capacity to get off on some flattering deception.

Maybe all friendship stems from that, not just when it extends beyond your own species.

Friendship. Tina had looked so lonely standing there, waiting for me to reach her. It occurred to me that she had all this time to spend with a total stranger. What then did that say about her life in Amsterdam? Chic apartment, walnut-veneer piano, knowing so much about van Gogh; yet you're not truly nourished by that sort of stuff. It isn't a substitute for friendship — illusion or not.

Back in the era after I'd been working as a stockman, having little or no means of support, I had tried my hand at various casual jobs: there were always the dishes to wash at eating houses.

Money left over from paying for my bed and food provided the stake for art dealing: that meant me buying up the pictures at auctions that nobody else wanted.

From time to time I augmented my stock with work by my own hand, with what I called 'Holt Internationals'. I did quite a good John Singer Sargent — a few pencil lines and there you had it, the Venice skyline. They usually picked up a sucker eager to take a punt. Somebody who thought he was smarter than the rest of the world put together, finding a masterpiece.

I was rather proud of my Sargents.

'That,' a friend of the period had pronounced, 'is the real art, Essington, the counterfeit. It takes the mickey out of the whole bloody job. You, you've got hidden talents.

'Forgery' — he'd gone on to expound an improvised theory — 'that's more like philosophy than art. It asks questions. You know, Kierkegaard, in Copenhagen, he counterfeited an entire life. He was free.'

That was how we all would have liked to feel, unfettered. Maybe that was why we tried all those philosophies: Zen, existentialism. Existentialism, for Christ's sake!

Later I got more confident with the counterfeit. I tried a few little throwaway Picassos, even a Matisse or two. Once I managed a Miro gouache that kept me alive and in style for a full twelve months.

You had to be careful. You could spend a few years getting gang-banged in the slammer for playing around with people's sense of judgement. They don't like it one bit.

Forgery, I'd enjoyed the game. Looked at my way it was a

continuation of the great tradition. In China it used to be the case that you weren't a master until you had complete control over the style of a previous master. You see — it depends on how you look at things. To be original, what does it amount to after all? Mostly it means nothing. Like, what could have been more original than Tina, her standing there in the park? An image so new to me that I could hardly believe it, even if she was so tenuously connected to this life.

Yet that was an image she'd grown sick of, to such an extent that she'd tried to destroy it by slashing her wrists.

No, as Desdemona and I approached Tina I was very conscious of walking up to someone who, by her own act, had tried to leave us all behind.

We ate together. This time Desdemona was waiting for us in the house on the canal. She must have been a nasty shock for whoever sprung the Vondel Park apartment door. She'd do that, in particular situations, just sit and watch for the action. Go into her body between the legs squat, and wait. Not even a growl, unless you put an ear right up against her chest. Then you'd hear something, sort of subterranean. She'd lower herself into that position, moving the front paws out a bit at a time, slowly, like an elephant.

When that door was sprung open there would have been an explosion of dog. I guess we had been lucky not to find the break-in merchant in a pile at the foot of the stairs. The odds were that wherever he was hiding out, at the very least he'd have tooth marks and ripped cloth for his pains. I suggested that Tina keep such details in mind, that maybe if she told the police, got them to check around the doctors, the hospitals, maybe they could come up with a case, something mauled by a dog.

Tina wasn't interested.

Why wasn't she interested?

Because it was too much, all too complicated. She couldn't manage any more of life at that moment. With Robert dead her perspective had altered. What use was it to worry about a door? What was a door? What would it matter to the dead?

When you were dead for such a long time.

Good point.

51

We were eating Indonesian. It is a specialty of Amsterdam. The most special is a *rijsttafel*. That was what Tina had ordered. To keep things international I was starting on a bottle of Sancerre. I figured I'd need it. From what she said there was some hot spiced food to be expected among the twenty-four dishes.

Tina drank mineral water.

Again the thin cigar. Tina wouldn't have been Tina without one.

And Amsterdam wouldn't have been Amsterdam without her. Unstable. OK. Still she was getting to be like a friend.

We watched each other, eyes picking up and missing messages.

Rain pelted down outside. It was Friday, the community was making preparations for Queen Beatrix's birthday. All Saturday there would be a street party, people selling things from improvised stalls like a giant garage sale. I'd been warned: the whole inner city would be packed, the celebrations continuing right through the night. Vondel Park may not be so bad, perhaps. In the centre, around where we were eating, bands would play, there'd be dancing till sunrise.

If the rain let up.

'Do you have a large family?'

I did not.

'So . . . what size of family? How many Holts are there?'

'Effectively, Tina, I'm it.' Obviously there were cousins, no way of avoiding that. A couple had even looked me up. Looked up my money would be more to the point. People are very simple creatures at heart.

Tina shook her head: 'That is not possible.'

'How many did it take to make me? One man, one woman, that's all.'

'But a family . . . it is what shows you where you are in the world. Where you are in time. It is your . . .' She ran out of English.

'Well,' I said, forming a little box about myself with my hands, defining its edges, 'this is where I am in the world.'

'There is your wife, as well. Her name?'

'Karen.'

'There is Karen.'

'At this moment the best we could say is half and half.' I described another box over to the side of the one I was in. 'She's here, her choice.'

The waiter brought a tray heated by candles; he moved the flowers to one end to make room on the table. Then the food began to arrive. Little dishes filled with goodies: chicken, fruits, egg rolls, kebabs, peanuts, meatballs, prawns; each drenched in some delicately spiced sauce. And there was steamed rice. That was to form the bed from which the meal would be eaten.

'With me it is the other way,' Tina said, helping herself to some rice. 'I have too much family.'

'The Carbentus clan went forth and multiplied?'

'It is a large family. It is like a world inside there. To be inside you do not need any other world.'

'And you're inside, attempting to see out.'

'You try to make a joke of everything . . . don't.'

'To keep from crying.'

'You still do it. What do you mean, "to keep from crying"?'

'I mean that there's only so much you can feel good about. The way you're building up this vast family you don't sound as though you're about to launch into a hymn of praise for its Christmas celebrations: warmth, laughter, party hats. You weren't making the large family appear to be a lot of fun. I was anticipating, that's all.

'Tina, I've been around. I've heard a lot of people sing the praises of the extended family, I even used to go out with a girl who was doing a life major in it; she had all the sociological and the anthropological and every other 'ogical language to talk about these things, yet the fact is she had it as some idea. The rest of the time she fought with her sister about who'd got what of her mother's silver. A lot of these things we say because the previous generation said them. The fact is nobody cares less about the family any more. Mortgage payments are enough. Who needs uncles if you've got debts?'

'You are cynical.'

'I should be. The problem with my wife is about families. She feels you have to have one, she wants to make one, be at the centre of one. You know, grandchildren crawling around her ankles.'

'So!' Raised eyebrows. She guessed what was coming. She gave voice to the guess.

53

'No, wrong. It's not me. It's not that I can't make babies. And that's not important either. It's that *we* can't make babies.'

'And!' Scooping out more rice. Topping it with some crisp-fried coconut and a meatball. She was moving to the front in the eating stakes. I'd been doing too much talking.

I went for the wine to cool down after biting on a chili, if that's what it was.

Tina laughed at tears in my eyes. 'That is *sambal badjak*.'

'I never was good with hot foods.'

'Families?' She prompted.

'I don't see why we can't accept it, Karen and I. OK, it's unfortunate, but we can still enjoy each other.'

'That is not the way your wife would like to live?'

I scooped up a curried egg, together with some God-knows-what. That went down in one bite. 'We're not talking about my family or my lack of one. You brought the subject up, Tina . . . your mob's the subject. Why?'

'Now I think it would have been better to say nothing.'

'You can't do that!'

'I can.'

'It's against the rules.'

'That is my point. There are rules. Ways of doing things. With the Carbentuses, they have their traditions. Until Robert has died he was the one to interpret these things. He was . . .'

'Head of the family.'

'That is what he was. We all looked to his word. Robert was a clever man. Where there were family interests, family business, he made the decisions. What he decided was good. It was the best decision.'

'Always?'

'Always.'

'That's not possible, not in business, Tina. You win some, you lose some.'

'Robert won all. Of course each of us has our private business. I speak now only of the Carbentus business. Of what was held in common.'

'Yours was?'

'My private business? It is my study, my . . .' She shrugged off the rest of the explanation.

There was a heap of food still on the table. A labour of

54

Hercules to get through it all. 'What,' I asked, 'is the Carbentus business?'

'How should I know? Property, investments in industries, I suppose. It is not my concern.'

'Until the profits stop flowing through.'

'I don't understand what you are trying to say. The profits did not stop "flowing through".'

I shook my head. 'It's not my affair.'

Tina smiled. 'I do not know how we came to talk of these things. As far as the family is concerned I am an outsider anyway. With Robert it was different. For the rest, I am . . . I am the result of a Dutch adventure.'

'Change subject.'

'Change the subject to what?'

'To anything you like,' I said, smiling, trying to break up the gloom that had descended over the little dishes, over the rice, the flowers, the half-empty bottle of wine. 'How about van Gogh?' I suggested.

'I have told you about him at the gallery.'

'What I can't work out is why Robert wouldn't finish up with a van Gogh? Why he didn't have a whole cellar full of them for that matter? Vincent sent pictures home, you told me that yourself. Sent them to his mother after his father died. They must have had quite a collection. Theo's widow, she would have been faced with storage problems.'

Tina puffed out her lips, French style.

'Tina, when Robert told me of his van Gogh he wasn't boasting. That wasn't the way things were. My feeling, looking back, is that he regretted it, regretted saying anything. You may not believe this but it popped out because we were looking at the stars. How's that for romantic? Right out in the wilds, nothing anywhere for miles, just the night sky. Then, out of the blue, literally out of the blue, Robert announces that he has a van Gogh. I believed him.'

Tina smiled now. 'If he had one, I have not seen it.'

'Could be part of your family business, part of the investments, the properties.'

'But we were very close. He would never have not told me about the picture. He knew I was interested in these things. Why should he not tell me?'

The waiter came. I indicated that we were finished, even with enough food still on the plates to feed an alley full of cats.

We walked back to the house on the canal, slowly, umbrellas up.

Tina was making coffee. I sat in one of the ladder-backed chairs, gazing about me, waiting for the brew to hit the table. What light there was came from two standard lamps, modern in style, one of which sidelit the over-coloured cubist picture.

Something caught my eye. I went over, took a closer look.

The flatness of the paint areas — it was particularly evident with the guitar shape — was disturbed by brush marks underneath. Like with the early van Gogh in the museum, this was a painting done over some previous work. What was underneath was of a different subject; those brush marks which I could detect weren't related to the final shapes, not at all, but nor were they very pronounced. If the composition had been painted over, say, a van Gogh, you might have been able to pick that painter's handwriting up with a frontal light, or in daylight for that matter. The paint of the cubist picture was as flat as the surface of the wall, it wasn't disguising much that had gone on one layer further down.

Yet it interested me.

After a while the making of pictures, and their history, can take over, deflect you from the image itself. But then it's also true that an interest in the technique and history of some work can lead you to reinterpret the image and reveal another level of meaning.

'She is pleased that we are back,' said Tina, holding the tray.

But I would have thought, from the way Desdemona was sitting, from the half-closed eyes, that she was lost in a dog dream and altogether very far away.

Chapter 6

Tina would have been lying in her bed — well, Robert's bed, I guess — breathing evenly, sleeping like a child, as rain poured down outside and the population wondered what was going to happen to the Queen's birthday celebration.

Over on Vondel Park the old Essington wasn't sleeping. Not a bit of it. I was tossing from side to side and alternating playing sleep-inducing games with attempts at catching the subjects scurrying across my mind's surface. Unusual for me. I'm normally straight out to it, the sleep of the innocent — deserved or otherwise. In Amsterdam I was convinced it was deserved. What a boy I'd been! Lust under control, only two-thirds of a bottle of wine down the hatch, dog safe and sleeping by my side. Even God would have been pleased.

No fear of the door being smashed down again. That had been fixed and an additional lock put on — some kind of ultimate design. I was safe and snug and warm. Maybe a fraction too warm.

I'd concentrate on waves rolling gently in to the shore. Someone said that the sea always returns. Who was that someone? Then it hit me — Dawn had told me that, quoted it in French. Starting from scratch Dawn had made herself the master of the language, and of the culture. She'd quote it at you. Make you know she knew. She would have made a good academic. All those pretty girls sitting in the front row hanging on each phrase of some diatribe against testosterone. And afterwards she could have had them three at a time, dipped in honey, chanting ideological mantras on the turn.

So waves didn't work.

I tried deep breathing, keeping it regular. That was going all right till the moment when I sat bolt upright with the sudden realization that it had almost put me to sleep. Stuff that.

I relaxed into thinking about what was in my brain in the first place — going with it. My mind oscillating between images of Tina and ideas of Karen. Always with Tina I finished up staring at the white scars across her wrists. Had she intended me to see them? Maybe that was why she relaxed, the secret was out. Maybe that was the reason for the strange dance as well — for those expressions of agony that had crossed her face as she pivoted in the room. The room next to the one in which I wasn't managing to sleep.

Somewhere, far off in the Amsterdam night, I heard a siren wailing. Desdemona groaned. What went through her mind as she lay there? What dreams?'

Karen had talked about adoption, that seemed to be the way she was drifting. She'd caught the idea from her mother — ever the practical woman, Mrs Christophe: there's a problem, there's a solution, that kind of thing!

Mr Christophe was French, from New Caledonia. One of the lucky ones, he thought, who'd escaped to Australia when the nickel price collapsed in the early Seventies. I started thinking about Mr Christophe. That's a sign of being hard up — when your father-in-law comes to haunt your dreams. Mr Christophe was one of the most forgettable men I'd met. Except he was a classic of his kind when it came to being a French colonial. It surprised me that when he hit Australia's shores he hadn't got a job as a prison warder. Fine, he'd brought enough money with him to make sure he'd never have to work. But since then he'd fallen for every shonky investment promotion invented.

You got Karen, you got the dad thrown in. Karen was worth it. She could put the world into a sentence and toss it across the room without noticing she'd done the trick. In our good patches it was like living with Eve without an apple tree to bugger things up.

Next I started to wonder about what the apple tree meant. No tree, no fucking? Had I got that right? Better to risk the tree.

Wasn't the fucking going to be great with some little kid's head peering over the edge saying . . . did adopted kids call people 'Mummy'?

It wasn't long before I'd populated the entire house, every nook and cranny of Villa du Phare, with adopted children. Turned it into 'a home' in the very worst sense of the word.

There'd been a moment when I'd teetered on the brink of 'a home'. That was after the news of my father's death came through. My mother fell into millions of tiny pieces which never went back

58

together again. And the word 'home' had been introduced to my vocabulary. It had stayed there. As things turned out somebody came to the rescue, a relative who popped me into boarding school.

Only then, lying in my Amsterdam bed, did it strike me: that relative must have been my aunt, Mrs Fabre.

That could have explained the inheritance as well. Not my charming ways after all. I'd been rewarded in middle life because I'd been saved as a little boy. Aunt had taken me on board all those years ago. Was it conceivable she'd always intended that I should finish up with the Villa, the art collection, the untold millions?

More sirens sounding. They give a man a feeling, those vehicles, unseen, belting through the empty night to some disaster, or from one. Some new capsule of tragedy transported at high speed.

Or just spirited cops having a bit of fun.

Thinking about Tina again.

About Madame Fabre — they still called her that around Villefranche and Cap Ferrat.

About Karen.

Wouldn't Aunt have been pleased at the way I'd negotiated the October stockmarket crash. What a clever boy, she would have thought. That was Karen's doing. She'd taken an interest in my millions, in preserving them. I guess that was the breeding instinct again. Looking forward to future generations.

Once she'd said, right after making love: 'Ess —' That's what she called me '— there's the pleasure and there's another thing. In the long run it's just as strong, the other thing. Sometimes,' she said, 'I feel that intelligence, our being able even to think about desire, is just a vehicle to transport genes.'

'How about worms?' I'd ask.

'What are you saying? Worms?'

'Does their intelligence transport genes?'

'*Touché.*'

I'd devoted a life to stamping out contractions of my name. 'Ess' I particularly hated.

That was till Karen took it up. Suddenly I could listen to her say 'Ess' all night long.

My unsleeping mind began to examine what it remembered of the cubist painting hanging in the house over on the canal. I'd noticed that on previous occasions, the way particularly awful

59

paintings stay with you. That was before the international art Mafia made a cult of dreadful art. They called it 'bad painting'. Clever that: by lifting a phrase, elevating it, you transform its meaning. 'Bad painting' had become high praise.

But the bad cubist work was out of place. There it was, hanging in my mind. (Was that the first light of day lifting the tones of the room?) I could see it hanging over there on the Looiersgracht, between the two nondescript landscapes. A silly thought struck me: Christ between two thieves.

Desdemona stirred, stretched — you could hear the bones creaking — she groaned, lay down again. Man had bred that size into the Great Dane; it was unnatural, a strain on the system. I was told they didn't live long. That made me particularly fond of Desdemona. (I never called her 'Des'.)

It appealed to me, the idea of the bad painting being like Christ. No idea why.

I must have gone to sleep.

Sun woke me, pouring in through the window. Sun and a face staring from a couple of inches away. Not an adopted child, but Desdemona. Her eyes saying: Let me out, I could do with a leak.

From Singelgracht in, there were stalls. It was like magic, they'd sprung up out of nowhere. And more junk for sale than you would have thought the houses could hold. Tina had explained: the people buy from one another, the same articles appear each year.

Except the food. Stalls making satay, pancakes, hot dogs, serving coffee, were interwoven with the junk piles. Jazz bands played on street corners, fighting for sound space against multimegawatt rock amplifiers thumping out recorded noise.

Desdemona and I wandered through the crowded city. For breakfast I tried a street-stall hot dog, not too bad, if you forgave the plastic bread to which Desdemona made no objection. I'm not too sure her teeth had a chance to try it out. Bomph. Like all her food, it went straight on down, untouched, untasted.

Early in the birthday party it was reasonable to assume that later things would get even more lively, that the streets would collect more celebrants. If that was possible. Already the bicycles appeared to be in retreat, the crowds were so thick — this was the day for foot soldiers like myself.

Junk has always been a weakness of mine. That was essentially what I'd traded in during my trading days, junk and forgeries. Good fun — the feeling of living off your wits. Not so much fun though when the enterprise failed to provide a living.

Karen warned that I could finish up that way again if I didn't concentrate. That was an exaggeration, of course. My inherited line of Degas monotypes, all by themselves, would have seen us through a whole string of cold winters. Then there was the Sisley landscape.

I don't know where Karen got the financial instincts from. Genetic? Her father's wasn't the line carrying the nous.

It would have been close to a full year since we'd had that particular argument. Karen putting the *International Herald Tribune* down on the table, eyeing me, calculating the moment. We were outside on the terrace. Full summer sun through the eucalyptuses, croissants, coffee, jokes about me going to fat, about the 'old man's build': huge trunk, skinny legs. We were fugitives from the summer crowd that fills the Côte d'Azur. Under house arrest, that was what it was like.

Well, I was. Most days Karen fought her way through traffic to the silk shop in Nice to rake off the cash on credit-card slips designed to home in from all over the world.

'Essington.'

The full name! Advertising trouble.

'The Scottish institutions have started going liquid.' Even the jargon, frightening.

What sort of way to start the day was that? Desdemona wasn't there to afford protection. She was down on the boundary fence chewing the fat with the poodle, name of Charlie, next door. Swapping dirty stories.

Oh for a dog's life.

We'd had this topic rear its head from time to time right through a strong bull run. Karen keeping tabs on things and on people. No faith in the advice we got from the money managers who'd come attached to the inheritance. Already, thanks to her, there'd been changes in the line-up. Now, suddenly, she wanted to take the lot out of their hands. She wanted to sell. Busting to do it. Convert all those long-term secure investments of Aunt's into piles of crisp new bank notes. She'd even worked out which country's notes to change them into.

61

'Since when have the Scots been supposed to know what's what?'

'Since forever. Ess, you owe it to Mrs Fabre. Try to think of it that way. To her memory.'

'I don't want to think about it at all.'

The result was that we sold up. Karen had picked the peak, almost to the day. It was weird. After that prices eased back but not so far, not enough to justify the drastic action. I started taking shots at the strategist.

That was a mistake because on a Tuesday in October there was the biggest fall since 1929. People jumped out of windows. A man in Miami shot his broker. The blood disappeared from the cheeks of the Australian beer barons.

And then Karen was buying the same stocks in again, only a lot more of them this time for the same money.

I remember her saying: 'That's the way it's done.'

Fuck me drunk!

And there I was in Amsterdam hunting through junk like a man desperate to turn a quid. I headed up into one of the less reputable antique dealer's streets where the shopkeepers had established outdoor stalls for the day in the hope of off-loading their buying mistakes.

It caught my eye, a small landscape in a mannered impressionist style — all the work of a chisel brush. Every country had its Impressionists and all over the place you find the locals in the late twentieth century trying to make claims for their home-grown followers of that Paris-based movement.

Some of those claims aren't all that ill-founded. There were excellent painters all around the place at the time. And nor was impressionism as discrete a movement as later art historians made it out to be. It was in the air everywhere; it was a manner of handling paint, the texture and the colour, that had got under way at the beginning of the nineteenth century.

What I was gazing at was a small painting that looked like it would have been produced by a second-generation Dutch Impressionist. Maybe painted before the First World War or thereabouts. Nothing exciting, but nice — just a road, some trees, a man in clogs. Much too nice to be stuck out on the street with the hot dogs and the assault of rock music. Some poor bugger had struggled over the thing, dared to hope that a quality would show up and catch the eye of some taste-maker — then or later. Instead he got me.

The painting cost one hundred and fifty guilders. I'd beaten the guy down to half. That was the pleasure to be had from those transactions. A kind of sport any two could play. My seller was keen, chances were the thing was stolen. The shop behind the street stall was right down the 'junk' end of 'antique'. Or did that signal a real difference: that my man was less a crook than his up-market friends? Honest antique dealer — a contradiction in terms.

That's best not fogotten.

People were going for the beer. I wondered if they'd be capable of keeping that up all day, and night. It turned out they were, and remained gentle with it. But I couldn't sustain the walking, my knees signalling collapse, my interest fading as well. And that despite barges chugging past, their decks crowded with revellers. Despite the food stalls — I was sated with quick snacks.

Steered by the crowd I found myself heading for Robert's house. Desdemona was keeping close, getting edgy at being pushed, albeit unintentionally. I tried my luck at the immaculate door. It opened, Tina dressed for the street.

'So!'

'I happened to be passing.'

'Then you must come in.' Not a great deal of joyous anticipation expressed in that. She was doing her duty. Not the warm companion of the previous night. 'But,' she added, 'I must go out.'

'Oh well, not to worry.'

'No, I insist that you come in. It has been thoughtless of me not to invite you. Vondel Park is hardly the place to be today. The festivities are here.' She gestured out the window, to the crowd of faces.

Passers-by didn't interest me so much; it was only a couple of minutes before that I'd been a part of the throng.

But Tina interested me. For an instant her features were set rigid.

'You aren't selling anything?' I asked, to take the tension out of her.

'I am not, though it is treason not to do so. Last year, I would have you know, Robert and I set up a stall. I made satay. It was Robert's idea. He thought it would be fun. I worked hard all the day. He talked to friends who dropped by. Dreadful, Essington. It was very dreadful.' Talking of time past warmed her up a little.

'Now I am going out to watch all the other people who are getting exhausted celebrating the birthday of the Queen.'

'I'll come along,' I offered.

'No, stay. Already you have done your duty. You must be tired of it by now. And your dog, tired also.' An attempt at a smile. 'You — what is it? — hold the horse while I am gone.'

'The fort.'

'I should not be long. I do not enjoy the crowds so much.'

I settled down in the window, trying not to look self-conscious as I demonstrated that, like any good Dutchman, I had nothing to hide.

But I couldn't stay there long. Not once the thought hit me about Amsterdam prostitutes, the way they display themselves in windows. Why, any minute I might stir the gonads of a passer-by and have to work out a price. I got up. The dog and I began to prowl.

On the next level there was a kitchen, a service room and another general living space, this one less sparsely furnished. And there were books. I ferreted among these and turned up a copy of Vincent van Gogh's letters, an English publication, one of a three-volume set. I'd selected the third, chronologically the last — Vincent writing from the south of France.

I took the book downstairs and settled in to read — dipping in here and there, getting a feeling for the artist. Of course I had heard about the letters, but till then had not read them — only excerpts quoted in other books. I'm not a great one for scholarship at the best of times.

I got comfortable. The painting, my recent acquisition, was resting against the wall. If the cubist piece was Christ and the landscapes the thieves, then the Dutch impressionist piece was surely one of the soldiers sleeping at the foot of the cross. Or Mary Magdalene.

Raising my eyes from the letters I could look across at the four of them — a mini history of art. They didn't tell me much though, except that there were more ways of killing a cat than stuffing its neck with cream.

A lot of what Vincent wrote to the long-suffering brother, Theo, was mundane stuff. How he was short of money, there was always that. Usually cunningly placed in the text, picking the moment. Often he'd start by reinforcing the notion of family: the death of an uncle, Mother's state of mind, his joy at hearing that Theo's wife, Jo, was about to have a baby. What good news that was going to be for Mother! But you could sense underneath that he worried about how these developments were going to effect Theo in his role as banker. Because it wasn't long before we got down to money again. He wrote a lot of letters, several a month. Hardly one without a request for funds. Even when he was conscious of Theo having a rough trot himself.

After the money gripes came descriptions of what he'd been working on. Often here he managed to raise the level of his concerns a fraction. He talked of looking at the stars while staying at Saintes-Maries-sur-Mer, of that sky being flecked with clouds of a fundamental blue, more intense than cobalt and, in the depth behind them, the stars, green, yellow, rose, white; glittering like gems, like opals.

Then you got back on to the money again.

Poor Theo. All suffering. Theo the younger brother who was equally subject to nervous disorders but who, wrestling with the vicissitudes of life, failed to use his health as a lever with which to move others: for him it was simply something to suffer. Theo, who was to die within a few months of Vincent and be rewarded with a matching headstone beside him in the cemetery at Auvers.

I got a feeling for Vincent's suffering, for his fear of attacks, of mind collapse, but I couldn't deal out much sympathy. He was suffering from himself. Some passages were genuinely tender, displaying a concern about others, but those were fleeting moments. Generally self-obsession prohibited him from looking over the rim of his own very particular world.

At the time that Vincent shot himself, not even managing to make a thorough job of that, Theo was a father of six months' standing; his son, baptized Vincent, was a sickly baby. Business was doing badly, as well. Right then Theo needed a dying brother like he needed a hole in the head.

Poor Theo. He got Vincent with a hole in the chest.

Vincent was always asking for canvas and paint to be sent to him. He asked for so many canvases of a certain size, say, size thirty. Or he'd have sent Theo half a dozen finished works, size twenty-five and size twenty.

Standardized formats. I'd noticed that as well in the pictures in the van Gogh museum. Vincent tended to use the same size over and over. He wasn't making the canvases up himself nor was proportion a major factor with him.

The painting I'd bought that morning looked to be a stock canvas. And, curiously, it had exactly the same dimensions as the cubist work on the wall.

The landscapes hanging up there on either side were longer, narrower.

Tina had stayed away a long time. I got sick of the letters, sick of sitting in the room. I tried aimlessly running my fingers up and down the harpsichord keyboard and got some head tilting out of Desdemona for my pains. Then I had another look at the cubist painting. I took it down. There was a wall safe behind, complete with keyhole. So what? I looked at the back of the picture. That was more in my line than wall safes. It was the standard arrangement of four stretched arms slotted together and tension put on the canvas by means of wooden wedges. It looked like a professional stretching job. Done a long time ago. The thumb tacks holding the canvas were rusted.

I compared it with the picture I'd bought. Yes, identical size. The stretcher looked to be of the same type. Neither of them had a maker's name stamp.

Up close there was the sense of a lot of paint on the cubist work, on the painting underneath, even though the ridges weren't particularly pronounced. And there was a slight stain of oil that had leaked through the ground to the fibres of the canvas itself. That wasn't supposed to happen. Not in the best circles.

The painting I'd purchased had no trace of oil migrating through the ground and sizing. Interesting. The cubist work was over something a lot older than itself. That was fairly unusual. Though there were artists who managed to get their hands on old paintings for the stretchers and for frames, it was unusual for them to work over the top of such a find. You didn't get a good bond between the paint layers, particularly where time has laid its patina of greasy soot over the older image.

Interesting all that, but was it enough to build a life on?

Answer, no. Not unless you went for art at the big-time level. There had been moments of exasperation when Karen had suggested that. I think it worried her to see me sitting on the terrace with my feet up on the chair she'd so recently vacated, settling in for my day. She felt I was letting life — the one great opportunity — slip through my fingers. Well I was, through choice. The last thing in the world I wanted to do was become one of those thrilling people on the other end of a telephone at an art auction. The whole room staring at the plastic instrument, waiting for the word to come that I'd gone up another hundred thousand.

It was rumoured that a lot of that telephone bidding came from cars parked outside.

To make money out of art you have to sell it. It is a push-over to buy the stuff, at any level — all you need is the cash. Selling is quite a different thing. They all have a particular enzyme, those who sell art, you can see it showing up in their physiognomy. Too often I'd confronted it, looked into those soulless eyes. The only good dealer I'd ever met was dead, killed. And he had been as dishonest as the day is long.

Anyway, even if you were good at selling, had the enzyme, what did you do when you got your hands on the great work? Me, I wouldn't be able to part with the thing. Those pictures I'd got from Aunt were going to hang on my walls till death parted us. And then . . . that was when the children came in on the act, seeing nothing but dollar signs.

What children?

The Holt mind going round in circles.

Unless, forgery — selling that was quite a different kettle of fish: fun, fun, fun! I hadn't let that career lapse completely since leaving Australia's shores. There had been moments. I'd even had a spell working with a master of the art, learning. I could have dropped my feet from that terrace table, after Karen headed off to the silk trade, and crept away to some secret room to conjure up yet another masterpiece with which to fool the experts.

That would have proved a satisfaction, of sorts.

But I guess I didn't have it in me. Necessity wasn't there to get the motors going.

Still, the idea of forgery is what keeps up my interest in the backs and the sides of paintings. I read them with almost the same attention as I read the front. And even with the displayed surface my mind will wander, searching out what is underneath. It isn't just obsession. The kind of thing you get to be able to see hidden under there might not have been detected since . . . well, at least since the Americans started to invade Europe at the end of the last century, hunting great art treasure.

It's estimated that sixty per cent of what they took back was either forged or misattributed. Misattributed is a polite way of saying what you're saying.

I went out. That would be all right with Tina.

I'd been inside too long. Quite an effort of will with, outside, beyond the window glass, every sign that Queen Beatrix's birthday was going along swimmingly.

Desdemona was keen for another try as well.

Sign of a good party: litter building up. There were plastic beer cups everywhere, popping under foot. Children were hopping on them, enjoying the crunchy kind of bang they made. Then more feet trampling them till they were a dust of transparent plastic slivers.

Great for the fish out there in the North Sea. Not that they'd been having much of a decade anyhow.

I found a table along the Keizersgracht where the sun shone, and if you were patient enough someone would bring you a pancake drenched in fake maple syrup, and a cup of coffee. I'd ordered three pancakes. We were a big pair, Desdemona and I, we needed to keep our strength up.

I gazed out over the canal at mostly private houses turned into banks and corporation headquarters. A barge passed, covered in advertisements for a local radio station. It was carrying a cargo of what looked like Amsterdam's media groupies. They were at one end, dancing with great self-awareness. Down the stern was the band and a singer with long, black tresses and tight pants so his balls stuck out. They stuck out even from my distance. On a bull that was a good thing, only you needed air circulating around

68

them to do the job. The guy was singing something between Latin and rock, some new ghastly hybrid. Crowds on the bridges cheered as they passed.

Desdemona growled. She wasn't liking her day that much. She looked haunted. Nature hadn't prepared her for a queen's birthday.

Of myself, I wasn't sure. Was I the great white hunter relaxing, watching the natives at their play?

I paid.

Standing up, asking myself in which direction to be aimless, I caught sight of Tina. There she was, right over on the far side of the canal. Not a chance in hell of getting to her, not with people packed around me like that, and a bridge to cross.

It had struck me before, the tendency to wear black — her mourning? From a distance it marked her out. Well, in my mind, at least. She had a black scarf tied over her head, making her look like one of the wives of the immigrant workers from eastern Europe.

That scarf hadn't been in place when she'd left me at the house.

She was standing on the second of several steps leading to a large varnished wood door. There was a brass plaque fastened to the brick wall of the building, telling the world what sort of office it was or, if not that, at least whose office it was.

She looked vulnerable and lonely among the crowd. Big me felt a need to protect her, to tell her that it was all right. Tina was turning her head this way and that. I wondered if she'd pick me out in the crowd. I went up on to the balls of my feet to add height, and waved. I saw a man approach her. They talked. He turned in the direction from which he'd come. She followed, her mien expressing reluctance.

What did I feel about that? Like a surge, I was jealous, cheated.

He was a short man, light boned, dressed in a well-cut, double-breasted dark suit. He wore a hat, dark brown with the brim tilted down front and back. The effect was elegant yet, at the same time, sinister. It made him look gangsterish, by association I guess.

I set out to catch them up. Not a chance. The crowd in that direction on my side of the canal had come to a halt around a car foolish enough to attempt to get in where no car dared. The roof was receiving quite a bashing. At front and rear young men had taken hold, they were rocking it good-naturedly. The driver had wound up the windows.

Chapter 7

Sunday, aimless. I wandered the streets, dodging the litter and hungover people. How did Queen Beatrix feel? I wondered. Would she also be going for the aspirin and the fizzy drinks?

Amsterdam, time to take my leave. One more visit to the Rijksmuseum and its van Gogh offshoot and then, come sunrise, I'd be on my way. Provided I could meet up with Tina, return the key, wish her well.

It decided to rain again. Desdemona had run in Vondel Park, lapped it several times over. She was prepared for the day of rest. I sat observing budding trees through the window, waiting for the museums to open up their doors.

I got to thinking about things in a vague sort of a way — 'things' being mostly Tina. Clearly there was something off balance in the Carbentus camp. Nothing I could put my finger on but . . .

The Holt intuition is no big deal, I'm just not the type who sees around corners. That understood, I still had the sense of something very wrong. There was Robert wanting to meet me after more than thirty distant years. And not simply out of curiosity — hadn't he been in a hurry? He'd headed all the way to Paris to make the contact. Why does a person suddenly get so excited about seeing a man with whom he'd once watched the stars under Australian skies? What was there about me that could be of use to him?

Answer, nothing; neither at first, second, nor third glance.

What did I have to be the big attraction? Well, there was always money, that's the big one. But who was going to pop out of the fog of thirty years and try and touch me for a few quid? The head of the Carbentus family empire? He wouldn't need to do that. The Dutch had riches pouring out of their ears. The whole world knew that. And Amsterdam provided the evidence as far as the Carbentus clan was concerned. Four storeys of canal house for Robert to call his own. Tina, the half-sister, over here in

71

fashionable Vondel Park. No, Robert wouldn't have been on the point of putting the bite on me.

My thoughts drifted to Tina. She was a puzzle, wasn't she? The woman who'd slit her wrists, who went up and down like a hotel lift. She was so charming you felt like hugging her, but the next minute her mind could turn, she'd act like she hardly knew you. Tina who was a part of a family that was too big, too heavy. A family so overpowering that she had needed Robert to keep her safe from it, from the pressure its members exerted.

Well, Tina hadn't put it like that, she'd only hinted. But that was how I'd read it between her lines.

And that other problem. People must have known how close the two of them, Robert and Tina, had been. And they'd all know Robert was dead. There'd been a funeral and a service; quite an event, Tina had said. I remember the grotesque question entering my mind: What of him was actually buried? From that living moment etched into my memory I had the idea of Robert totally obliterated — the particles which had constituted his being blasted to kingdom come. Yet, you'd think: shouldn't there have been more evidence of caring relatives nicking around to look after Tina?

While I'd been in Amsterdam all I'd witnessed of her social life was one meeting with the dapper little man, and that an assignation, something to keep hidden, it seemed.

Even the bloody phone didn't ring; well, not while I was around anyway.

Naturally I'd wondered about both Tina and Robert failing to get married, neither of them taking the plunge. Nothing so odd in that, I guess. Only, usually there is someone in a person's life. It's the way we are made.

Unless that someone was each other?

Which had crossed my mind more than once. Two children with years separating them — eleven years or so — only 'half' brother and sister and spending the first part of childhood without any contact.

It could fit. Would possibly even explain the woman's strange intensity. Explain the slashed wrists as well. A terrible burden to find yourself over the line, beyond what's acceptable, your passion taboo.

Even in enlightened Amsterdam.

Some kind of a picture of relationships was forming in my head. But there were other elements to place in there as well. Elements like the van Gogh painting. Could you have a van Gogh painting and your half-sister not know about it? Even if they had sold the work years ago, it would have been a subject that cropped up from time to time. 'If only I still had the painting, think what it would have fetched.' That sort of talk.

I was sure Robert hadn't made the story up. I'd been over and over that, it just wouldn't have made sense. Not in my terms.

Funny the way I kept on thinking about the Carbentus bit of the family. Eurocentricity, is that what you'd call it? Or was it me concentrating on the paternal line — that was what Dawn would have caught on to as quick as a flash. There was also a maternal line; maybe they could have been the bunch causing the problem. In Tina's case there was a Javanese family. No sign of how strong those connections were, although some ties still existed between Holland and its former colony. Ties more substantial than the occasional meal of *rijsttafel*.

And there was the other child, the one who'd stayed over there, Haryanto.

Of course, back there somewhere was the fear that I was thinking about all this because the mind was following the hormones — because it was always drifting off in Tina's direction.

I had a bite on my way to the Rijksmuseum. I needed it. And a couple of glasses of beer. That seemed to be the national drink. I took it in a *bruine kroeg* — one of the traditional Dutch pubs. Not too much action on account of the party that had been. I sat by the window watching rain and the occasional bedraggled character wandering past.

The museum was close to empty as well. Spot on opening time, I was first in through the door.

I finished up sitting in front of a big Rembrandt double portrait, *The Jewish Bride*. It got me. Late Rembrandt — I'd come to Amsterdam unprepared for the mastery of it. He moved the paint in every possible way — rubbing it, brushing, stippling, building a surface of lights and darks seemingly illuminated from within.

You couldn't have forged that. Not in a lifetime. It was all done like an autograph, a completely personal handwriting, his particular touch.

73

I left the Rembrandts and headed through underneath where the museum bridges the road — a shelter for dishevelled buskers. I gave a handful of change to a man doing something on a saxophone over the top of a battery-operated box making drum sounds as accompaniment.

I was obliged to sprint the distance to the van Gogh museum on account of the intensified rain. There was something in particular I needed to check up on there. One of my obsessions: to establish for myself Vincent van Gogh's standard canvas sizes. I also wanted to have another look at the brown picture of the cigarette-smoking skull with the painting underneath showing through.

Afterwards, I bought a heap of postcards at the desk and headed back for the apartment.

Things being quiet and the streets near empty I decided it was safe to pick up the car from the long-term park I'd found after bringing Desdemona back from the kennels. Then I could leave it in front of the apartment in Vondel Park ready for a quick getaway in the morning. I'd be out of the city before the traffic became congested, maybe enjoy a relaxed breakfast somewhere along the big road heading south for the sun.

Amsterdam, it got eight out of ten. That was a high score from me. I'd never really managed to be a city boy. Maybe that was why I'd become too contented out there on Cap Ferrat. Sniff the perfume of the trees, pretend the sea stretching out before you was scorched grass — you could be in the Australian bush. If the poodle next door would shut up its yapping. That dog had become possessive of Desdemona. Chances were, with us away, they'd had to put it under sedation.

For an early departure the trick was to pay my respects to Tina while bringing the car around.

Driving, I braved the narrow streets that sneak along between the buildings and the water, managing to avoid killing a cyclist. I even found my way to the house. After several tries.

I knocked on the door.

Perhaps I should have rung. The departure plan had come together so quickly that I'd shifted into go without a thought for social obligations.

I knocked some more, stood there, hands on hips, looking up

74

for no reason other than I suspected that that was where she'd be. I could see in the window the ground-floor room, empty. Just space and then the harpsichord over on the far side.

And the three paintings in place.

No Tina. Curious. Well, she was moody, she'd gone into her shell. Yet a feeling, nothing I could trust, but a feeling none the less, that the house wasn't empty.

I drove away.

That was all right. I could leave the key in the letter-box with a thank-you note. Together with a final set of regrets about Robert.

I dozed off early, slept till dawn. Then up, a face rinse, no shave, threw the lot into the suitcase, picked up my souvenir, the painting, and trundled down the stairs. No names on the mail slots; it took a moment for me to be sure I'd got the number right before posting the key.

Beautiful Tina, goodbye. Keep happy.

Ten paces to the car. It was distinctive, my car. I'd picked it up six months earlier from this man who did property developments overlooking the Villefranche harbour. He'd managed to go bust the way those people will. Do not shed a tear, they come back again just as quickly. The car was flashy, silver, with the paint oxidizing on the roof and bonnet. It was also a heap.

Ten paces it would have been from where I posted the key. I had the painting under one arm, suitcase in my hand. Ten paces right into the arms of a pair of small and nasty-looking men. One of them knew my name!

He said: 'Mr Holt?' As though it was a question.

'That's me,' I answered. Like I'd been trained.

'Do you mind?' the same man asked. He took the suitcase and the painting.

Desdemona was standing right behind me. I guess she was watching the action, waiting to spring.

I asked them if they'd like the dog to kill them.

The one elected as mouthpiece advised that if the dog attacked they'd shoot it. He asked me to hold it by the collar, just so we could all be sure that it would stay alive.

I held Desdemona by the collar.

They were so cool, so on top of life, the pair of them. They were being professional, like a dentist would be, or a lawyer.

75

I asked how they knew it was me.

'Mr Holt, we've always known.'

Trying to be funny, to keep the conversation light: 'Always . . . since I was a . . .?'

'Shut up.'

The accent — Dutch, I guessed. But they weren't the tall, happy blond chaps who'd been getting drunk all over town a couple of days before. These men were neat, small. Nor did they look like they'd recently drunk more than is good for the human unit. Eyes bright — even, I might have thought, intelligent.

Good dressing, conservative. People who earn a lot for what they do, and invest it wisely.

Curious what you fasten on when knowing someone's got a gun pointed at your head.

'The dog goes in the boot.'

'She won't fit,' I protested.

'Why don't we try?'

I reached to get the key out of my pocket. That was the hand not attached to the dog.

'Please do not bother, Mr Holt. My friend will get the key.' Followed by having my pockets patted, the key extracted. What would it have been? Five-thirty. You'd think someone would pass. The trick was to make things go slow.

The man opened the boot, searched it, told me to put the dog in. I paused, glanced at the gun, a clumsy-looking weapon. You certainly wouldn't want to be hit with anything that came out of that. Apart from killing you it would make a terrible hole, unaesthetic.

I kept calm, it must have been the early hour. I felt as though I wasn't actually a part of the action. I put Desdemona in, as reassuringly as possible. I didn't want her to die, she was my friend. She looked at me as the lid came down. But she trusted me.

In Australia graziers carry their dogs everywhere in the boot. Sometimes, outside pubs, a hundred degrees in the shade, you can hear them scuffing about in there.

In a sense it was their mistake putting Desdemona in the boot. She was what was keeping me under control. As soon as the lid closed I could feel myself start to vibrate, I could sense anger rising through me like a tide.

'Do you mind if we take this for a moment, Mr Holt?' Always polite but firm. English much better than Tina's. The man arranged his words in perfect order. Tina had a few little faults that were soft to hear, and droll.

'And would you oblige by standing perfectly still in front of the car? We do not want to create a spectacle.'

I stood as I was told while the voice-box walked off with the painting. He took it to a car parked on the far side of the road, handed it in through the window. A minute or so passed and then the painting came out again. I was starting to catch on. They reckoned I'd stolen something.

They made me get down on my knees and go through everything in the suitcase. God that felt bad. There's something about the inside of a suitcase. It makes your life look less than you might have hoped, reduces it to tat.

The one who talked patted the sides, the front, the back of the case. He didn't find what he was looking for. And I was getting confident. I didn't have whatever it was, so it was starting to look like their problem, not mine.

My car door was opened and the talker started poking about in there, feeling under the floor mats, sliding the seats back. He was looking a bit flustered; he had gone red in the face, was getting hot. His little mate was losing concentration the way people do when they see the boss's perfect plan coming to pieces. I screwed my head around to get a look at who was in the car over the far side of the road. No chance. It had those smoky windows that certain people think add something to their image. Makes them feel like Haitian dictators. The chill grey light of an Amsterdam dawn glittered off their surfaces.

The man was even further inside my car, and grunting. So I went for his mate who was now peering over the road as though expecting some signalled instruction. I banged him very hard on the side of the head, a hammer blow. He pivoted, half lost balance. I stepped around behind him, locked an arm across his throat, got hold of the gun hand, with gun. I held it pointing at where the other man was easing himself back out of the car.

Over the road an engine came to life and whoever it was that had taken a look at my painting departed.

A black Mercedes.

I wasn't in total control of the situation, not with us both holding the gun. But then they weren't in a great position either. The chances were I could force pressure on the trigger, get a shot in. I don't think they wanted that.

I dragged my captive up against the wall of the apartment block and set about choking him. I was just that much bigger than he was, it was easy. Particularly with the gun turned around now, and sticking into his stomach.

'Hold on, Mr Holt. We don't want anyone hurt,' the other man said.

'Only my fucking dog.'

'To avoid trouble, that was all.' He had his hands out, calming the waters.

His mate lost a lot of strength all at once. I let him slip but kept hold of the gun.

'Now, Mr Mouth,' I suggested, 'how about you shut up?'

It worked, not a word.

The keys were still dangling in the Maserati door. I got the man who'd come that far unscathed to put them in the boot lock.

'What's it worth not to open that lid?'

He was looking scared now. That was good. He was doing penance. They have to learn, they have to get to know what it feels like to be made to kneel in front of a suitcase, to go through the contents.

I said: 'I'll tell you what. How about we've gone half-circle, now it's me on top? All seems to have come right between us. But the dog . . . it has had less than justice. Why don't you just tell her you're sorry? Face to face. Animal's rights.'

'Jesus!' he said.

His friend had made it back up on his feet, looking sheepish.

'Or, you could tell me who was in that car.'

They both got that look of people who'd rather die than tell you what you want to know. A look that lies. There are not so many heroes. The thing is to push them hard enough.

Desdemona did the trick.

In the boot she was like a bomb waiting to go off. Turn the key and cop it.

The person in the Mercedes was a man. His name was Cornelius.

'Who Cornelius?'

'Cornelius Carbentus.'

I felt some disappointment when I learned that there had in fact been two people in the car. The other one was Tina.

So disappointed that I forgot to ask what it was that I was supposed to have stolen.

Tina being in on that action: a pin prick to the erotic balloon that had never quite filled up, much less got off the ground.

Chapter 8

'I'm dotty about it.' My joke, the picture was built up out of dots.

'God! I could have hoped for better than that.'

'Not from me you couldn't.'

'Let me put it this way, Ess . . .' But the words failed her.

'No,' I said, 'I like it, I really do.'

'There're six of them. I went to town. I mean, those people, they were so enthusiastic about the idea.'

'I'd hope so. You didn't have any trouble with the notion of commercialization?'

'What's so commercial? They do what they like doing and they get paid. Every design will have the name of the artist running along the side. No . . . they were pleased. You've got to remember, there's a lock-out in Australia. They're 'Aboriginal Art', that's put over to the side, right out of the way. It's not real art.'

'That's the way arties look on the stuff — it's an embarrassment.'

We were out on the balcony at Cap Ferrat. Karen fresh off the plane — if fresh was a condition applying to anyone who'd just sat in a seat breathing stale air for twenty-six hours. She was anticipating trouble with sleep cycles, and shuddering at the hint of bags under her eyes.

There were the six canvases removed from their packing tube. One was pinned up on the wood of the terrace pergola; the others were rolled together on a table.

Rebecca, who kept the house going, joined in the viewing. She was holding her hands behind her back while shaking her head from side to side, wondering at the mysteries of art. There was no way of knowing with Rebecca — of knowing what she thought about anything, let alone the paintings of Australian Aborigines.

I'd belted home; well, tried to, the Maserati had had ideas of its own. While the motor was alive I listened on the radio to results from the French elections; politicians being interviewed, analysts getting paid to tell you what every street drunk already knew. That was when my mind wasn't wandering back to Amsterdam, to things I didn't understand about my stay there. Things like who had broken into Tina's apartment? I asked myself that question over and over. It couldn't have been the two men who stopped me going to my car. The dog would have been on to them like a shot the second try. And, anyway, they were working for Cornelius and Tina. No need to bust the lock. No need to break in either.

So there was someone else involved. Someone else after . . . were they after the van Gogh, if it existed? Or what? Or had the door been busted by a drug addict? And was it simply a coincidence that it happened so close to my confrontation with the gunmen on their picture hunt?

What kept on niggling at me was that they had been looking for a painting. Then, what painting would you try so hard for?

Of course, whole slabs of life never make sense, they aren't meant to. Or we fail to discover the logic in them — maybe that's closer to the truth of the matter.

The car got me as far as Avignon. That was where it coughed, spluttered, died, resurrected itself for a couple more kilometres and then gave up the ghost. I rang through to Rebecca's other half, Renardo, and then was obliged to potter about killing the hours until he came to my rescue.

I arrived home in true style, in the yellow Bentley Continental with the sloper body that had been my aunt's pride and joy. Since her death there had been confusion over its ownership. I held the documents and paid the bills but Renardo, who'd driven for Aunt while Rebecca kept house, remained impossibly possessive about the machine. If I'd stood up for my rights in the matter the household would have collapsed. I'd been drilled in the niceties of the master–servant relationship while sitting at the old lady's bedside, watching her die. It all came down to me accepting certain responsibilities: Rebecca and Renardo stayed with the house, the house stayed with me. There was to be no parting till death.

They were good to me, both of them; tolerant, like you might be to a delinquent son. I'd grown fond of them as well, though I couldn't train myself out of regarding them with some awe.

81

They'd given me most of the French I spoke and had infected it with a strong southern accent — the inflections Cézanne exaggerated when he went up to Paris and encountered chaps like Manet, Monet, Degas and Renoir in the Café Guerbois. (That was where he is supposed to have said: 'You ask what am I going to exhibit, M. Manet? I tell you, a bucket of shit.') It's a nice sound, southern French; I enjoy it out of the mouths of Renardo and Rebecca, it has the ring of truth.

Rebecca said the Papunya painting made no sense to her but she was sure that it was very nice. No doubt she and Renardo would have a good laugh about it later, when we were out of earshot.

'It's ravishing,' Karen exclaimed. She'd slipped into the French she'd learnt from her father and polished up like a silver chalice.

'But what does it mean?' Me still playing the fool.

She laughed. That came easily to her, broke up the doll-like features, now a fraction bruised by the flight. She dropped the lids over green–blue eyes, scrunched them up, put a finger to the side of her head, mimed screwing it into her brain: 'Mean! Ess, I wouldn't have a clue. But neither would the man who explained it to me either. He just kept on saying that what it meant was too secret, too fragile for anyone to know. I asked what they were doing selling the stuff to galleries and collectors then. So he switched to a lot of claptrap about Marxist economics. Even little old me knew he was talking rubbish.'

Croissants would be rationed now that Karen was back, and there would not be a sign of *pain au chocolat*. She kept pretending she was going to fat. Crazy talk. People like Karen moved around too much, too fast, to put on weight. She thrived on action, even beneath the fatigue you could see the excitement, the thrill of life written on her face.

'And then he was trying to lay me.'

'Who? Where was this?'

'Not to worry, Ess, we slept with an unsheathed sword between us.'

'Unsheathed!'

Laughing, she came round, wrapped her arms around my neck, pecked me on the cheek like you would an injured child, a kiss to make it better. 'You're my Essington,' she said, 'I don't forget it.'

'Who tried?' I asked, obstinate.

'The fucking bureaucrat or whatever he was. A failed English-man with a beard going matted at the ends. He was the one who went on about the spirituality of the art and all that before the sudden switch to talking about excess value and the way capitalism exploits the artist. He's the one exploiting the artist! He's trying to keep them down. You know, Ess, it seemed to me that they were his pets — that was what he wanted them to be at any rate. I'd ask one of the artists a question and my Englishman would pop up with the answer.'

No more croissants but Rebecca brought out another jug of coffee. She was pleased that Karen was back. Rebecca thought husbands and wives should stick together.

'Then he's grabbing me by the hand, telling me I've got lovely tits. Lovely tits! For Christ's sake!'

'He told the truth, Blue.' That had become a familiar name, 'Blue'.

'The truth! Don't you start, Essington Holt.' She laughed. 'And you've got . . .' A pause while she thought about it. 'You've got a . . .'

'Enough!' I said. 'An aching in my heart.'

After he'd picked me up beside the dead Maserati I'd said to Renardo, him immobile behind the aged Bentley's wheel, his face too long, too gloomy, too grey to be true: 'Plasticine. A few hundred kilometres and then the bloody thing melted.'

'The Maserati is a great car.' He went on to tell me of those he'd watched racing in Monaco during the great days of the Grand Prix. 'Then,' he assured me, 'they were real cars.'

'I'd bet it was the car and not the apartment blocks that sent him bust, Molena.'

Molena, Renardo assured me, he was a good man. Sound. He would come back. I should wait and see.

Renardo knew about things, about people. He was related to most of them in that part of the world, except the hundreds, and thousands, the millions, of blow-ins.

Renardo wouldn't want to be related to them.

As we headed into the light that trails behind the setting sun, and then into the darkness, I thought about my departure from Amsterdam.

The gun, I'd tossed that into a canal. Made a small ceremony of it, parking in a side-road just outside Amsterdam and walking up on to a bridge separating one chunk of factory farm from another. Desdemona had watched the thing fall out of my hand and hit the water, sending out an expanding sequence of concentric surface corrugations.

You wouldn't want to be caught tootling over a border in a clapped out Maserati coupé with a short barrel Mauser .38 revolver resting in the glove box. It wouldn't look good. A Great Dane in the back was bad enough. Not that I got stopped, not even going into France where they still had an interest in controlling who entered the country—a hangover from the terrorist bombing spree they thought they had quelled, keeping Paris safe; that was up to the pre-Presidential number that had taken out my friend, Robert Cornelius.

I had come up with only one explanation for the little men's aggression: the van Gogh Robert had told me about. It had to exist. Tina's claiming lack of knowledge of it simply hadn't rung true, and thinking it over—those mood changes as well—I found myself starting to suspect a game going on there.

Yet, if there was a game, how about the scars?

Robert had got in touch with me, with the Australian. But if they knew I had a connection with art — with megabucks art — it was conceivable that they reckoned a van Gogh was the reason for the contact. It figured. They couldn't have known who'd seen whom, and when, in Paris. Robert and I might have spent the morning together before the bomb went off. I could be in possession of a whole lot of information about the painting. Assuming it existed. I could even have known where it was. On the off-chance that the rest of the Carbentus clan weren't in on the same secret.

There was the possibility that Tina was the only one kept in the dark. By Robert — her beloved Robert — as well as by everyone else. Thus paranoia about the family. Out there in the cold, the colonial-born, part-Javanese relative. Inside, nice and warm, all the blue-eyed beauties with a line going right back through the great Vincent to bookbinders to the King in The Hague.

That didn't make sense, not with a Cornelius Carbentus in the car. Robert's father's name. A family name that cycled through the generations?

But then Tina being part of an attack on me — that didn't make sense either.

The one thing I became certain about was that I'd discovered the van Gogh that Robert had mentioned. The realization hadn't come in Holland; not with the slow Holt mind, not a chance of it. It began to dawn on me while killing time, waiting for Renardo to show up. Suddenly I'd have put money on the idea that the cubist picture hanging in the canal house, between the predictable landscapes, was painted to obscure a van Gogh underneath.

It was the only answer to the question of why in those neat, those uncluttered and elegant interiors, there was such a painting on display. That house had been sparsely furnished. And owned by someone who chucked junk out. By someone who wouldn't keep a thing for sentimental reasons. There was no way he would have clung to a bad painting that looked so out of place. OK, the other two, the landscapes . . . but why not hang them? They were undistinguished yet they did the job, they said 'picture' nicely, and with manners. Even better, they said 'old picture'. Most probably that was what they were, perhaps worth a few quid. The sort of thing people in Australia like to show when they've made their pile, so that it looks as though the family has history, wasn't just discovered under a cabbage leaf.

If I was right about the cubist work, then it was a joke. And it appealed to me. There was even the possibility that they'd sell the house and contents. That the van Gogh could finish up out on the street some Queen Beatrix birthday, begging a buyer.

No, it was good.

Karen spent the rest of the day sleeping, half sleeping or simply lying about. She wasn't a believer in the discipline advocated by those who worship jet lag: staying awake to get back into your time zone. If she wanted to sleep she'd sleep.

She did.

We had lunch together, Karen looking groggy. When I suggested a swim from the rocks by the lighthouse she gave the idea thumbs down and popped off for a bit more dozing.

Frustrating that. I'd been hoping for some resolution of the problems existing between us. Instead all I got was a sleepy kindness. Which was OK but inconclusive.

Karen didn't seem to mind the inconclusiveness of things. Me, I went for solutions.

Dawn might have written that down to maleness.

While preparing to receive guests for dinner, though, our conversation did get around to babies.

'I had a look at the conditions for adoption, Essington. From the Australian end. It would have to be through Australia because of our citizenship.'

'Then forget it.'

'Why do you say that?'

'Twenty years on we'd still be in the bureaucrats' grip . . . and no baby.'

'That's not the way to look at it, Ess.'

'Oh yes it is, if you want to deal with Australian bureaucrats. They're the worst, Blue, I've heard you say as much yourself.'

'The only ones we've got.'

'You mean it? You're serious?'

'Of course I'm serious. Ess, I don't want to grow into a . . . what? Into someone like your old aunt. She had you, that was something at least. But only you. What did she do the rest of the time? Sit out here with her bloody paintings and that yellow Bentley, getting herself driven here and there. What kind of a life was that?'

'We don't choose.'

'Ultimately, maybe not. Yet we can have a lot of effect along the way.'

'You're going to go ahead with this?'

'I was . . . Ess, I don't want to talk about it now. I'm screwed up in the head from crossing the world, and Dawn's coming. It's a serious business. And yes, I'm serious about it.'

'You're putting me on notice.'

'If that's the phrase.'

'It's no good, I can't sleep.'

'Small wonder, you've been out to it all day.'

Moon over the water out there beyond the trees, its long reflection picking up the ripple caused by a warm breeze off Africa. A leisure cruiser had up-anchored and was departing Villefranche-sur-Mer. That was the way they did it, those ships — mostly Greek or Russian — they let the passengers have their fish meal at one of the line of restaurants along the stone wharf and then off to the next port of call, leaving nothing other than a slick over the bay's water as a sign that they had passed our way.

The ship's lights heading for the moon's reflection.

It was nice just being there, Karen there too — killed Amsterdam.

We'd stepped through the window on to the balcony outside our upstairs bedroom. I moved a couple of cane chairs from the shade into the white opalescent light.

'Some night watching?'

'Sure.' Ruffling up her hair in her hands. 'Yeah, sure Ess.'

We'd been in each other's arms for an hour at least, almost dozing off, content. Then Karen had come awake again.

'I saw that,' I said.

'What?'

'*The Night Watch*. It wouldn't go on silk as well as the Papunya pictures.'

'Don't suppose it would.' Not much interest in the conversation. Well, not in that conversation, at any rate.

We sat in silence.

'Ess.'

I reached across, held her hand.

'There's a catch,' she said.

'A catch?'

'You're too old.'

'We know that. Still, I try.'

'For adoption. You have to be under forty.'

I froze.

Karen went on: 'I asked about that. They won't budge. They say they've got more couples than babies anyway, miles more. You being too old kills it.'

I couldn't think of a thing to say. There wasn't any way around that. You are the age you are.

'Unless?' I asked.

'We got unmarried.'

'Karen, that's called divorced.'

'Well?'

You could sense her finding this hard to do, hard to say. So it bloody well should be.

I was taking it as badly as could be expected.

Out to sea the ship's passengers, in search of some new paradise, had crossed the moon's glitter.

Sail on.

I said: 'I don't think that would help the cause. Adoption bureaucrats might not like age but, I can tell you now, they hate divorce. You ask them. Ring them . . . it's office-desk time in Aussie at this very moment. Give it a try.'

I'd let an edge creep into my voice. Couldn't help it.

Karen said nothing.

Then she said: 'I think I could do with a cigarette.'

Karen wanted cigarettes at that sort of time. Three or four a year. She said they did something chemical. I went downstairs and fetched an old packet.

'They could be stale,' I said as I stepped back into the moon's light.

Karen had walked over to the iron railing; she was leaning against it, facing in towards the house. Her head was thrown back, she was looking at the stars.

'Out there,' she said, 'the stars . . . fantastic.'

'I know.'

'You know?'

'I stared at them for years, while I was getting too old.'

'Essington!' She ran across and hugged me. 'It's just that I feel so bitter.'

'That's all right, Blue.' I sat her down. 'Here, have a smoke.'

'I don't feel like one any more.'

'A drink?'

'OK, a drink.'

A couple of glasses into chilled Chablis, tongues and brains lubricated: 'Anyway,' Karen said, 'there just aren't Australian-born babies coming up for adoption. It seems the most likely is from some other country and then there's all the blah blah blah. You know, regulations. Even the age problem . . . they say that forty-seven is the cut-off. But there can't be more than forty years' difference between the age of the would-be parents and the baby.

'It was terrible. I know they have to be careful but the forms were all written in this language, making it sound like a trade or something.'

'Depends how you look at it.'

'What do you mean by that, Ess?'

'Weren't there countries that shut down on having children adopted out into places like the United States? They felt it was a

88

fad, to have this pretty little exotic baby: take the Doberman down to the lost dogs' home, replace it with a cute little Thai kid.'

'Maybe it was. Essington . . . do you think it's a fad with me?'

'No I don't, not at all.'

'Then, what?'

'Well, like I've tried to say before, Blue, there are some things you've got to live with.'

'That I will not accept. Live with! Now I do feel I need a cigarette.'

I pulled one out of the packet, lit it, passed it across. Karen drew in hard. 'They always talk about what you should do . . . what you should live with, Ess. What the fuck should I live with? I should live with what I want to. Who's going to be more right than that?'

Reasonable question.

The cigarette was going down like it was an explosive's fuse.

'There're always people telling other people what they can and what they can't do. Like the bloody Pommy up there trying to organize the lives of the Papunya artists. Would have come out to Australia without a clue in his mind and then he lands some cushy job that allows him to indulge his belated colonial fantasies. All because he speaks with a plum in his mouth! Because he's inbred back to some robber baron.'

The cigarette was out. The glasses refilled. Go on like that and I'd have to trot down for a second bottle.

'Dawn was in good form,' I said, to stem the tide.

'I hate them.'

'I liked all that about sex roles, about society defining what's a man, what's a woman.'

'They sit up there in their nasty-looking buildings and write down what they reckon ought to be the regulations. Most of the time it's them struggling to fill page space, that's what determines the regulations.'

'Dawn's story about the hermaphrodite,' I prompted.

'I don't care about any hermaphrodite. I don't care what sort of genitals they've got . . . that's nobody's problem. People work it out. Essington, what I want is a baby. You know that, I know that. We can't ignore it then, can we?'

'No, Blue, we can't ignore it.'

'But we can't do anything about it either. They've got their regulations, haven't they? They've determined what's best. They do it from averages. That's what it's about, you know . . . average performance. Us, we're no more average than the rest of them. We're we. We'd have about as much chance with an adopted child as anybody else. I mean, the kind of people who are going to sit down and take it, what sort of child are they going to raise?'

'You were going to sit down and take it, Blue. It's the geriatric husband who's the problem.'

'Oh, Ess. I'm sorry about that. I didn't mean it.'

'I only just miss out.' I'd recently had a birthday. Forty-eight years young. Karen had been in Queensland visiting her parents. Part of a long world prowl in search of a way to satisfy this need of hers. The Papunya painters had provided a rational excuse for the trip.

It was her need. I wasn't at all sure I liked children. Wasn't certain that I'd tolerate one about my feet. Not that I wouldn't have tried.

'Those are the rules. There are a lot of other ones as well. You lodge this much money then that much, you get interviewed, you get into line, you get interviewed again, you pay more money . . . average time up to three years.'

'Up to!'

'That's right. I think they said it depends on the country. And there aren't many countries that allow it. Mostly South American.'

We drank up the wine, Karen went for another cigarette. Usually the need was satisfied by the first couple of puffs, then out. I went down for the second bottle. When I returned Karen had moved back inside. It had started to get cold out there: the African heat bank had run out.

I said: 'I liked that bit of Dawn's about the final doctor, the one with a scientific interest.' The hermaphrodite of Dawn's story was going to be burnt, protesting innocence. Innocent of what? 'Was it burnt for being like that or for having been to bed with a woman?'

Karen, shaking her head, not interested in my chatter: 'I don't remember, I really don't, Ess.

'The doctor argued the civic fathers into a stay of execution. When would it have been, Blue, which century?'

'Jesus! Don't ask me.'

'So he poked and sure enough he found a tiny recessed penis, touched it with the end of his finger. And it ejaculated! "Thick and white like a man, not watery like a woman."'

'Did Dawn say that?'

'She was quoting, I think.'

'And at our dinner table!'

'Standards, Blue, they're slipping.'

I guess I dozed off. Karen sat perched up on the end of the bed. When I woke up, minutes or hours later, no way of telling, she was rocking herself, like an elephant . . . or like a baby in a cot.

I thought to myself that there had to be some other way, and then went back to sleep.

Chapter 9

'Was it thick and white or watery?' Karen had her coarse side as well. Obviously the description had stuck in her mind. Such a simple way of sexing the species.

I got an image of giants in white coats conducting the test, holding the people up by their ankles, throwing them into the appropriate pen. The rural background coming out. We used to do that with sheep and cattle.

We were waiting to board a plane for London. Nice airport already jamming up with the summer crowds.

There hadn't been any way of getting Karen to settle down. The thought of adoption was upon her. Thus the trip to London, chasing after possibilities. We were going to check out a couple of international humanitarian agencies to see if there was something between adoption and the long-distance fostering schemes that you see advertised — usually with some big-eyed kid looking like he didn't have a hope in hell of making it through to puberty.

I'd been talking about my Amsterdam experiences. Karen hadn't asked before and I hadn't felt inclined to volunteer the information. For one thing there was my ambivalence over Tina. Even if Karen couldn't give a damn, I still had the right to nurse a private guilt over ideas that had drifted about in my head and come to nothing.

Tina's presence in the car on that last morning hadn't completely cancelled her out. I guess because she seemed to have so little control over herself. I'd more or less assumed that she was with Cornelius Carbentus — the mystery man — because some kind of pressure had been applied. I had an idea for Cornelius: tucking his head under the Holt arm and hammering my fist into it till he said he was sorry. But what did they have over Tina? Was it simply money? She being the poor relative just hanging on? Or was it to do with Robert?

'Watery?' I didn't catch on to the thought behind Karen's reference to Dawn's hermaphrodite story, not at first. We were in the queue — well, in a French approximation of one — waiting to climb on board. She was getting at me about Tina. I asked myself: why stay innocent when you had to put up with that?

A week had passed since I'd got home. There had been the problem of getting the Maserati back. Up near Avignon, where it had expired, they'd demonstrated an unwillingness to take the motor to pieces; instead, the garage concerned got as much money as it could for the towing and investigation. They had managed to replace a water-pump gasket along the way. There had been enough hours in that time to rebuild the entire bloody machine.

I'd rung the previous owner, Molena. He was still to be seen around the bars and restaurants, looking about as close to going bust as the Duke of Westminster.

Molena named a mechanic who'd serviced the car before. The man specialized in the great marques; a lot were brought to him from Monaco. Molena was the born middleman. He would even go along to see the mechanic with me, just to make sure the man knew who he was dealing with.

'A magician,' Molena assured me.

'With that heap, he'd have to be.'

'It's not that bad, my friend, not so bad at all. A car like that, it breaks down from time to time, but so does a great racehorse. We are dealing with creations that are too fine, too perfect for the rough and tumble of our life.'

A poet. Molena was a sweet mouth. That was the kind of talk that had got me buying the bloody thing in the first place. That and predictions of it gaining value while you drove.

Molena was a man of medium height who liked to dress in the most elegant casuals money could buy. Cream colours with touches of pure blue in the Moroccan-made slip-ons. He had me feeling shabby, gave me the impression that I was emitting too much body odour with the excess heat I still couldn't stop producing.

Molena wore a perfume, spicy stuff, so he'd smell nice for the ladies. Molena didn't know what Napoleon knew, that God made the attractions work through body odour. Cover it up and you were liable to sleep either alone or with other out-of-nature neurotics.

Molena had never watched a stallion running with the mob.

On most other things, though, I'd bet he was ahead of the game.

Confident eyes: a kind of open stare that could have been misinterpreted as honest.

He had the big dark eyes of the boy on the bike from the Marais. The one that had got himself blown up, poor bugger. I was getting over that, managing to handle it.

There wasn't any way of disliking Molena. Something in his make-up wouldn't have allowed it.

I'd got into telling him about my life. Was it a collapse of psychic resistance? Did I think I was making a friend? That's the hardest thing for a settler in a foreign land, to make a friend from among the natives. They'll be helpful, polite, attentive; but at the end of the day it was you and them. Three years in France and I'd hardly managed to put a foot inside a local's house.

I was assuming Molena was local. Most of them sported Italian names. Historically, that corner from Nice east had been Italian country.

Life had sometimes felt a fraction lonely out on the Cap, failing to mix. I'd had a world coming to me, but mostly that was an Australian world. People on their global trip, hunting a bed. Friends of friends.

It was a curious feeling, and very artificial.

Even Karen commented on it. She'd thought things might change when we had a baby. That baby would be a kind of link between the worlds.

There I was with Molena and no child. We were sitting at a bar in behind the beach. It was my regular watering-hole. The waiter knew me. Always there was an ice-cream container of water waiting to be served for Desdemona.

We were drinking coffee, Molena musing out aloud about the over-supply of apartments along the coast. Then telling me how he'd spent his whole life trying to get away from the Mediterranean. But never managing to do so. It was the sun, he concluded. He'd been brought up drenched in it. The moves away had led to periods of depression. He'd tried Paris, set up a business there, working with the media — he left that vague: 'media' — doing well enough. But he'd returned for the sun. He said he despised himself for it.

I ribbed him about the car. We laughed. 'Italian steel!' he said. 'But . . . genius!'

'I don't need genius like that.'

I ordered a jug of house rosé. It was good drinking. Especially while chewing on the tiny local olives. It made me think of poetry. No poem in particular but poetry in general.

Later, me and the wine were telling Molena about the trouble with trying to adopt a child. I'd put the whole thing one person removed. Telling him about this friend, about how hard it was. And how you'd think with the number of people in the world with nothing to eat, dying, that there'd be some system for sharing things about — either the people, or the food, or both. It wouldn't matter how bad life was once you were adopted, you'd still be ahead of dying of starvation. That was my argument.

Popping another olive into the Holt mouth. Ordering more rosé, another half-jug.

Molena said that he thought there were other ways to approach the adoption problem. Said to keep him in mind if my friend was interested in learning about them.

'And have the child melt down in Avignon, like the Maserati?'

'Quality assured, Essington.'

We'd got that far, him calling me Essington. It felt good. I decided I liked Molena.

Renardo liked him as well. That was good enough for me. Around those parts Renardo Pinci was respected for his judgement.

We were into our seats on the London plane, Karen and I. I didn't mention that a few days before the roof had blown off a model just like the one we'd boarded. Karen wasn't sure about air travel at any time. She did a lot of it but had to shut off half her mind to sit there. I don't think she believed in the principle involved, didn't think air got displaced; she thought that was just words.

'And other than romp about with this perfect Javanese lady, comparing body juices, what did you do, Ess? Assuming you had the energy left.'

'No problem with the energy. We had vestal virgins to towel us down between bouts.' I wasn't going to let Karen, still enjoying her twenties, get away with talk like that.

'Ageism.' That was what I called it. 'The balance of the time I bear-hugged small affectionate men.'

'Bi-guy! A turn-up for the books.'

'Well, like Dawn said, it's really just gradations all along the same scale. "Our sexuality is ill-defined in ultimate terms." Wasn't that the line?'

'Where did you find the little men?'

I told her about how they found me. I hadn't been going to talk about that either.. Karen already had this impression of me as a man programmed to home in on trouble, as one who even had the knack of conjuring it up.

I didn't see things that way at all.

So I didn't tell her about the van Gogh. Going after that would have been a no, no. Absolutely.

London had sun. That looked nice: red buses shining in its watery light, people coming out of themselves.

The parks looked good as well, with the trees half-way into leaf and narcissus out all over the place — even along the railway line from Gatwick.

Karen had done the arrangements so we were booked into somewhere flash, with Hyde Park over the road and Mayfair tucked away behind. I could never see the point. A bed, in my book, is a bed, is a bed, is a bed. Why pay quadruple for one over another?

'Because it only costs you half anyway, Ess, it's off the tax.'

'Half's still too much.'

'Shut up.'

I shut up. It was the same old argument. We'd be having it when Karen was shoving my wheelchair over a cliff.

I was not to go along for the making of inquiries about adoption. That had been decided. Karen knew what she was doing and she didn't need me leaning over her shoulder getting the whole thing arse about.

I set out to look up my old friend, Grantley Simpson. It was an inspiration. Nice to follow up inspirations. I headed off for his tiny office in Old Bond Street.

Grantley is the Degas expert. You want to know about

something the artist did, some technical trick — and Edgar Degas knew them all — or when it was that he said he'd spoken to intelligent people about art but they didn't comprehend.

Grantley knows the lot.

He knows all about the Degas monotypes I'd inherited from Aunt. He'd spent hours examining them, grinning his shy smile in appreciation.

I drew a blank in Old Bond Street.

That, I guessed, was Mrs Thatcher's economics. The south of England was being bought and sold over and over, the prices shooting up with the action. And there were a lot of good addresses getting a face-lift as well. The poor were turned around, headed back up that north road they'd descended in the days of Dickens.

Money was king. And Grantley Simpson had been banished. It is one thing to know all there is to know about Degas, none of that adds up to owning one of the buggers. Non-acquisitive, Grantley had never seized the opportunity.

I ran him to earth miles out, direction Heathrow. He was living in one of a line of terraces on the main road. Shabby was the word. A landlady type opened the door. She looked me over like she was hoping for a sex criminal. I asked for Mr Simpson, put on my best voice. Gave my name.

'Where're you from?'

'Australia, one hell of a bus trip.'

'I'll bet it was that. Did they take that corner fast, down there by South Africa?'

'Thought it was going to turn over.'

'I expect you did. You know what I say? I say they go round there like that for no better reason than to put the wind up the passengers.'

What I'd taken for a scowl was just her way of observing the world through spectacles an inch thick.

'You'd be a bit weary then,' she added, 'come in.'

So in I went.

'We are very fond of our Mr Simpson,' she said. 'Wouldn't want him to get into bad company, would we?'

'Then I'd better leave.'

'Wicked as you might be, I couldn't turn out one who's travelled so far. Mr Simpson!' Screamed. And again: 'Mr Simpson!'

A plump woman with a face randomly modelled out of putty. Her hair going thin and patchy. Someone who'd had chemotherapy. She had a ring on her finger and was dressed for housework.

'Thank you Mrs . . .?'

'Simpson.'

'You don't mean . . .?'

'No, I do not.'

'A happy coincidence.'

'No coincidence either. Grantley Simpson!' Calling louder. 'He'll be out the back, I shouldn't wonder. That's where he does his work, down the back. I'll just poke my head out the door and see if I can't call him.'

I was standing in the parlour. Knick-knacks all over the place and the walls covered in nondescript prints under soot-smeared glass. There were antimacassars on the chairs, nicely placed and all decorated in the same way. I could smell the damp working its way up the walls. It had begun to creep across the carpet too, as mould.

Makes you wonder, I thought. Then they came in the door, the pair of them.

It took Grantley a moment to place me. Maybe because I was standing with my back to the front window, to its thin, white, lace-edged curtains through which filtered the already-filtered sun.

The recognition took long enough for Mrs Simpson to allow doubt to cloud her time-ravaged face. Then Grantley said: 'Essington!' and sat down. We all breathed out.

'Tea, will it be then?' Mrs Simpson asked.

'I'd love a cup,' Grantley said.

'Me too.'

'Well,' said Grantley, looking sheepish I thought. That was the trouble with getting rich, one of the many, it made the rest of the world act like they thought they'd failed in some way. Either that or downright resentful.

Grantley was viewing me over a pair of half-glasses. I could have sworn that the cardigan was the one he'd worn the day I first met him three years before. Maybe a bit more darning on the elbows — grey into moss green. He kept on touching the glasses with the tip of a finger as though to stop them slipping down his nose.

'Gone a bit long-sighted. Had to get myself a pair.'

There wasn't anything all that new-looking about the specs. Chances were he'd bought them in a junk shop. I'd heard they were all pretty standard, those reading glasses. People got them at around the same time of life. If I was a reader I'd have to get a pair like everybody else.

'How long have you been out here?'

'How long have you been in London?'

'Arrived yesterday,' I said.

'Well.'

'Couldn't wait to see you. Popped along to your old office . . . you'd vanished, you devil.'

'I'm afraid there wasn't a choice in the matter. If it hadn't been for Margery here it's difficult to say where I might have finished up.'

'When we introduced ourselves I thought you'd gone and got yourself married.'

'My brother's widow, Essington. And a fine woman.'

'I can see that.'

In came the tea, and biscuits decorated with pink icing.

We went out to lunch — I insisted. We took a taxi, went to Heathrow, established ourselves at a table in the restaurant at Terminal Four.

'Well, this is nice,' said Margery. 'Grantley, you and your posh friends.'

'There isn't anything posh about Essington, I'm afraid.' Grantley gave me a sly grin.

'Just rich,' I said. 'Never even made a cent of it myself. Inherited wealth, Mrs Simpson, they ought to tax it out of existence.'

'Not till we've eaten, Mr Holt.'

I asked Grantley: 'What's all this about your posh friends?'

'I'm afraid that's Margery's joke, Essington. It's more a question of where have they gone?'

The waiter arrived. They pick them for the smart restaurants. Snobs mostly. They look down on you. Perhaps there's a school where they're taught that. With us three the young man felt he could really look down a long way, like he was peering into the abyss.

For openers he pointed out that there was also a café in the

99

airport. I thanked him for that. Then he handed the menus out, giving the wine list to Grantley, the oldest male.

'What would you like to drink?' I asked Margery.

She raised her eyebrows in reply, as though requesting guidance.

'You name it, we drink it,' I said.

The waiter rolled his eyes.

'Do they have Chateau Ausone?' she asked.

I asked the question of the waiter. He took the wine list back and scanned it.

Eventually he shook his head.

Margery laughed.

I eyed the waiter, beckoned him over. 'Relax,' I whispered so they could hear it in the stalls, 'we're here to enjoy ourselves. And take warning, today you don't have an act that we can't top.'

'Fine then,' he said.

'That's better, isn't it?' I looked to Margery.

'Lovely,' she said. 'Some nice Saint-Émilion, would they have that? Really, I couldn't give a tinker's curse.'

The waiter trotted off the way they do. We went through the menu in silence, Grantley tapping away at his glasses to keep them in place.

I asked him about work.

'Well, to tell the truth, Essington, the question should be: 'What work?'

Margery watching her brother-in-law over the top of the menu.

'But, Grantley,' I said, 'there's a boom going on, an art boom! Surely there's Degas paintings changing hands, authentications, catalogue notes, all sorts of things? That huge Degas exhibition in Paris at the moment . . . the Grand Palais . . . is that where it is?'

'Do you think they'd make up a plate of chopped fresh vegetables?' Margery asked, an embarrassed smile on her face.

'It's what they're there for.'

'Then that's what I'll have. The rest looks very nice, very tempting, but I think for now I'd better stick to the fresh vegetables. Would it be too much, do you think, if we asked for rather a lot of carrot?'

I knew the score, I'd seen it before: chemotherapy, and then diets with crossed fingers.

'I'll just cheat a bit with the glass of wine,' she said.

'Are you certain about the wine, Margery?' Grantley asked.

'Grantley Simpson, it's my own death.'

'Yes,' he said. A small grim smile playing at the corners of bloodless lips. Parchment skin creasing its flaky surface, like he had scurvy.

Grantley had several fresh scars where he'd cut himself shaving. They went with the felt slippers he wore.

'I'm not what they're looking for, Essington. Not these days. The collectors, they're quite a different type. It's this change in the world. I really couldn't say if it's for the good or for the bad. What I do know is that it's real. People are different. It doesn't matter who you are or what you know, if you've got money and it shows, that's what counts.'

'Sometimes I think it's more democratic,' Margery said. 'But it's been no good for you, has it?' Patting him on a frayed sleeve.

'I'll have the sole.' He looked pleased with himself for making a decision.

I had a bloody human casualty on my hands. Two of them probably. That was the way with history, it didn't give a stuff. Bureaucrats were history made mortal; me and Karen with her baby, we were against the league. What we needed was a gigantic and disastrous war someplace. That would be history working for the would-be adopters of children. Right now nothing was on a big enough scale, so they felt free to stick to their rules, and let the people rot.

I couldn't instruct a man to smarten himself up when he knew more about Degas than anyone else alive. But I was sure that that was what was needed. Well presented, Grantley would have been top of the list for the private-collection curator's jobs being created all over the place. The October stockmarket fall hadn't put the frighteners on the big, big operators. They were just getting a second wind, really setting about redistributing the wealth.

The waiter took the orders and didn't even kick at having to ask his majesty the chef to chop up some vegies. He'd found a bottle of Chateau Cheval-Blanc; those globe-trotting businessmen really do themselves proud at airports, the way they spend money that should go into dividends. I said that would do.

After the serious stuff of eating, and once coffee was served (tomato juice for Margery, her third), I brought up the subject of Vincent van Gogh, asking Grantley what he knew about the painter.

'Not, I'm afraid, a great deal, Essington.'

'That means more than most people.'

'I'm sure it does,' Margery interjected. 'They were always alike, Albert and Grantley: studious, devoted to their fields.'

'Albert designed aeroplanes,' Grantley explained. 'He worked on the Delta Wing. There wasn't anything he didn't know about that. Not that it was a success of course.'

'Well,' I said, 'Degas was, and van Gogh. Maybe the Delta will come back some day.'

'I believe it has, Mr Holt.' Margery had trouble calling me Essington. She must have thought it sounded dangerously familiar. I'd force her into it, she'd drift back again, revert. 'The Americans have this thing they're working on, a cross between the Delta and your boomerang. I read about it in the paper. Albert would have been overjoyed to see that. All his dreams come true.'

'You have to go with the market a little, Grantley,' I advised. 'Perhaps you can't just stick to Degas any longer. Your knowledge, you could apply it right across the board. You know that . . . pigments, types of paper, all that stuff; together with your ability to see. I mean it's the big thing, isn't it? You told me yourself: "You look, the quality speaks to you." Your words.'

He shrugged, obviously not wanting to hear.

'It's his eyes as well,' Margery warned, an exasperated tone. 'He believes he's going blind.'

'Blind! Because he needs reading glasses! That's bloody Degas again, you know that don't you Grantley? Degas! He did his late great work going blind. Grantley, listen to me.' He'd fixed his face in a stupid smile, like a kid caught measuring his dick. 'Grantley . . . Bloody hell! what's the use? Excuse the language.'

That to Margery.

'No need to worry about language with me, I've heard the lot. Said most of it in my time too.' You could see Margery barracking for me. It had obviously been eating away at her, watching Grantley throw in the towel.

'When did Albert die?' I asked, to end a long conversational lull.

'A year and a half ago; seventeen months and twelve days to be exact.'

And then she'd got the cancer. They wrote about that: cancer triggered by an emotional shock. Maybe losing a brother had taken what little stuffing there was out of Grantley as well. They can be like that, scholars, no go in them. That's why they take to books in the first place — reading things, writing them. It's a technique for ducking life.

Only life has a way of coming along and knocking at your door.

'I think I've got a job for you.'

There wasn't any way out of that. Not with Margery looking on. He must have owed her something in the way of support, for keeping the ship afloat. Even if that something was spiritual.

'And it's van Gogh.'

'Van Gogh.' He said that wearily.

'It's something, Grantley Simpson, and it's right down your alley.'

'Checking out a lost work,' I explained. 'The only problem is that I have to find it first.'

Now he wore a fixed smile. Like someone acting happy at the foot of the gallows.

'I'm going to find it, don't you worry about that. Well, it's more or less found. Now its just a matter of getting my hands on the thing.'

'So exciting,' said Margery. 'Grantley, you old fraud, you always make art sound so dull.'

'Because it is, Margery. Except when this young fellow comes charging about. It's still dull, it's just that his energy creates an illusion.'

'That's what they do with blobs of paint, Margery,' I interrupted. 'Create illusions, much more exciting than anything I can do.'

'Well, Grantley?' She set him under her steady gaze.

'Van Gogh!' He threw up his hands in despair. 'What would Degas say?'

'"Atta boy", that's what he'd say, and you know it.'

'What can I . . .?' Still protesting.

'The job starts from now, the research. I want you to get all the information you can, so that we are able to establish for certain that the thing's real. And restoration techniques, I think we might need a lot of those.'

'I am not a restorer.'

'We'll see about that. What's a van Gogh worth these days, Grantley? I know it's beneath your dignity to think about vulgar little matters like that. But wasn't the last one to go to auction sold for . . . was it thirty million quid? So how about five hundred for the first week's work. And —' Here I gave Margery a little nudge '— the same again against expenses, then a whole basketful of the stuff on completion?'

Chapter 10

Karen was still at it the next day so I did a bit of footwork around the dealers and auction rooms in New and Old Bond Street and thereabouts. They are all of a kind, the operators. I don't think I'll ever adjust to them, precious types who'll do or say anything to stay in business — mind whores.

I can accept the need to turn a quid. Not that I was ever good at it myself. I guess it's the fundamental dishonesty of the dealers, the way they use phoney erudition, philosophy, yelps of aesthetic joy, even friendship, to make a sale — that's what sickens me. Selling watches outside an East End pub, claiming they haven't fallen off the back of a truck, that's honest by comparison.

Still, it's the art spiv's lack of respect for the truth that makes the forger's job so simple. Slip a fake into their hands and you've got the blind leading the blind — eager sellers, eager buyers, getting the artworks into their system.

I was asking about Degas drawings. They surface from time to time, mostly horses in England. He did a lot of horses. I'd acquired one of them when last in contact with Grantley, a little study, about one-foot square, just under three thousand pounds. With Grantley at my side I'd snapped it up with confidence.

Now I was asking for works by Degas and being given the spiel on the big Paris show: how values were going through the roof.

I wasn't a real buyer. I was trying to drum up a bit of support for my old friend, sticking my oar in. They mention a work, I ask if it's been passed before the expert eye of Grantley Simpson.

Grantley who?

They roll over the staff pretty quickly in those places. Young men in a hurry, eager to put Mummy and Daddy's money into a shop front of their own. What an ambition, running a shop!

Could be I did the old codger some good, more likely I didn't.

Along the way I bought what you might call a pornographic print by the London-based artist, Ron Kitaj: a modern Degas

105

admirer, beautiful draughtsmanship. If I remember rightly, two girls doing something with a man's erect penis. Was it pornographic or erotic? Or both? I thought it would go well with the Degas monotypes I'd inherited.

It was a lithograph. I took it rolled, in a cylinder.

Karen had got somewhere and she hadn't.

Where she'd got made my hair stand on end.

'Essington, it's not just a solution, it's a worthwhile thing to do, a humanitarian gesture.'

'Bullshit it is.'

'I never believed you'd respond like this. You are the bitter end. You know that?'

'At least I've still got my marbles. What do you want to become . . . Josephine Baker?'

'Josephine . . .? I don't care who. It makes sense, it helps people.'

'That's exactly what it doesn't do. It's a wank, that's what it is.'

'A wank! You . . . you wouldn't know what a wank is. I mean you're that far off the mark half the time, Essington. I'm in there getting something together and what do you do? Buy dirty pictures.'

'You don't like the Kitaj, I accept that. It wasn't so much money, Blue. I bought it . . . the man's only one of the biggest things in London.'

'So is that prick. It's revolting.'

'I'm sorry. How's that? I'm sorry I bought it. But that isn't what we're talking about. We're talking about your crazy idea of a foundation. We don't need a foundation.'

'You don't give the thing a chance. You leap on it. Essington, have you so much as bothered to consider what I'm saying?'

'I don't need to . . . since you haven't. It's a desperate move, that's what it is, by someone who's so locked up about something that they can't see the wood for the trees any more.'

'Can't see the . . . I'm trying to do some good, for Christ's sake, and you're off buying pictures of cock sucking! Essington, apart from anything else that's old man's art. The adoption people are right. You're too old. You don't even know what's going on. People don't do that kind of thing any more. AIDS has killed it. And if you don't mind me saying, good riddance.

106

Nobody's interested. It's past, it's all been tried and the consequences are a disaster.

'I'm talking about the future, about a future for the world's children.'

I picked up the Kitaj, tore it down the middle, doubled up the paper, tore it again, kept on going till I couldn't get it in to smaller pieces — till I just didn't have the strength.

'How many children are you going to save, Karen? Six? Are you going to save six? And how do you intend to choose them? The pretty ones, or ones born with deformities; black ones, yellow ones, green ones? Is that what you like about it, the selection, playing God? These people you've been talking to . . .'

She wasn't even trying to interrupt. Tearing up the lithograph had done the trick. Pornographic or not, she was shocked. I threw the pieces over the carpet. That was what you paid for in Mayfair, the deep-pile mushroom-coloured carpet. Big deal!

'They've got their problems,' I continued. 'So they like to work them out by doing good. Or, more precisely, by conning other people into doing good while they draw comfortable salaries, take holidays in Portugal. Think for a minute, why don't you? If you still have it in you, think about the good. What fucking good? You lift a few children out of their families, their society, take them to the south of France, have them injected for every disease ever invented, get them educated — the liberal arts . . . why not the liberal arts? So they get to be what?

'So they get to be like everyone else over this side of the equation. Have you ever stopped to wonder if that's what nature intended? Karen . . . OK these people need food, maybe need a system that allows them to grow food. They need medicine, I'm not going to argue against that. But they don't need to come in their sixes to the south of France to learn to talk through their noses and pick a good wine without too much tannin. That, Karen, is what they do not need.'

She was picking up the bits of the drawing. Staring at me, holding them in the palm of her hand.

I said: 'Careful, it's still pornography, dangerous.'

'I didn't mean you to . . .'

'Oh yes you did, Blue. Tomorrow we can burn the books.'

*

107

Not much said on the trip back to Nice. Not much said there either. Lots of being off at the shop with Dawn: solidarity. And me up against it, being stubborn.

That weekend Mitterrand won another term as President of the Republic and Chirac resigned as Prime Minister.

I drank too much wine at the Bar Plage, then repeated the act the next day. Even Renardo started to look at me strangely, as though he was weighing up the chances of having a word on the subject. Desdemona got an undeserved kick in the ribs for being between myself and a doorway. That surprised her. Surprised me too.

Then I got the letter, postmark Amsterdam; I opened it. Shaky writing in lines going up and down like mountain ranges. Letter forms leaning every which way. It was from Tina Carbentus. It could have been from a child — the sentences.

Jesus, I don't think I've ever read anything so sad. In essence its message was that by the time I'd got through to the signature she would have joined Robert. She thought they'd be happy together over on the other side.

Small chance of that.

She said she was sorry that we hadn't said goodbye. Asked me to forgive her. She said that she knew what was going to happen as I tried to leave but there was nothing she could do about it. Nobody would listen to her. They had forced her to go along. Not being specific, just 'they'.

She wanted God to protect me.

So do we all.

Back to the dissipation. I stayed for a long time in the sun at the Bar Plage, watching rubbish jettisoned from ships of the US Sixth Fleet get landed and then picked up again by gentle, innocent waves. As I sat there I didn't think about Tina Carbentus. Nor did I think of Karen and the agony we were both going through. Then a rock concert got under way on the deck of a destroyer. There'd been launches passing backwards and forwards between the ships, and taking girls out from the shore. The amplifiers were megawatt, the music more like a weapon of war, even from where I was sitting. Electric fuzz.

Desdemona pretended we weren't being bombarded with it. She had her muzzle resting on my lap as though sensing the lostness of my mood, doing what she could. She didn't succeed.

Oh hell!

Do something with yourself, Essington. Get out there, give the world a nudge. That was the thing you knew. When in doubt, act.

Amsterdam. The plane coming in to Schiphol Airport. A clear day so you could see tulips in their colour-matched patches making so many flags of the earth. I'd brought one suitcase and in it the painting I'd purchased on the day set aside to celebrate the birthday of Queen Beatrix.

Very efficient set-up. Straight from the plane to the train and into town. Into the central railway station surrounded by its quota of smack freaks and weirdos. People from all over the world who'd drifted in because they'd heard that it was a good ride.

I carted my suitcase to a hotel, the first I came across. A big American-style affair run by some international chain. Exactly what I hadn't been looking for.

I didn't ask about the cost, I just moved in. Bugger it. They told me I was rich. I was going into training. An evening meal, I ate it with all the trimmings. Then I went up to room seventy-three with its enchanting view of row upon row of well-laid bricks. Still, lack of a view doesn't make much difference in the dark. I looked up Carbentus in the book. Wrote down all the family's numbers and probably a few of people totally unrelated. Then I called Tina's apartment.

No answer. I hadn't expected one. That was the sad thing. The call was made out of hope — or was it curiosity? I tried the canal house. Nothing there either. Both vacant, so that was something I now knew. Nothing much to make of it but I knew it.

The problem was to get into that canal house, Robert's house. I didn't have an answer to that one.

I rang a Carbentus with a lot of initials, the first of which was a 'C'.

A woman answered.

'Can I speak English?'

'Of course.'

'I'd like to talk to Cornelius Carbentus.'

'I will get him. Who will I say is calling?' Right first time! It could get to be my day before the hour came when we turn to pumpkins.

'My name is Essington Holt.'

Silence.

Sounds of the telephone changing hands.

'Mr Carbentus?'

'Where are you ringing from, Mr Holt?'

'Nice, Mr Carbentus, the Côte d'Azur, it's good down here, warm.' I figured that since someone else had answered the phone he wouldn't know the difference.

'What can I do for you, Mr Holt?'

'First, Mr Carbentus, you can apologize.'

'Apologize? What must I apologize for?'

'Fine, forget it. The other thing you can do is tell me where you buried Robert's half-sister. I want to have flowers put on her grave. You may not know it, Mr Carbentus, but we Australians are a sentimental people: we like to remember, and to do what's right.'

He'd been spluttering away through that little speech. When finally able to get a word in he said: 'There is no grave, I'm sorry to have to disappoint. My cousin is alive and recovering from an accident. If you would like to see her . . .'

That gutted my argument. But maybe not my play.

Tick, tick, tick, the mind hunting a response. 'Mr Carbentus, you wouldn't have an address, a phone number for where she is?'

'Indeed I do, if you would wait a minute I will get it for you.'

'This is costing!'

'I will be as fast as I can, Mr Holt.'

When he came back he asked me if I had a pencil. Old-fashioned that, 'a pencil'. I said yes. He said that was good. Then he gave me the details.

'Thank you, Mr Carbentus. Oh, and by the way, how are your little friends?'

'My little friends?'

'Goodbye, Mr Carbentus.'

The businessman type. They keep their wits about them, watch every word. That's the way they make money. But their brains — they've wrapped them up with the kitchen scraps years ago. They are children with the imagination removed by surgical incision.

I slept like a log.

Ate breakfast with two boiled eggs and a ton of toast; three

110

cups of coffee. I felt like Popeye after a dish of spinach, even using the stairs to return to my room, taking them in pairs. I arrived red-faced and panting at the door of number seventy-three.

I tried the hospital telephone number. It was, Cornelius assured me, a direct line to Tina's room. Well, we should see.

'Tina?'

'Who is that?' Very cautious.

'Essington Holt.'

'Essington!'

'I got your letter.'

'You did?' Flat.

'I'm pleased to hear your voice. I can't tell you.'

'That is nice to say.'

'I mean it,' I assured her.

'From where are you ringing?'

'Are you alone in there?'

'Why do you ask?'

'Cautious, that's all.'

'You are in Amsterdam? How did you know to ring this telephone?'

'I rang around, made inquiries. You know, Tina, this is the world out here, no secrets.'

'You sound the same,' she said. 'You are — how should I tell you? — you are so different.'

'From what?'

'From everything.'

'And is that bad?'

'No,' without a hint of hesitation, 'that is very good.'

'The house on the Looiersgracht, are you still in residence there?'

'I am in hospital.'

'I know, but.'

'Well . . . I expect so.'

'I liked it,' I said.

'You want to stay there?'

'Is that possible? Do you have a key I could get?'

'You are crazy, Essington Holt. After what has happened to you. I was watching you that day. I saw you and the two men that they had waiting for you.'

111

'I know, I know. You said in the letter. Tina, I don't want to go over that. I understand that you were being leaned on.'

'Leaned on?'

'They were making you do things that you might not otherwise have done.'

'It is true, Essington.'

'I said I understand that. They are after the van Gogh painting, aren't they? You don't have to agree with that. I'm just letting you know what I know. It might assist you in some way, to know that I'm on your side — on your side and Robert's.'

'That is our side.'

'It was like that, wasn't it, Tina, you and Robert?'

'It does not make you angry?'

'It's not my business. That's your life, your memory.'

'You are . . . is it like a breath of fresh breeze?'

'I only wish a whole lot of people thought that.'

'Your wife . . . what does she think?'

'That's a question I'd rather you didn't ask. The key?'

She told me how to get it, from the desk at the small hotel around the corner, on the Prinsengracht. She would ring.

'Tina, one more thing. Do you mind if I don't come to see you for a few days? I'll ring. I'd prefer it isn't known that I'm in town.'

'They will see you at the house.'

'That I will try to get around.' Futile intention.

The front door was the only access. I decided that there wasn't a lot of point in hanging about trying to work out a way inside undetected. If they were crazy and under-occupied enough to watch for my return, then so be it. I went in through the painted door, saw the three pictures in place, headed straight on up to the next level.

I rang Grantley.

I thought about Tina lying there. I wondered how she'd tried to do it this time. There is no certainty like a leap off a tall building. That way you avoid hospital as well. A gun, well you'd think . . . except Vincent van Gogh had managed to botch it: taking two days to die, spending the last one sitting up in bed smoking a pipe. That, after shooting himself in the chest!

Imagining Tina, it was with her wrists bandaged. Again.

I guessed she felt ashamed of herself. She'd sounded tentative on the phone, uncertain of the response she could expect. And why not after the car episode?

I decided I didn't like the Carbentus clan, made it a blanket decision. Fuck them, every man jack of them. You might have thought they'd have produced a soul, someone from among their ranks, capable of holding that woman's hand, a person who could tell her at least that it was all right.

Then, on the other hand, your suicide is your suicide. They make their own rules.

I got to thinking of Karen. Our clash in London. Never before quite so nasty, not the two of us together. Something had been fractured as a result of that. Time, I guessed, would let me know exactly what that something was.

They could fill Villa du Phare with kids if they wanted, if it brought harmony. Was it too late to say that? If it brought Karen back on to an even keel. What she was into was something I obviously couldn't even start to understand — the entire landscape was different out there in female land. There were boards around its horizon to keep me out.

I got stuck into a bottle of Dutch gin — drinking thimbles of it as chasers to beer I'd found in a well-stocked cupboard.

I was going to get stoked.

Oh yes, that was very clever. One, two, three, down the hatch.

Karen standing on my feet. Us two dancing out the windows and on to the balcony. All of Essington, all five-foot-four of Karen, standing up on her toes on my feet, head tilted, lips slightly apart, watching me with those alert green–blue eyes. That long neck . . . us naked — being noble savages — Desdemona following the action, trying to understand.

Come on, Essington!

I ripped the top off another beer. Tossed down a gin.

The phone is a kind of prop for loneliness, for disorientation. Well it always is for me. Dump me somewhere unfamiliar and I'll reach for the hand-piece, start dialling numbers. We're all mad in our fashion. Why not indulge it? So, why not fill the house with children? With anything that Karen had in mind.

Shouldn't that be what love is? Not some kind of capitalism. Not the exercise of power.

'Karen!' The instant the receiver lifted at the other end.

113

It was Rebecca. Mrs Holt was not there. I recited the number at the canal house and the one at the hotel. I didn't ask for anyone to ring.

There had been calls from Molena.

Rebecca didn't know what he wanted. She gave me his number. Probably that the Maserati was declared dead and they were concerned about funeral arrangements. Still, I liked Molena. I rang him.

'Essington!'

'I'm in Amsterdam.' I realized at the start of the conversation that I'd developed a need for this cool spiv — my friend; I didn't want it to be otherwise.

I had the beer in one hand, the phone in the other. I was telling him about Amsterdam, hamming it up, making it sound flatter than it was, putting tulips behind every passing ear.

Molena said: 'The Dutch girls, did you notice Essington, they laugh, they have the big laugh, loud?'

I said, no, that I hadn't.

'Oh, but they have. I was in love with a Dutch girl. A very tall girl . . .'

It felt good, talking to this friend about girls. I took a big swig at the beer; I reached over, filled the thimble with gin.

Good, good, good.

'She was called Sophie. She would put her arm about my shoulder, called me her "little friend". Essington, we made love in English. Me . . . you know . . . I hardly speak a word. We managed. She was a wonderful girl, Sophie. Her hair was thick, gold, it glistened like the stalks of wheat.

'But she could not marry me, Essington. Her parents wouldn't permit it. They told her that I was a dago. That I was just a blonde girl's fantasy. They sent her to America.'

'That's a sad story, Molena.'

'It broke my heart.' He laughed. He had a good laugh. 'Essington,' he changed tone, 'I've a business idea, it may interest you.'

'Business? I'm not sure . . .'

'Babies, Essington. You said you had a friend who wanted to adopt a baby.'

'I did, did I?'

'You mentioned that they were having problems with officials, with paperwork.'

114

'They were?'

'I have a business deal that could solve the problem for your friend and make money at the same time.'

'We're not talking about snatching?'

'Are you trying to offend me?'

'Molena, I look on you as a friend, as a good friend. I don't want to offend you, nothing is further from my mind.'

'What I have to propose must have trust each way. Nothing written, but trust, Essington. It is the only way to do it. And I am able to assure you that only the very best interests of everybody will be considered.'

I could only half concentrate, still I caught the gist.

'You're on, Molena, long as it sounds reasonable.'

'More than reasonable.'

'It looks good . . . you're on. I'll tell you what, I'm getting back there in around four days. We'll work it out from there.'

'I should go ahead, put it together?'

'Long as it's as you say.'

'Essington . . . you don't mind me asking, are you all right?'

'I'm a little drunk, that's all.'

'You want to talk this over some other time?'

'Put it together. But, like I said, it's got to feel good . . . for everyone.'

I celebrated with another gin. Maybe I was going for the clear fire-water a little faster than I was going for the beer.

Claude Molena, I liked the man. It was very sad about his lost Dutch love. Passing into a stupor, trying to figure out something I could do about it, some way to get the girl back for him.

Except I didn't know her name, did I? Sophie — by itself, that wasn't enough.

'Grantley,' I'd said, 'there has to be a way of you letting me know that you've arrived, to expect you.'

'I've seen it on television,' he said. He was really going downhill out there on the edge of town, watching the telly. That wasn't Grantley. 'You let the phone ring so many times, then put it down and ring again.'

'How many times, do you reckon?'

'Why not three, Essington?' It was good to see him getting into the spirit of things.

I'd noticed in London that he'd elected to disregard Karen's gesture of a couple of years ago. She'd given him a cake of soap. Making no joke about it. Gave it to him gift-wrapped.

The clean Aussie girl, two showers a day.

Grantley had missed the point altogether, but took no offence; he'd said thank you. Perhaps he had the soap still, wondering what to do with it.

As agreed the phone rang three times. Well, maybe three times. God alone knew the number — God and Grantley — because I only woke as it stopped.

Then it rang again.

'Hello?'

'It's me.'

'Grantley, let me think.' With what? 'You've got money?' I asked.

'A hundred pounds.' And proud of it.

'The camera?'

'I've got that as well.'

'Good.' Still trying to get the brain to function. 'Change the hundred into guilders.'

'I have done that.' Indignant now at being taught to suck eggs.

'Then get a taxi to here.' I gave him the address. 'Should cost you about fifty of the local money. Oh, and Grantley . . .'

'Yes?'

'Hang on. No . . . I can't remember what I was going to say.'

'You were going to ask if I'd bought some film.'

'Have you?'

'Of course.'

Two minds, one thought.

Chapter 11

My five hundred as wages was gone, together with the money for expenses. On top of that Grantley had dived into those of Margery's savings that were standing in the way of her pension benefits.

All this cash went into the fares, the spending money he'd changed to guilders, and an Olympus camera with fifty-milli-metre lens featuring a macro facility. There was also a light-weight tripod. That was left over from when Grantley had sold his own Nikon. In his game you need camera gear as a tool to record what you're looking at, using the photos as a memory prod when searching after detail. Well, that's what they say, and what they do, as well. Except Grantley, he relied on his memory. That Nikon of his had seen very little use.

Of course Grantley was a terrible purist, constantly bemoan-ing the way photographic reproduction had eclipsed real contact with works of art. In the late twentieth century people were even buying the stuff from photos, he'd complained. I knew it was true, particularly the market in new art, in the 'bad painting', where nuances of surface, tone or colour made little or no difference.

We photographed the frightful cubist composition using a tungsten film and every movable light in the house to illuminate a small room at the back that we set up as a studio, a room that wouldn't give off a telltale glow into the street. We took the painting at every plausible exposure on three films — one of them colour negative, for prints. The other two were for transparencies. All that work was just to make sure there was sufficient reference material from which I could slap up a copy of the work to slip into place on the wall should that prove necessary.

Before Grantley and I went out for a meal I took a look at the canvas he'd managed to rustle up for our little game. Perfect:

aged stretcher, the dimensions were right, the fabric appeared old, dusty, discoloured. Not an easy thing to find, not without a picture on its surface. And this one even had the prepared ground for painting old enough to be turning yellow.

He told me it had been a lot of trouble finding the thing. In the end he'd resorted to making it up himself.

'The rust on the tacks?'

'Salt water.'

'How are the mighty fallen! A forger no less, Grantley!'

He just shook his head, looked a little dazed. Because what I'd said was true, too true. And he wasn't doing it just for the money, although I had the feeling that his sister-in-law would have had a word or two to say on that score if he'd refused. He, poor bugger, was doing it for friendship.

Dangerous stuff.

In the cold light of day I wondered if I had over-prepared for this forgery work, if I'd allowed for too many possibilities. The idea, my idea, was to use three paintings: the three-card trick. And, if we were hunted out of that house before I'd got things arranged as intended, it was going to take a lot of photographic colour fidelity to put myself back into the game. Because that was when I'd have to turn up with a replica of the cubist work so that it could take its rightful place over the door of the wall safe.

I looked out the second-storey window and over the canal. It was still early, the sun hadn't made an impression on the general blanket of mist. On the water itself the retired hippy type who lived on the barge tied up opposite the front door was getting about, half pace, picking things up, putting them down somewhere else. His cat following at heel.

Over the far side a car pulled up and a man got out of the passenger's side. He looked across at the building I was in — a glance only — and strolled off in the direction of the Prinsengracht. The car rolled on the other way, heading out of the town centre. The driver might have been familiar, but then again he might not have been. Just a face behind the wheel. Could be he was a small man like either of the two who'd taken a poke at me on the previous visit.

You can't afford to let yourself get paranoiac.

Grantley was on his back, snoring lightly. I shook him awake,

118

indicated the bathroom, living optimistically, and trotted into the kitchen to make coffee.

I left him to examine the painting we'd photographed the night before, while I went off shopping. Instructions: no answering phones, no opening doors. Had he got that right? Yes, he'd got that right.

I made for Leidsestraat, trying to get in amongst the main shops at that end of town. I dropped the films off at a processing place — the fourth I'd tried — that guaranteed getting transparencies back the same afternoon. The prints were no problem anywhere, but transparencies required a different kind of processing with not so many outlets that could handle it quickly.

Then I traipsed off looking for an art-supply shop and a hardware store. It was a couple of hours before I made it back to the house.

I saw him as I approached the street door. He had moved over to our side of the canal and was chatting to the barge dweller, who now had the cat in his arms. I paused for an instant, considered, then crossed over to the pair of them. I said hello; a civil being with a civil tongue in its head, that was me.

'Hi there,' answered the barge dweller. A native of the US of A. Convivial enough, though he gave me the once over, reading what there was about the Holt features to be read.

The other man, the one I'd seen earlier alighting from the car, he smiled — nervously, I might have thought, as though I'd caught him doing something that he shouldn't have been doing. He told me that it looked as though it might clear up.

I certainly hoped so.

The barge dweller wanted it to be sunny too.

We were agreed. There ought to have been more of it, sunshine.

'Ah, well,' I said, 'can't just hang around chatting. There's work to do.' I held up the plastic bag from the hardware store.

'What is it you are about?' the man who had got out of the car asked, but not seeming all that interested in my reply.

'Painting,' I replied. 'Me . . . I'm Vincent van Gogh reincarnated.'

'Well,' said the American, 'keep your ears on.'

Jesus, he laughed at that. Thought it was terribly funny.

119

'What's that you said? I can't hear you, I've got a bandage over my ear?'

It was an old joke. I winked at the watchman, if that's what he was. He'd shoved his hands deep into the pockets of a military-style quilted jacket. Not knowing what to think of such mind-blowing repartee, he slouched off. He said it had been nice to meet me. He said the same thing to the barge dweller.

Inside the canal house my friend Grantley was sitting at the second-storey window with the spectacles slipped right down to the tip of his nose, down to where it formed a little rosy lump. He was making clucking noises with his tongue. Well, that was until I pulled out a packet of biscuits I'd bought, those and a carton of milk.

What would he like?'

He'd like a nice cup of tea, his very words.

I made him one while he continued to peer at the canvas, mainly at the back.

'Well, Grantley, what have we there?'

'Difficult to say, Essington. The only thing we can be sure of is that what is visible is not necessarily its most significant property.

'You see here, on the back —' His finger traced the lines where the oil had leaked through the ground into the fibres of the canvas — 'that would indicate there is a painting under this monstrosity. One that was painted with too much medium, or the paint was applied very thickly. They both amount to the same thing, both would produce a similar result on a poorly prepared commercial canvas like this. Both locate a lot of oil in one spot.'

'Oil which will travel, migrate?'

'Given half the chance, indeed it will. It will work its way through any layer it is able to penetrate. It's in the nature of the molecule. While the surface of the oil-paint mix is reacting with the air, forming a skin, what is underneath remains relatively fluid. It will migrate, true enough. The skin, of course, delays the drying underneath. It is a problem with thick paint.'

I knew from previous experience that I was going to have to endure a lot of being lectured at. That was the way Grantley carried on when there was an audience: he bent over his work, fiddled about, thought out loud, making the connections.

A lot of what he was going to tell me I would already know, but why interrupt? It could be that I would be acting the know-all at just the moment when he was offering something completely new.

Passing the cup of tea, strong as he liked it, to tan his insides, I asked about my theory. How was it standing up?

It was doing fine. 'Mind you, it's an act of vandalism of the very worst kind.'

'Unless it was done properly, by someone who knew what it was all about.'

'How likely is that, Essington? By the way, what lovely biscuits.'

You'd have thought he had worms. I gave him another though, to keep him at it.

'If it was done properly, Grantley, wouldn't it be the perfect way to preserve, as well as to hide, a painting? No air, no light.'

'Could a barbarian do a thing properly? Only a barbarian would shut a painting up like this, lock it away so it couldn't perform its purpose, so that it can't be viewed.'

'Or it was done in barbaric times.'

'A possibility, Essington. Still, I fear we are about to discover some terrible, irreparable damage.'

'And, even worse, the damage will be of no account. What we find under there may not be what I think it is.'

'Precisely.'

Stage one of what I'd decided on was to paint a copy of the cubist work over the landscape I'd bought from the street stall. And we didn't want to destroy the original until that had been done, just in case there was a stuff-up of some kind. As to how good my reproduction would need to be, there was no way of telling. Had anybody ever bothered to look at the thing anyway? Grantley hoped not. I suspected not. Nobody, that might be, except Robert Carbentus. And he wasn't around to raise objections.

If there was a problem with time or my short patience, getting final detail right could be done from the photographs. No chances had been taken, something had to come out from all those exposures we'd tried.

I was fiddling about in the rear room where we'd taken the photos. The drawing came first, getting it right before starting to paint. The window was open to disperse the fumes of the acetone

121

solvent waiting to evaporate out of a line-up of little cans of hobbyist's colour I'd bought — that was just as soon as the lids came off. I had the full range of those colours available and was hoping that they hadn't changed too much since the cubist painting had been originally made.

Carefully, using a ruler and Chinagraph pencil, I drew a grid of squares over the original. Then I drew them again, the same proportions, over the weakish impressionist-style landscape.

'Why did you ask me to bring this canvas from London, Essington, if you don't intend to use the thing?'

'For safety's sake. Didn't want to be caught short. I still can't say if we'll need the thing. But, Grantley, better sure than sorry.'

That wasn't the entire truth. Yet, at that stage, how much did I know of what I intended? Really, I was improvising as we went along, and because that was the method, I'd played safe, making sure I had enough of everything. And, up my sleeve, there was the three-painting-trick idea. But keep it to yourself, Essington, that's the way.

Using the same system as I'd been taught in Geography at school where we applied it to drawing maps, I copied the picture's outlines from the original, working square by square. That way you don't develop a collective distortion; you can go back and check that the copy has the elements in the right places. In the old days artists used that method for drawing from nature, looking through a frame squared up with a grid of taut wires. They even had a headrest so the viewer's position didn't vary. The poor devils had been labouring to turn themselves into cameras, that's what it amounted to.

While working at the drawing I pushed a litre can of acetone solvent over to Grantley and asked him to have a go at a corner.

'A moment, Essington. I am a scholar, not a conservator. Distinct categories, I'm afraid.'

'Not out in the real world they're not,' I said. 'There isn't the time or the space for demarkation disputes out here.'

'I simply wouldn't know how. Even if it didn't go against every instinct, against all my training.'

'You know how, Grantley. You can wash dishes. We're going to wash this painting. It's a cinch. Go for it kid.'

'No.' Obstinate old shit.

'Fucking don't then!' I could have forced him to drink the acetone, that's how I felt — the old Essington flash point.

Self-control. I kept on drawing, working my way across the uninspired design.

Grantley sulked.

'Have a look out the front window then,' I suggested. A make-yourself-useful tone. 'But not from downstairs. See if there's a character watching, would you? And a man on a barge. Just check up on them for a minute or two. It might keep your mind off tea and biscuits.'

'Watching?'

'That's right, Grantley. They think we're on to something.'

He shuffled off. I noticed for the first time that he'd done Holland the courtesy of removing his slippers, fitting himself out instead with down-at-heel, rubber-soled fake brogues. The only thing they lacked was a lace in one of the pair.

It wasn't long before he was back. No sign of the boatman, but a man in a jacket like I'd described was leaning against a wall over the canal. He seemed to be gazing at the front of the building we were in.

You could see that put the wind up Grantley.

'As long as he doesn't come in before we get out,' I commented, as casually as I could.

Grantley asked if there was a cloth, perhaps he'd try the acetone.

Psychology, Essington.

The room where we were working had a tall window giving on to a kind of no-man's-land between buildings. For what served as garden down there a weed had pushed through a crack in a few square metres of concrete. A lot of dispersed cool light came through the glass and fell on to the long trestle table I was using to support the canvases.

It wasn't so cramped. It was hard to tell precisely what the room had been used for. Wooden shelves of various dimensions covered one wall; these were empty except for the occasional randomly placed tin or bottle of some household cleaning fluid. Things like brooms and vacuum cleaners were shoved against another wall. Yet it was much too large for a broom cupboard. Big enough for a bedroom. Perhaps, if it wasn't for the Queen's

123

birthday each year, it would have been filled with a bachelor's junk.

Now it was filled with acetone fumes: Grantley rubbing gently at a corner of the composition, directly on the crudely painted key-pattern edge of what was supposed to represent 'tablecloth'. It was vanishing under the solvent.

The painting was done in lacquer. That was what you'd use if you wanted to cover another one underneath. Lacquer, it came off like nail polish when rubbed with acetone, it's what nail polish is.

'No more, Grantley. Wait till I get further along the track with this.'

'I do hope, if you're right in your supposition, Essington, that we don't turn up one of his Paris works.'

How was that for stuck up? 'Getting choosy are we? Not so long ago you didn't expect we'd get much at all under that lot. Then you were too hoity-toity to have a go.'

'That was before I actually set eyes on that man over the canal. Then, suddenly, I thought to myself: Someone else is thinking in the same way that Essington is thinking. That fellow over there is being paid so much an hour.'

'Mercenary, that's what you are, Grantley. And I thought you'd dedicated your life to aesthetics.'

'"There is no wealth but life" — Ruskin, Essington.'

Pleased with himself, my partner shuffled off to make another cup of tea. I guess he wanted to take one more peep out the window. I hoped he wasn't getting himself seen. The trick, I always thought, was to look as devil-may-care as possible in life. It kept the opposition on edge.

'He went completely to pieces in Paris.'

'Who did?' The biscuit didn't taste so good with an acetone nose. They reckoned that was the worst thing you could do, eat and use the stuff at the same time. Cancer!

'Van Gogh.'

Grantley was dunking.

'Up till then he'd been working in a particular style. His dark browns, you know the work. Realist, in a fashion. Realist subjects, certainly. And then he went to the art capital, to Paris. I always had the impression it was in Paris that he lost his way and

124

also, I believe, it was the sophisticated city itself that dealt a final blow to his mental health. The van Gogh mind, never reliable mind you, Essington, became a catastrophe.

'His brother, Theo, was an art dealer there, as you know. He was a successful member of an important dealing house. What is more he had made contact with the most advanced of the younger painters. That was how Vincent, the older brother, came to meet those people who now, when we look back, we see as the great painters of the age. It could of course have been as simple as the fact that he drank too much. There seems to be evidence for that conclusion.'

Grantley poured another cup of tea — for himself. The sure sign of the addict, not to offer it around.

'He hunted about for a style. Madly ambitious, always. That is an essential difference between so many of those artists and my beloved Degas. He was such a civilized man. Ambitious for his art but a private man, keeping himself to himself. Happy to look back at the great past to find his models. And he was a major innovator, Essington . . .'

'And anti-Semitic.'

'We must forgive genius.'

'That would be up to Dreyfus, wouldn't it?'

Grantley shrugged.

He continued while I put the finishing touches to my copy of the uninspired, but luckily simple, drawing: 'Van Gogh was to try to imitate each of those brilliant men in turn. He stole their subjects, he stole their system of paint application, their colour. Totally eclectic, mad with ambition, deeply frustrated because he wasn't getting anywhere. Perhaps that, Essington, was the explanation for the drink.'

'"Hats off gentlemen, a genius,"' I muttered as I lifted the lids off my row of cans.

'Schumann.'

'What?'

'Schumann, his line, I believe. On Chopin.'

'You scholars.'

'Mind you, Essington, we are talking about a product of northern Protestantism. Van Gogh was brought up in a small town, surrounded by poor peasants. He came to Paris, a man who had already suffered a severe nervous breakdown. Imagine him hobnobbing with the likes of Lautrec for instance, an aristocrat. The lot of them so comfortable in their bohemianism . . . all except Gauguin, the restless soul in search of an escape from our civilization.

'Van Gogh simply did not fit in. He knew it, his new acquaintances knew it. Exactly how much he was suffering while trying to arrive as an artist can be seen in his Paris self-portraits. In these we see him examining his own madness, trying to understand it. It was the man in those self-portraits with their strong paint, their crudely expressionist marks, who packed up and made the journey to Arles.'

'Where he lived unhappily ever after, Grantley.'

'Where he had two amazing years of production and then could take no more. He was forced to retreat north again to a village outside Paris.'

'Where he shot himself.'

'Where he shot himself, indeed.'

I'd been getting the colours down during the lecture. Making notes of all the values in the original rather than attempting to render the finished product straight off. That could be done later, if necessary, from the photos.

Time was the thing. Those people out there, they were watching. That, I felt sure, was because of my meeting with Robert in Paris. They believed it had taken place, and now reckoned I knew where the thing was. They were providing lots of opportunity for me to find it. But keeping tabs on us at the same time, so I couldn't get away with the prize.

That was going to be the big trick. If I was right, if it was a van Gogh under that guitar and tablecloth and frightful colour — it was the colour that seemed to point to the idea of lacquer in the first place — then the main difficulty would be in getting the picture out of the country.

Not only could the Carbentus clan try and stop me, they also had the law on their side. No one in Holland wanted a work by their belatedly favourite son slipping over the border. No one at all.

As I got the colours established I prevailed upon Grantley to rub out a bit more of the painting. Not that we were revealing a lot of anxious, full-colour brush strokes. Not a bit of it. We were getting down to a general dirty brown.

126

'I'll be remembered as the man who destroyed a van Gogh with acetone.'

'The way things are, Grantley, you're not going to be remembered at all.'

'I don't care so much about immortality. But my professional reputation!'

'Cruel as it sounds, there isn't so much of that left either. I went around, tried to drum up a bit of business for you, did some consciousness raising. They don't remember, Grantley.'

With dignity: 'I have my publications.'

'It's a new world out there. They chew things up then spit. No sentimentality any more. All those bright young men waiting to boot you out of the way. You've heard of that expression, "wasting space"?'

'I am pleased to say, no, I have not. Well, that was until you've been unkind enough to introduce it just now. Have you considered, Essington, that you have something of the bully about you? A trait that you might do well to watch, if you don't mind my saying.'

'If I do?'

'Who was it that said . . .?' Finger jabbing the glasses, thinking.

'Grantley, enough quotes for one day.'

'I'm afraid it's gone right out of my mind.'

'The Lord be praised. Now get into it, won't you? Rub on.'

His reluctant hand wet the rag with acetone; he applied it to the vanishing picture.

I was mixing up a nasty mauve for the key pattern when I noticed that I'd traced a variation in its geometry. That was where Grantley was gingerly rubbing away on the original. It was gone. It hadn't registered while I'd been drawing the copy. That must have been while I was listening to the scholar's dissertation on van Gogh in Paris. The wanderings of the mauve line, turning its right angles — suddenly it struck me that they formed the letters 'P' and 'L'. Like a signature. But carefully hidden. The person who had made the painting wanted to be remembered.

For what?

Someone should have been able to make something of those initials. We'd rubbed them out. Not to worry, they were safe and sound in the photographs.

I had backache. Stretching, rolling my arms over in their sockets, opening and shutting my hands. I wandered about. Out the front window, still the same man. He was now on our side of the canal. A hell of a job, a real argument in favour of going on to higher education. He had a blank, stupid face, and shoulders like a weightlifter. No neck that I could see: the head grew straight out of the shoulders. Bloody lucky they hadn't recruited him for the street confrontation of my first visit. '

I gave Tina a ring. She was fine. Just fine, Essington. She sounded tentative on that subject. But not at all on the fact that they knew I was in town again.

'They wonder what I want?'

'They know. I can't convince them that they are wrong.'

'Tina, would you do me a favour?'

'What can I do from a hospital bed?'

'You could think.'

'I fear there is too much thinking already. That is what the doctors are trying to tell me.'

'Then maybe what I've got will be good for you. Get your mind on to something else. That's what they say, Tina. Get out of the cycle, the bind.'

'You must want to do that.'

'You don't?'

'I do not know what I want.'

'Then try and think of this: Did Robert ever say or do anything that might indicate that he had, not necessarily a van Gogh painting, but something valuable in the house?'

I caught a sigh, expressive of nothing so much as lack of interest.

'Tina, there is a man outside at this minute, he's watching. There has to be a reason for that, doesn't there? Don't you understand that?'

'A man outside the house? You are sure?'

'Nothing more certain.'

'You must be very careful.'

'It's this Cornelius, isn't it? He's after something. He thinks I at least half know where and what it is.'

'But, Essington, this is a crazy thing. Cornelius wouldn't hire a man to watch you. You aren't mistaken about this person? Or perhaps he is a man who has nothing to do. He is

128

watching another house . . . a jealous lover, for instance; a robber.'

'I talked to him.'

'You have talked with him? Then why do you ask me?'

'I didn't ask you, Tina. What I asked you was to think back about Robert, about the painting. He told me he had a van Gogh. Why would he invent that? It has gone somewhere. Nobody knew Robert as well as you did. You must know something . . . maybe something you've forgotten. It happens.'

'You are suggesting I lie to you?'

'I'm suggesting that you should hunt about in your brain, that's what I'm suggesting.'

'You sound angry now.' Like a child!

'Fucking hell! Angry! Tina . . . now listen. Can you concentrate? Do it for your own good. The painting?'

'He was unhappy.'

'So are we all.'

'He was dreadfully unhappy.'

'Since when?' I thought of the face I'd glimpsed in the Marais, examined it. Hardly unhappy.

'Terribly. He had been unhappy for months.'

'Because of you?'

'No. We were happy, Robert and I.'

'Why then?'

'I cannot say, or I would have been able to help him.'

Sure, slitting her wrists must have helped him a lot. That was the way to go, building up a chap's confidence in the idea of the continuity of things.

'How many months would you say?'

'I could not be exact. Essington, it was so painful. Painful to remember.'

'It wouldn't have been money by any chance? You said he looked after the family finances.'

'Money? Why should it be that?'

'I've got to go now, Tina. Keep your chin up, won't you? And, if you think of anything, let me know. Tell you what, I'll ring tomorrow. I'm not taking calls here, I prefer it that way. You see, I'm afraid of what I might hear from the other end.'

If the clan cross-examined Tina then that call I'd made to

her might buy time. As far as they were concerned I was still hunting the van Gogh.

Me, I was convinced that we were only a layer away.

Grantley had about four square inches of the lacquer removed. What might at first sight have been thought the brown of one of the northern van Gogh paintings, turned out to be nothing of the kind. You could see that by turning the picture over, examining the back. There was little correspondence between the brown and the marks where the oil had soaked through the canvas fibre.

Grantley was poking the surface very carefully, investigating the texture. He asked me to take a look.

It was rubbery.

That felt good, full of promise. I'd thought that if there was a van Gogh under there it would only be because it was in hiding. Therefore the telltale pattern of brush strokes would have to be hidden as well. I'd assumed a filler, some chalk mixture — chalk and a glue. That would have explained the curious sense of thickness of the canvas.

But the filler wasn't chalk, not at all. Instead it had a gelatinous feel. Gelatine — sculptors sometimes use it to make flexible moulds. Or they used to do, before the age of plastics.

It could make sense. Coat the painting with a layer of gelatine. Not a bad system. That would make two layers, each with a different solvent required. Acetone for the final painting, the disguise.

I guessed hot water for the gelatine.

The phone rang as it had done half a dozen times that morning. I let it ring out.

Chapter 12

The canvas we were working on was sixteen inches by twelve. Grantley postulated that this pointed towards it being a Paris picture, or earlier. He said that although there were many exceptions, once Vincent went south the size tended to increase.

That kept Grantley wondering about the quality of what we were set to discover, if it turned out to be a van Gogh. Funny that, Grantley going on about quality. Any van Gogh would have been beyond my wildest dreams. And him worrying about the Paris pictures — bloody old woman.

I was more interested in following through with my initial hunch. If I found a painting by Vincent I was going to be more than happy. Even if it was only some canvas on which he'd scraped his brushes clean. I had a lot of mind invested in the venture. I'd walked out on a difficult situation at Cap Ferrat and now I was hoping to pick up a compensation prize. I needed that, for self-esteem as much as anything.

What's more I seemed to be getting there. The satisfaction? To be right, just for once.

I got Grantley to concentrate on working the solvent all around the edges of the canvas so they'd be clear of the lacquer. Meanwhile, I kept on with the reconstruction of the vanishing monstrosity.

Grantley had demolished the packet of biscuits and was on to his God-knows-how-many cup of tea. We were well into the post-lunch period, me trying to go faster all the time. The guard was in position and still on his lonesome, although there had been a moment when he might have just finished talking to a well-dressed man in a soft-brimmed brown hat who I caught sight of sauntering off into the distance. Or was that Holt fantasy?

Just a thought.

I still had to solve how I was to collect the photos. That was a problem: not to get followed, heavied.

And then the other problem: how much time were we going to be allowed? What would happen once it ran out?

My impulse was to keep up the pace. To get on with it. Grantley wanted to eat biscuits.

Anyway, we were out of biscuits.

I was for immersing the picture. If it was gelatine then the way I worked it out the water would soften it so it peeled off like a sheet. There couldn't have been all that much adhesion between it and the painting's surface. More likely it was just stuck there by virtue of surface tension.

Unless it wasn't gelatine.

'Grantley, this isn't the National Gallery, we aren't on salaries. Nor do we have the rest of our lives to play about vying for the golden handshake.

'Essington, I must register my disapproval.'

'Did you get that down, miss? Grantley, this isn't a meeting, there aren't any witnesses. We just do the thing. The world's got by without this painting for a hundred years. We stuff it up trying to reveal it, what's lost? The way you're carrying on people wouldn't try to assist at a birth! As far as this painting is concerned it's this or nothing.'

'Or it goes to its rightful owners.'

'What are you trying to say? What owners? Nobody gives a fuck for it. The real owner's dead.'

'Why are they waiting outside then, Essington?'

'For the bloody van Gogh! But not for the picture, for its monetary value, that's all.' So loud by then that they might have heard me right out there in the street, they might have even become worried. 'Which doesn't, at this point in time, exist. Not as far as they're concerned it doesn't.

'That's a moot point.'

'Bullshit, Grantley. They're out there waiting for me to find the thing. I find it, then it exists. Finders keepers!'

'It doesn't belong to you.'

'Who the hell does it belong to? Name them. Just give me one name, Grantley.'

'This fellow, Carbentus.'

'That fellow Carbentus is dead, like I just said. Anyway, I don't have the time to argue. Either you help or you don't. I'm dunking it.'

132

'I do wish you'd think about it, Essington.'

'You just wait, Grantley, wait till the gel lifts off. Then we'll see what you've got to say.'

He left the room. Distancing himself. They'll do that.

I filled a trough that looked like it had suffered neglect since the installation of the washing machine and dryer. That was in a small laundry off the room where we were working. I tested the water, just about the right temperature, tepid, and then I added detergent as an aid to penetration.

'I read somewhere, Grantley,' I called out, 'van Gogh used to wash his paintings to get rid of excess oil. What were they?' That brought him back in through the door. The chance to blow his trumpet.

'At that time the commercial manufacturers of artist's paint added non-drying substances such as tallow to lengthen the shelf life of tubes of paint and to make for a better plasticity.' Like being with a book. 'These inhibited drying, particularly if you applied the paint in the manner of van Gogh. He would squeeze it directly out of the tube, often mixing pigments together on the surface of the canvas itself. We can see this through the use of microscopic photography. We are able to examine the way in which the layers of pigment smear across one another. With palette-mixed colour, of course, the dispersal of one pigment into another would be considerably more even.'

I was agitating the water, rubbing at the brown layer with my fingertips. I could feel it dissolving, and at the same time expanding as it absorbed the moisture.

Getting somewhere.

Grantley had forgotten his moral indignation. Scholarship excused all. It will do that, an overtrained mind; it can't keep with issues for long. It's much more interested in facts, getting them filed into some sort of order.

I had to add more hot water from time to time, to keep the temperature up. The whole shebang was going limp, frighteningly so. There was the danger of everything coming away from the canvas — the van Gogh, if one was there, and all that rested upon it. Better not to think about that possibility.

Then I got it. It began to lift, the whole bloody thing. Unbelievable! Underneath, first just the ends of pale blue-green brush strokes — rough, quick marks. Then more of the same

133

thing. The original ground showing between the paint. Yellow appeared next. The chrome yellow that, according to the experts, changed hue in time and gave the sunflower paintings their mysterious colour intensity long after the artist had died.

Oranges and browns began to take the form of a beard.

'I do believe it is a self-portrait.' Grantley had no qualms now. 'From the Paris period. A sketch, I should say.'

He tapped away at his glasses with a hand wet from making the irresistible gesture, from touching the new-found work.

'I truly believe this to be the most remarkable day of my life.' As he said that he took the glasses off to dry the lenses. Wetting his hands again he had to repeat the process.

'My, my, my.'

'How do we get the fucking thing out of here?'

'Oh,' he said, 'it is quite remarkable.'

I was holding it up by then. There were bits of the covering still attached. Small scraps. But you could see what we'd got. There was Vincent, pale blue-green jacket crossed over at the neck. He wore a yellow straw hat and was smoking a pipe. The eyes, their expression, wan, that was how I'd describe it. Two sad brown-black dots crudely popped into place. Behind the head the canvas was filled in with random strokes of impasto white.

'The first thing we must do, Essington, is remove the tacks. When that painting dries it will become too taut, it could even tear if the fibres are rotted. Often they will weaken at the turnovers. Standard practice these days is to introduce reinforcement at that point.'

'I thought you were the ignoramus on conservation.'

'Theory, Essington.'

I'd bought pliers, a screwdriver, the lot. I went for the tacks, pulling them like rotten teeth. I'd already worked out that the trick would be to take the thing away rolled.

We weren't out of the rough yet, pretty quick smart something had to be hung downstairs over the safe. We had to do that before the invasion. There would be an invasion. No problem about it.

I managed another hour's work on the copy of the cubist painting. Most of the original had been saved, held together by the gelatine; it was lying out on the worktable, somewhat the

134

worse for wear, while I was brushing in the copy. The slowest part was the key pattern on the tablecloth, where I'd discovered the initials. That and some fiddly stuff up the tuning end of the guitar's neck.

It wasn't completely finished but enough was painted for the work to be placed in the frame that had been around the original, and thus around the obscured van Gogh.

We were still under observation. What I wanted was to go out. But how to set up the house for the visitors I could reasonably expect to drop in during the outing? I'd decided it was best not to leave Grantley behind to hold the fort against the world. He wouldn't have been able to manage it, and he would have been talking about the painting we'd unearthed before you could say Jack Robinson.

I'd swear I was watched as I hung the painting over the door of the wall safe. But that was from across the canal, so our guard wouldn't have been able to make out anything more than a general sense of movement behind the window glass. Upstairs I laid everything out on the worktable: the untouched, but old, canvas, the solvent, the pots of lacquer colour and a set of tubes I'd bought — a new style of artist's colour made out of a mixture of oil and synthetic resin. They are supposed to give the effect of oil colour but have a drying time of only a few hours. You can apply them any way you like, and they thin with water. The perfect medium! Made me wonder why everybody wasn't queuing up to buy.

I rang a cab.

When it turned up I was waiting inside the door, watching at an angle through the front window. I don't think the guard had a clue we were about to bolt till the moment when we came out through the front door, head first, and straight into the car's back seat.

'Schiphol.'

He took off slowly along the canal but went like a bat out of hell once he'd got on to more open roads. I don't think the cab caught a green light but we didn't stop once.

Grantley was sitting there looking upset. We'd fallen out again, I'd offended his sense of what was right. And now, without the chance to object, he was being deported. The camera

135

was hanging around his scrawny neck, the bag with his meagre belongings was crumpled at his feet. He was departing without having visited the Rijksmuseum, that was what he resented most.

I couldn't be bothered explaining that he was going for his own good. I'd deliberately neglected mention of my early-morning thrills on the last visit. Not because he would have got scared — though he would have, who wouldn't? — but because I didn't want the deal to sound any more shonky than it was.

I tried to explain: 'The law! What do you think it is?'

Him holding up those yellow hands, the long fingers that had never gripped anything hard. Flapping them at me, as though he was warding off attack from an angry rooster.

'Grantley, the law is for the people who make it. Always was. Rule number one is to remember that little fact. The law's useful, but it stinks.'

'Please, Essington, spare me the philosophy.'

It wasn't till we got to the airport and I was steering him towards Departures that the tension between us flared into full-scale war.

'After what we've achieved . . . what we found . . .!'

'It will destroy me, Essington. I must ask you to drop the idea.'

'You're asking me to throw the whole bloody thing away?'

'I'm asking you to consider me, to consider my position.'

'You're safe, couldn't be safer. That's why I want you to do it.' I knew that there wasn't any point in offering money. That would have put him off altogether, wounded him. He wouldn't have talked to me again. Not to the rich man who could buy his way through life.

I owed him money anyway. That had been our deal. But now was definitely not the moment to write out a cheque.

So I bullied: 'You've got to fucking do it!'

'Have you ever considered your language, Essington? What it says about your sensitivity to other people's feelings?'

'I don't have time for feelings. We're lucky to get you on to this flight, it's the one chance to take the painting out, to keep it safe. Don't blow it, Grantley. For God's sake, don't blow it.'

'To ruin my career.'

How could I ask: 'What career?' He had his pride.

'An old man has the right to hope that people will remember him with a respect sufficient to value his opinions at some time in the future, Essington.'

'"Old man" talk now! I beg you, Grantley . . .'

What a load of crap! In the future people were going to care less than they do now; there was going to be more and more jostling for space; life would be a case of holding the space you got, loading it with consumables. No doubt about that.

I was thrusting the painting — still very damp and rolled in a sheet of plastic — under his determined nose. 'Take the damn thing, Grantley. Do you want me to crawl?

'It would lower my opinion of you even further.'

Bloody hell!

'Imagine if we reversed positions, Essington. Would *you* get on to that plane with a stolen van Gogh under your arm?'

'I would, after what we've been through.' Calling on his team spirit.

'It's not only my reputation, you understand, I have to think of Margery. She has been very good to me, that woman, at a time when life hasn't been easy for her. Can you imagine what effect it would have if I was to be placed in one of our gaols?'

They were calling for London passengers.

Grantley turned and bolted. Ungrateful old devil. It took me hours to get a glimpse of his point of view.

A lot more hours to forgive.

I kept a look out around the taxis. Nobody waiting there, nobody watching. I headed back to Amsterdam, this time with a gentler driver.

We talked about tulips.

Big thick Essington, on your own now. It had been the feature of my plan to get the van Gogh out with Grantley, providing we unearthed one. Now, riding in the taxi, I was feeling sympathetic towards those dictators who have people shot for failing to obey orders — in the democracies we call them 'the army'. I could almost see things from Grantley's point of view but . . . well, he'd really upset the applecart. My applecart. Very frustrating, people not doing what you expect them to do. People thinking for themselves, having their own ideas.

Their own blasted ideas!

Now I didn't have one, not an idea.

I had one wet, rolled painting though. How long could it last, wet like that? Not long. Mould would develop. I'd end up with a van Gogh mushroom. To dry it gently, that would take a couple of days. No chance of that.

I didn't come up with a proper answer. Instead I gave the driver the name of the hotel near the station where I was still shelling out for a room.

The man on the reception desk looked a little apprehensive about my roll of plastic. There was a steamy appearance to the packet; he didn't think that looked too good either. It took me a lot of guilders to have it locked away in the hotel safe. I told him that the contents were important to me. That they were only to come out of the safe if I asked for them.

In the end I got him to write out a receipt.

Up in room seventy-three I ripped the bed to pieces so it looked like I'd spent the night there with a women's hockey team. I drenched the towels, wet the bathroom floor, generally messed the place up. I didn't want anyone thinking I was paying for an unused room. That sort of prank can get people talking.

People start to talk and you can never predict how far the talk will spread. Even as far as a Carbentus ear.

I made it to the processing place just before closing. Picked up the shots, both the prints and the transparencies. Then a couple of pastries and off back to the canal house. I had the idea it would be a pain in the neck for the watchers when they saw that my old pal, Grantley, didn't make it back with me.

It could have been the kind of information that would cause them to want to get into some hard talking. Still, up to that time they'd seemed in touch with reality, acting fairly gently, gently. As though they didn't like trouble any more than I did.

It was impossible to tell if the house had been inspected during my absence. I managed a wave out the window at a man in a heavy blue overcoat who seemed interested to find me back in residence. There wasn't any sign of the day guard. Maybe he was still off hunting for the taxi. Shouldn't have been too hard to find, he would have taken the number. And he would have been told that we'd finished up at the airport. With the radio hook-up of taxis, I guessed I'd only just got clear of Schiphol before the whole lot of them came looking.

Keen, the Carbentus clan. So would I be if I thought there was a van Gogh waiting to be picked up at the end of the day's work. I still was keen, and I'd picked it up. Only trouble, I hadn't got it out. Not yet I hadn't.

I went back to work. The phone rang. I'd got used to that. Ignored it. It rang again when I was sitting checking the remake of the cubist painting against the photos. They were the only evidence I had left. The original had gone down the plug hole in little pieces before I made the fruitless run for the aeroplane.

The photos were what you might call overkill. But then things could have finished up otherwise. It could have been that they were all I'd have to go on for the remake. And they had their uses, checking the painting's detail, getting it right. The mind plays tricks: no matter how right you think you've got an image, there'll be mistakes. And you can't pick them. Not even looking at the thing reversed in a mirror.

Stubborn old sod, Grantley, I thought. But I was starting to understand his fears. Amazing how it settles the brain cells, a spot of painting; it increases the potential for philosophy. I didn't want to be his downfall, things were going badly enough for him as it was.

Grantley had been a help, no doubt about that. He'd checked out the painting, examined the quality of the pigments. He was in no doubt as to the approximate date that it had been done. He said you could tell from the quality of the pigments, by the way they were ground. These things had changed a lot over the years, particularly with the development of modern industrial chemistry and the demands for colour to help sell cars. Finer pigment particles, that was one thing; the other was synthetic varieties of earlier hues.

No, Grantley had been in no doubt, the painting was done at the right period. It followed that it was a van Gogh, if only because nobody else would have dared to paint like that then. Dared or bothered. What was it that Cezanne had said about him? He'd called them 'madman's paintings'. Not so many people back then wanted to be slotted into that compartment.

It would have been about ten o'clock when I rehung the now

139

completely finished cubist painting up on the wall, covering the safe. I'd managed to get a little bit of age on to the surface by feathering over the lacquer's shine a kind of grease–soot mixture that I'd collected out of the oven's distant recesses.

The pastries were eaten but I was still feeling decidedly peckish. The coffee was finished, so was the milk. I was stuck with black tea. Much too sophisticated for my childish palate.

I went for it all the same.

Keep up your fluids, that had been Mother's advice.

The man in the overcoat was standing outside, eating something out of a paper bag.

Maybe they'd figured that Grantley hadn't got off with anything: if he had why would I still be there, buggering about inside Robert's house? Maybe they felt confident as long as I was in place. I would have put money on the notion that they'd taken precautions to avoid a repeat of the flight to the airport. Not hard to do, of course. All that had to happen was for the authorities to be alerted that a van Gogh was about to be smuggled out. That would be sufficient.

Grantley may well have been right to resist the role of courier. They could have been waiting to pounce already. Maybe he was frisked as he went on board. But people like Grantley do not like to be searched, particularly when they've just been standing up for tired principles, and protecting their reputation. I was sure that under such circumstances he wouldn't breathe a word, but would instead play the role of the outraged citizen, tight-lipped.

The phone rang.

I had a sudden thought about Tina. I answered it.

The voice wasn't unfamiliar.

'Cornelius Carbentus.' That was what it said, introducing itself.

Chapter 13

'Mr Carbentus . . . can you think of anything we can possibly have to say to each other?'

'Mr Holt, you are at present on my family property, illegally.'

'That's where you're wrong, Mr Carbentus. I'm here on the insistence of Tina Carbentus, half-sister to the house's owner.'

'Late owner.'

'At the risk of being unfeelingly pedantic.'

There was a pause.

'Mr Holt, I am not ringing to argue with you. In fact, quite the opposite. We have no disagreement. A friend of my recently deceased cousin . . . why should I have cause to be arguing with you?'

'A question that's passed through my mind more than once.'

'In fact, what I wish to propose is that you and I meet together, that we take the occasion of your visit, use it as an opportunity to get to know one another.'

'Whatever you like, Mr Carbentus.'

'Tomorrow morning, early, would that suit you, Mr Holt?'

'I wasn't planning anything special. That'd be fine.'

'Could we make it eight, how would that be?'

'That would be fine. Tell me, these hoons you keep posted outside here, watching over me. Do we really need them, Mr Carbentus? What is it you're expecting me to pull? That's what I don't understand.'

'To pull? Nothing, nothing at all.'

'Then?'

'Mr Holt, as you well know, things aren't always what they appear to be. I am charged with certain responsibilities. Particularly since the tragic death of my dear cousin. There are interests which must be protected.'

'That doesn't explain how I fit in . . . Wait a second, are you trying to get me to believe I'm being protected?'

'You could be, Mr Holt. Indeed, I do believe that would not be so very far from the truth.'

'Watched, more likely.'

'Tomorrow, we can pursue these topics in the morning.'

The call from Cornelius Carbentus made it all the more important that I get the third picture ready, just in case I had to perform the three-card trick.

Art is illusion. It's getting people to believe in some new, some invented reality. Even just for a moment. For long enough for it to seem wonderful in some kind of way. So I started wading through Robert's books, looking for the model. He was strong on van Gogh, that was his suit. Not just the letters. There were books of drawings, books devoted to the paintings that had been executed before arrival in Paris. Several large coffee-table volumes boasting glossy covers with one or other of the master's best-known works reproduced there — full Technicolor. There was the popular novel, *Lust for Life*, and even a book of stills from that film showing Kirk Douglas impersonating Vincent, pretending to be totally consumed by . . . by a kind of Hollywood nothingness-angst.

I was looking for a reproduction of some painting to suit my purpose. Because I was a little tired, I guess, I'd go for one, mark it with a slip of paper, then find another which seemed more suitable. Not able to make a decision. There were a lot of reproductions to hunt through. And only so much time before Cornelius Carbentus was going to be standing there on the stoop, huffing and puffing to blow the house down.

Nobody was out on the streets. But there was a car beyond the canal. The second time I checked it the interior light was on. I figured I was still under surveillance.

A warm glow out of the windows of the barge. I guessed the owner was snug inside with his cat, listening to . . . would it be Bob Dylan on worn vinyl?

The light in the car went off again. No flies on Cornelius. He was looking after his interests. Why shouldn't he be? Life —how you tell the story depends on whose side you're on. Me, I'm on my side.

That's sanity.

I put three books out across the floor, pages held open by more

142

books acting as weights. There was a picture of some flowers with cut stems resting on a table, that looked easy enough. There was another, a copy of a Japanese woodblock print done with some oriental writing, black on orange, down both sides. And a third, a self-portrait, not so different from the one we'd uncovered, only he looked a lot grimmer in this little number and there wasn't a pipe stuck in his mouth. The self-portrait was the worst-quality reproduction, it was in a pre-war publication. It was listed as 'private collection, Dresden'. I figured that more or less guaranteed it being out of circulation. Not much survived the fire-bombing of Dresden.

Being destroyed was a mark in its favour.

I was making up my mind, pondering, when I picked up one of the books I was using as a weight. The title was in Dutch, I had no idea what it said. But inside there were a whole lot of pictures reproduced, the work of a number of different artists. I recognized a couple by Mondrian, but nothing else. Mostly geometric abstractions; or surrealist with unlikely juxtapositions of naked women, pieces of fruit, machine parts. There was also a third category: paintings that were cubist, one way or another.

Artists' names were printed underneath each reproduction. One reproduction caught my eye on account of the way it was done. Crude cubism — you couldn't tell about the colours though: the block-making was so dreadful and the register out by miles. The artist was Pieter Loos. I had a bit of a hunt around the composition. There it was, the 'P' and the 'L' worked into some decorative wallpaper behind a skew-whiff Chianti bottle. My man, discovered! Maybe, one day, I'd have the chance to look him up. Anyone painting that badly had to have a nice soul, that was the way I looked at it. Look at me, I was the exception that proved the rule.

Tantalizing. How I would have liked to find out why. Why Pieter Loos made such a picture on top of a van Gogh.

I worked all night, me and the reproduction of the self-portrait from the Dresden collection. It was crudely painted, like the one in the hotel safe, with lots of ground showing through. I had the quick-drying paints, tubes carefully selected so I didn't use any colour that wasn't in Vincent's basic palette. I kept a heater going for the drying. And the oven was on low, that was to plonk the

143

picture into, if and when I was getting desperate. It didn't take all that long. The trick was to get the bravado up, slashing the paint across the canvas in much the same manner as the master would have done, to keep his hand away from his ear.

I was finished when light was coming up into the sky. The paint itself was passably dry. I scrubbed a little of my oven mixture, gone soft in the heat, over the surface and worked it into the texture of the canvas. A mistake. It was too greasy for my purposes, something I hadn't anticipated. It wouldn't take the lacquer colours.

I went through the shelves, the cupboards, selecting and trying out an assortment of powders, hunting one that might work, that might get the fat out of it, roughen up the surface a little. I got the best results with a white substance out of a cylindrical pack which had a kitchen sink printed in bold outline beneath the brand. I rubbed that into the residual grease, cleaned it off, then had another try.

Luck. It worked. The lacquer took. But by then I was behind schedule.

That final version, my second, of the much-abused composition that had hung in front of the safe was applied to the canvas pretty slap-dash. Nothing to be proud of at all, not even old Pieter Loos would have approved.

Still, I now had the third card ready should it be required. Next, to get out of there.

I had meant to make the trip in the dark. Too much time wasted getting lost with myself before I'd made the selection, before I'd got started on the painting. Too much time figuring out alternatives, being indecisive. The simple explanation was that I'd been dog tired at that stage. But by the time the sun came up I was well over some threshold, into a second day; I had passed through the need for sleep and come out on to the other side, riding on my nerves and too few pastries. Not the right state of mind for a negotiator. Nothing like it.

There was a door opening on to stairs from the second storey where I'd been working. The stairs led down to the few square metres of concrete where the weed had been mad enough to push its head up, searching for light. That was the back of the house.

I went down those stairs to join the weed. I held my latest cubist work, wrapped, under one arm. With my free fist I knocked hard on a door.

144

Knocked hard, then knocked again. Shades of Robert the Bruce — stage directed by his spider. Or was that Flora Macdonald?

What is it? 'Knock and it shall be given to you?' No, that couldn't be right. Well it was. No problem about that. The door opened. An enormous man with a head celebrating the idea: hair.

'Wrong side,' he said, Dutch English, accented American.

'You can say that again.'

He did. Through the acres of beard.

He was standing, filling the door. I was being examined by twinkling blue eyes. The twinkle not altogether kind.

I was explaining myself, the foreigner who had come out of the rear door and couldn't get back in again. I didn't add that my head had a clock inside it with the seconds ticking away.

Staying with the Carbentus family, was I? More crafty eyed. Yet, at the same time, the outward impression of the fairy-tale dwarf who grew. Grew! A gigantic man. A human mountain!

The truth, Essington.

'Robert Carbentus, he was my friend in the Carbentus family. Now he's dead.'

Tick, tick, tick.

'Dead?' Acting the surprise. As though he was the man not to know of a neighbour being blown up by a bomb that had made the headlines all over Europe.

I told him about it, putting myself into the picture as I described it.

Even that didn't get him out of the doorway. The Dutch, you can look through their windows but there wasn't a chance, or so it seemed, of getting through the door. And how could I fell him?

He wanted to know what I had in my hand. I'd wrapped the painting in some rather crumpled brown paper that I'd dug up. That wasn't a disguise though, there was no way that it could be taken for anything other than a painting.

The honest foreigner who'd locked himself out in the wee hours of the morning with a painting wrapped in brown paper under his arm!

That was the fairy tale.

'Well, well, well.' He was saying that mostly to enjoy the timbre of his own voice-box, his particular hybrid English. A hand had reached out, fingers opening and closing.

145

Of course, I thought, I could go for a kick to the balls. It doesn't matter how big they are, if you can get them in the balls. Only would my toe find its mark, that delicate pair of gonads tucked away under all the blubber?

I gave him the picture.

Big hands too. Like the god of lumberjacks. Dressed for the role: a giant's blue jean overalls buckled over a thick, plaid shirt. The paper was torn off my little gem.

That action made me think of bears.

Then the painting was held out at arm's length. He grunted. 'Loos,' he said.

'Mine,' I replied.

'Not whose.' Still the knowing twinkle in his eyes. He was playing with me, the bastard. And for all I knew Mrs Giant was nattering to the police on the blower while I was being kept unhappily occupied.

'Loos . . . Pieter Loos.'

'That's the one.' The problem when you're caught out is that everything about you expresses guilt. I could feel it like a substance that had been smeared all over me. And I could feel his eyes taking in the presence of that substance.

Cunning eyes, like those of a lizard after insects, expressive of nothing.

Examining the picture. 'An artist without talent.'

'You reckon?'

'I know.'

Nothing like certainty.

Time running through my fingers.

'Yet a brave man.'

'Is that so?' How could I, standing there, be interested?

'A very brave man . . . an artist, no.' He gave it back.

It never occurred to me that you could find a brave artist. That was like a contradiction in terms. Vincent, he hadn't been brave. You only had to read the letters to see that. It was his brother, Theo, who'd had the brave streak.

What could I do?

The painting had been passed back to me. 'A very brave man.'

I wasn't interested in how brave. I wasn't interested in 'brave' at all.

146

I couldn't figure out a way to be brave off my own bat. Certainly not a useful way. Killed, the man would still block the door. You'd have to break the body up into bits to move it clear — use a chainsaw. I had neither the means nor the inclination to kill anyone.

It was cruel the way he kept on with his story. He'd bring his enormous hands up into the air, fingers half closed into fists at the end of arms with the dimensions of a bullock's hind legs —there was that much meat on the bone.

'Of the best family, a banking family, a grand house on the Keizersgracht. A tall man, handsome. A ladies' man, you would call him. And didn't the ladies love him.'

I couldn't concentrate. My mind was spinning about inside itself, looking for somewhere to go, to get away from that voice. When I eventually brought it to a standstill, stopped it, I was still hunting for a path around, or through, that body full of words. No chance.

Tick, tick, tick.

'So his career prospered because the ladies liked the man. He was a nothing . . . a no-talent. You would call him a pretty face. That would be the term, Stateside.'

Stateside!

It struck me then; the man was put up to this. An extension of Cornelius's watch. He'd got the neighbours working for him, as well. I was being filibustered into a corner. It could be the Loos story was a load of crap, told to fill the time. But why? And how did he know to tell it? Pieter Loos?

Tick, tick, tick.

'Well collected, favoured. In the books, the exhibitions. I could never believe it. Me, I was twice the talent.'

A painter then! And modest.

'In America I was to prove my talent. But, here in Holland before the war, they only had eyes for Pieter Loos and his kind.'

Who'd want to have eyes for this creature, for my gigantic gaoler?

'You right there, Henk?' A male American voice, the real thing this time, coming from somewhere inside the house. Two of them!

'All under control.'

147

There wasn't any question about that, not with the giant having an assistant.

'You've got a visitor, ask him in.'

'I'm getting around to that right now.'

Again I had the painting taken out of my grasp. It was held in his clenched paw; he waved it about like a flag. 'Friend,' he said, 'please excuse my lack of manners, do come in.' Still that knowing look in the eyes, and me with the feeling that games were being played.

That's when I saw the second man. It was the hippy type off the barge. Wasn't that a coincidence?

Tick, tick tick, more minutes passing. I was a prisoner of some unspecified type, and for what kind of reason? The meeting was looking a lot less than a surprise for these two, these two what?

In its confusion my mind scanned the plan I'd concocted. The van Gogh, the original that was supposed to be secure in London, was beginning to compost down in a hotel safe. The first copy of the cubist composition was in place, doing its job — well, something had to go right — it was hanging over the safe next door. Only someone had to see it there before it could be considered to be out in the world. The third card — that was the one with which I was hoping to do illusionist tricks; hoping that, if the worst came to the worst, it would buy time while I got the hell out of Holland — along with my own good self, it too was trapped with the giant.

I had thought that maybe I'd be able to pass it over to some dumb official, telling him what it was, where I'd found it, in simple language. Use it to put myself in the clear so I could cross the border. With it I could prove the whole van Gogh story to be a concoction of Robert Carbentus's imagination, something he'd told me about years before to big-note himself. A prank, nothing more. A Dutch joke. They had caps and ovens and treats, why not jokes?

It wouldn't take all that long to prove that my van Gogh was the fake it was meant to be. Done when? Done by which hand? It really wouldn't matter. Once they cottoned on to the fact that it wasn't by Vincent, then the whole story could be put to rest. So the third card was the trump. I'd had complete faith in the thing, in its capacity to get me through doors, across lines drawn on a map.

148

Now it was being waved about like the daily paper. And at the end of that multi-kilo arm.

Jumbo threw the painting over to the aged hippy. 'See what I got given to me.' Not just an accent overlay but he had a tendency to phrase like an American. 'By Pieter, the one I'd told you about. By Loos.'

The man off the barge examined their prize, looked at the back, smelt it. 'New!'

'Curious, isn't it? Pieter dead so long and up springs this little number, smelling like a car straight off a Detroit assembly line.'

Me standing there, having to listen to that sort of shit. Eight o'clock, the time to meet Cornelius, would have passed.

'Quite a find,' said the man off the barge.

I couldn't put it together, not with the pieces rearranged so suddenly. The two of them, not at all fazed, as though they already knew more than I did. It didn't make sense. There had been those men watching, employed to watch. If that was right, why then were there two more, one in front, the other at the back? Covering the entrances? The giant at the back, the one called Henk, he would have fitted in fine with the men on shift out the front. Yet it wasn't one of that pair who was with him now, but the hippy.

OK, I'd seen one of the watchers talking to the hippy, but it hadn't been that kind of conversation, you could tell. I hadn't got the impression of people who were working together, who were in league.

I couldn't make sense of anything.

Outfoxed.

'Robert mentioned to me that he was off to see a party, name of Essington Holt. That, friend, would be you. He figured you might be coming back with him. That there could be a bit of business to be done.' I looked at the giant with genuine surprise.

'He told you that?'

'That's what he said. Worried he was, wasn't he, Albert? He was in a fix. Worried sick with it. Had to work out some solution. That was when he lighted on the idea of you. Thought you might have the contacts. He imagined you could set up a deal of some kind.'

'What deal? What's this you're talking about?' I had already given up on Cornelius. That worry was past — well, for the moment, at least. Unless these two were his mates, then I could

149

expect him to come skipping in through the giant's front door at any minute. I was concentrating on putting myself back into some sort of psychological order. The ticking inside my head had stopped. There wasn't anywhere I wanted to take that painting to any more.

All of me was in the room with the two men. That was more like it, I began to feel complete: the old Essington. My brain functioning, trying to put things together, building its own solutions.

'Robert had a notion that you had contacts, Mr Holt. Because he knew of your collection. Told me about it. Quite something, it seems.'

'He was wrong there. All inherited, not mine in the true sense. I didn't put it together. A collection, in the true sense, it should be your own taste.'

'He said that was what you'd done over the years, made a trade in paintings. That you knew about the market, even that you'd been involved with an art fraud a year or so back . . . forgery on a big scale.'

'Accidental, like tripping over a banana skin . . . that doesn't mean you know how to grow the things.'

'You do know, Mr Holt. This is the evidence.' Pointing to the painting the second man still held in his hand. 'Not too bad. What would you say, Albert, if you couldn't smell it?'

The barge man, Albert, was thin. He had that worn look attached to so many products of the Sixties revolution. His face was grey to yellow, there were deep lines where his cheeks had drawn in. They said hashish would do that for you. Whatever it was, it had happened. Maybe just from sniffing flowers like Ferdinand the Bull.

He was also tall but . . . they were Mr Fat and Mr Thin. A thing like that could have set them talking in the first place, established the relationship. I once knew a Mr Heron who married a Judith Crane. We reach out for friendship, for connections. It's a very basic need.

'You call that evidence . . . evidence of what?'

'Forgery.'

'Forgery!'

'Forging a Pieter Loos.'

'Wait a minute, even assuming I did that fucking picture, that's

150

not forgery. There are people copying the masters all day long, all over the place . . . public galleries, art schools, out of books. It's one way to learn. That picture there . . . it's a copy by whoever. That's no forgery.'

'Playing with words,' said Albert.

'Bullshit, "playing with words". If you can't see the difference then forget it. We're talking about intention here, about what you try to do with the picture . . . that's when forgery starts.'

'He does know, Albert, Robert was right. The right man.'

'You've got the wrong man.'

'Got? Mr Holt, we haven't got you. You knocked on our door.'

'Henk was kind enough to let you in.'

'Then let me out again.' I reached for the painting.

'That we cannot do, not so soon.'

Cornelius Carbentus, when he rang, had implied that the watchers were there for my own good. I started to wonder which watchers he was talking about.

Then I started to wonder quite what it was that he had meant by 'my own good'.

The giant: 'I must insist you sit down for a short time, that you make yourself comfortable. Perhaps you'd like a cup of coffee?'

I sat, declined the coffee just out of bloody-mindedness. Albert took up the offer, repeated it, this time I saw reason.

It appeared instantly out of an adjoining room. I needed it, I could tell that from the way I rose to the aroma.

'Mr Holt, I'm going to tell you what this business is all about. I have the feeling that before his tragic death Robert neglected to do you that service, that he left you in the dark.'

'He never had a chance.'

'Oh, really?'

'Is that true?' Albert like a chorus in a play.

'Really,' I said dryly.

'He died there in Paris.' The giant was acting out the search for plausible explanations. 'He died, and you just happened to come on up here to visit him anyway. Yet you knew he was dead. Spiritualism! Albert, are we slow? Mr Holt was communicating with the soul of the dead.'

151

'Go fuck yourself.'

'Hey!' Big hands up again, keeping me calm.

'For the moment let's forget the explanations for your behaviour, for our behaviour, Mr Holt.' The half-clenched paws still raised in the air as though suspended on a puppeteer's threads.

Lowering them, he continued: 'First let me tell you something about our hero, this Pieter Loos. On that subject I am the expert. You see, he was my brother. Older than me, my brother, and the reason that I'd been forced to try my art on the far side of the Atlantic. Even though Pieter was dead, he had left enough of a shadow to keep me obscured. It is a problem with families.

'Pieter's shadow was cast long on account of him being a hero and because the women loved him. His art, as you have seen for yourself . . . who could study it more closely than a copyist? Is that the word you'd prefer? His art was of no value whatsoever. Always on the spot, at the right dinners, sure he was. Or undoing an influential suspender.'

'So what's changed?' asked Albert.

I was listening to the voices of bitter men.

'Nothing's changed,' the giant continued. 'Nothing at all. For Pieter, however, something did. For reasons of his own — totally of his own — during the days of the Nazi occupation he got himself arrested, taken away by the SS. He was never seen again. No facts to check, nobody knows a damned thing. But, since then, he's become the hero. We all needed those. Suddenly he's done this, done that. If the families Pieter is said to have helped . . . if they were added up I tell you the population of Amsterdam would be . . . well, infinite, even with the Turkish workers.

'His art, that also enjoyed a vogue in the years directly after the war. It finally slipped out of favour with the revival of expressionist tendencies and the emergence of a new generation — young people who were sick of old stories.

'I was sick of them already. I was working in New York from 1948. I was making my own world, my own reputation.'

You could see what that was. The room was adorned with four large canvases each slashed with black gestures over neat rectangles of pure primary colour. I guessed they must have been the work of the native returned. He let his eyes wander slowly over them with something like adoration. He was letting me know what was what where quality is concerned.

'As I told you, our family was rich, established. Friends with the Carbentus family. Social equals. That meant one hell of a lot more then than now. But the connections were sustained. Me and Robert, we weren't so far apart in years. We'd always been friends and then, later in life, we find we're living back to back. Never in each other's pockets, as the saying goes, but close enough as friends. When there is a problem, we talk about it together. Try to help each other. It was me who took his sister, Tina, to the hospital a couple of years ago when she'd tried to kill herself. A very tragic thing. It hit Robert. It had a very bad effect on Robert. Hurt him deeply.'

Albert following every word, scrolling suitable expressions across his face.

'Then, less than twelve months later, he lost so much money in the stock market crash that he's worried sick. Trouble sleeping. He is depressed. That was when I was able to be of the most assistance. To offer my support. Isn't that right, Albert? Try to work some way out of the money bind.'

'What are friends for?' asked Albert.

'You see, it wasn't his money, he was managing it for the family. It was money held in common between them. Money tied up in some way. It was Robert's grandparents' fortune. Somehow he was left in charge of it, him and an old lawyer employed by the family since forever, fellow name of van Vliet.'

'This,' said Albert, 'was to be the salvation.' Indicating the painting, my painting.

'Salvation,' echoed Henk.

'How's that?' Making it sound a genuine question. What access was I supposed to have to the mysterious workings of the Dutch mind?

'That is what we were hoping you'd explain,' said the giant. Still that look in his eye.

It hit me, the full beauty of it. Albert, at least, believed that he had the painting, the van Gogh. That was why he regarded it as Robert's hoped-for salvation. They hadn't been fooled by the fresh paint over the top, they'd been taken in by it.

That was a run to me.

Only one, but something.

I kept a straight face, hiding new-found hope.

'That,' said Henk, 'was supposed to have gone missing in the early days of the war. Before the war to be precise. Before the German invasion of Holland. Robert's father had been in Indonesia when the Germans came, so he stayed there. Nobody ever set eyes upon him again. Nobody, that is, until Tina appeared at the end of the hostilities.

'Robert had talked of the painting as a boy, after his father had gone away. It was a proud secret with him but, of course, he had to share it. He shared it with me. I must say nothing, I must promise, holding my hand over my heart. That was how it became our secret.

'I honoured my promise. Mind you, I knew nothing, only that there was a painting.'

He kept on going, taking no heed of time. We were served another coffee by Albert the barge dweller. He was the giant's Sancho Panza I guessed, enslaved by his friend's property; and by his belonging, his nativeness.

After the war the story was that the painting had been hidden, but discovered by the Germans. That it was stolen, taken back into Germany. Nobody knew who took it, whether it was an officially sanctioned theft or, like the hands and heads of so many Gothic angels, it had been snatched by some enthusiast, or maybe just a simple souvenir hunter. The spoils of war. You want to get something for risking your life.

Nothing more was said about the van Gogh. Robert never mentioned it again. Not directly after the war nor right up to the time he took off for several years of travel. Nor did he mention it after his return to take up responsibility for the administration of the family investments. Or, if he did, then Henk certainly hadn't heard about it over there in the United States.

So I was the only person who had been let into the secret of the family's continued possession of the work.

That, the giant explained, was one strong legend to grow up among the families, the legend of the missing van Gogh. Of the loss of the famiy heirloom.

A second legend, over on the Loos side, was that Pieter, the artist, had done more than assist families. He had worked with a small group of art lovers to hide paintings belonging to private collections. That he had made many works vanish for the period of the occupation. These had re-emerged after the allied victory, and taken their place again among the furniture and families of the Dutch bourgeoisie.

The two stories, side by side.

Then Robert's investment disaster in the October crash. His making contact with me. The fatal trip to Paris.

Where did Henk's loyalties lie once the news came through of Robert's death?

When Cornelius came around looking . . . what was he to say? There was young Cornelius, the next generation. A dedicated businessman. For him the past was forgotten, the future was made up of transactions. A 'new person', life was money and position, that was the beginning and the end of it. Cornelius, who'd long suffered the knowledge that his uncle, Robert — a man whose life was a public scandal because of the intense relationship he was believed to have with his half-sister — that this uncle was also permitted by stale legal decree to mismanage the family money. Cornelius, how impatient he must have been to get his hands on that money. To be able to touch it with his magic wand. Cause it to redouble and to multiply.

So, Henk must have told the young man the story.

At the same instant that I had turned up on the scene. And worked my way into Tina's confidence. I had then spent time in the house, poking about. And, what was more, returned a short time after my initial visit. Like someone driven, someone in a hurry.

'So that was why I had the gun pulled on me?' I knew the answer, I knew that was why. Still it had now come out, all in one piece. It made sense. That was the first time the whole thing had been put together.

And that was why out in the street, in front of Tina's apartment over there in Vondel Park, Cornelius had driven off at the first sign of a form reversal. He wasn't a crook, didn't have the stomach for it. He was a respectable young businessman in search of what he believed to be his property. Well, I guess he was right. Some fraction of it must have belonged to him.

'Had a gun pulled?' Genuine dismay.

'He didn't tell you that side of his honest little scheme.'

155

'That side could never have existed, not Cornelius.' Henk looked to Albert for confirmation. The emaciated head shook in the affirmative.

'That, friends,' I said, 'is where you've got it wrong.'

Chapter 14

To walk out of Henk Loos's house and get around to the front of the Carbentus house on the Looiersgracht meant that you went half-way around the block. The painting stayed behind in Albert's safekeeping. Which went to show how trusting you can get. I wouldn't have left a van Gogh in that character's hands, not in a month of Sundays. To make the point I kicked up quite a song and dance over letting it go: insisted on promises, on hearing empty declarations.

Henk kept on going over two things: how clever it was for me to find the work in the first place and what an inspiration to copy one of his talentless brother's paintings over the top. Who else in Amsterdam, he asked, would have known what that painting looked like? Let alone who it was by.

A reasonable question.

He wouldn't countenance the idea of Cornelius getting involved in violence. Even once convinced of the truth of my story of the stick-up at Vondel Park, he wasn't going to accept that the two thugs had been working for Cornelius.

He could never believe that.

He seemed to have a high respect for businessmen, and wasn't seeking disillusionment.

We came to the Prinsengracht, headed along underneath the budding trees, then turned into the road running between Looiersgracht and its houses. That was where we ran smack into one hell of a commotion. There were people all over the place, a lot of them looking official. Henk charged forward, clutching my wrist in one of the great paws. I had no option but to be dragged along in his wake.

The door of the house was open. There was a policeman on guard, keeping the sightseers at bay. An ambulance was standing by, with men in white coats dragging a stretcher out of the back.

Henk had talked us inside.

I wish I'd never been there. I wish I'd left the whole bloody thing alone. That I'd stayed in the sunny south, sipping the pink wine at the Bar Plage, walking Desdemona along the narrow path that led off Cap Ferrat and past the Villefranche children's water-slide's gleaming blue plastic.

She was lying where she'd fallen. On her back. There were bandages on her wrists, that was sad in itself — not that the thought occurred to me till later. She was dead, but not by her own hand. By some terrible hand. The head was smashed like an egg. Like the fragile thing that it had been in life. The forehead was collapsed, her features were covered with blood. She was spread-eagled, but with an ugly twist to arms and legs which rendered the whole final gesture into a scream made physical.

Holy Christ!

The professionals were taking it in their stride.

Upstairs there was another body, with life still resident, just ticking over. It was Cornelius, that was how I met him. Through blood and his half-closed eyes. He'd been shot, from what I could see, three times — one was a head shot. He'd made it most of the way to the door I'd exited by two hours earlier.

Henk had gone white. Blood that had filled his face from the exertion of getting around the block had now vanished. The features it had filled were sunk. He'd lost size. And, I suspected, he'd saved my life. Saved it with his long-windedness.

Twice now, when members of the Carbentus family had met death, I'd been a bridesmaid. Never, thank God, a bride. Not so far.

Standing, looking down on Cornelius's face while a doctor worked feverishly setting up a portable life-support system, I got a mind-picture, a detail that hadn't registered while I'd been on the ground floor. Up on the wall above where Tina was lying, and above where her blood was so terribly splattered, there was a gap. The first copy of the Loos painting was gone. There were the landscapes, each a fraction askew but still in place. The centre picture was gone. The door of the safe was closed, looking as though it hadn't been disturbed. There had been an irony in that, in the safe being there, failing to arouse interest. But right then I wasn't registering ironies. I was in shock. Numbness gathering me in its cold arms.

158

Abstracted, I scanned the workroom where Cornelius was lying. Mostly it was as I'd left it. Except the photos were scattered about, somebody had sorted through them at speed.

So, it was the photos that had pointed to the Loos painting below. Whoever was responsible for the carnage had picked up a lead that way. Why would anybody take so many shots of the one painting? That would be the question presenting itself to them.

It didn't answer the other question though, the big one about the terrible beating that had crushed Tina's delicate skull. That was more like an act of rage: like someone gone berserk. It was a crime of quite a different kind to the shooting upstairs. And totally unlike the confrontation I'd endured on the last morning of my previous visit.

I couldn't think. I couldn't try to work anything out. Stunned, we stood mute, the giant and I. Our minds resisting taking it all in. I saw the soles of Cornelius's shoes, new, just the hint of abrasion. I found myself wondering if they pinched.

I saw my cup, filled with cold tea. A still life unaffected by the violence. A witness only to its own existence.

I wanted to be out of that room, out of the house, out of Amsterdam, Holland. Karen could fill the house with children, I'd change them, bathe their wounds. Anything for sanity, stability, for the celebration of the fact of being. All her instincts had been right. Mine, totally wrong. I was sorry. Terribly sorry.

Sitting propped against a wall, head held between my knees. A firm hand on the nape of my neck. Opening my eyes I saw shoes and trouser cuffs. Looking up I met the eye of a professional face.

I must have fainted.

'Just sit, rest,' it said. Then it was gone.

Cornelius was being moved on to a stretcher, strapped into place for the descent down the steep stairs. A man in a white coat was holding inverted bottles at the end of plastic tubes. I can still picture that medico's face: young, the smooth golden skin, the nose with a slight turn-up at the end. It was a Dutch face. I thought of van Gogh's peasants. Of how this man's ancestors could have acted as models for the young artist.

Cornelius on his stretcher, I saw him as some mythical hero being carried to his rest, surrounded by white-coated priests.

I saw him also as a victim of my stupidity, of my meddling. What did I imagine I was doing?

What was I going to do with the picture?

Confusion.

That which had begun as a game, as a puzzle for me to solve, had ended so terribly. And me, lured into the mystery of the thing by Tina's curious imprecision when talking about Robert's van Gogh, by her denial of any knowledge of the painting's existence. That, more than anything, hadn't rung true. With her, always that sense of something held back.

Precisely what it was, or why, I couldn't say.

What had she been protecting, keeping? And from whom? From me? Possibly from me, from the stranger poking his nose in where it wasn't wanted.

Yet it didn't fit.

I thought about her face, tried to lock it in there, at the centre of my vision, so I could extract answers from the image itself.

It was wearing a black headscarf. The eyes weren't looking in my direction. She was in profile, expressionless. There was a man standing with her. The man in the soft brown felt hat. Lightly built he was. Elegantly dressed too. It was not a Carbentus profile.

Who then?

'Who?'

I looked up. Henk was standing there. 'They want to talk to you.'

Bloody oath they would. Two bodies, one dead, the other so close it could hardly matter, and me at the heart of it all. Sure they'd want to talk with me — forever, most likely.

That was it, the answer to the question: Who? There were the other families. Tina, like the rest of us, she had a mother and a father. Then there was the other son, Haryanto was it? It is common enough for one family to dominate, to hog the scene. Nobody bothers to contemplate the second network. Let alone the third. That's the way they cultivate family trees. Heavy pruning.

And it happens when people marry out of their class that it's the dominant group which forms the recognized family.

'OK,' I said, getting to unsteady feet. 'I'm coming.' I couldn't

160

recall fainting before. It was weird. Time gone, vanished. Like a ticket blown away by the wind.

I felt cheated.

Then, later, I became frightened. Very frightened. And, I decided, I was going to get the hell out of there. But first I was going to have to do a lot of talking to the police.

Henk was carted along too. But in another car — I guess so we couldn't work out a story, standardize our information.

I was honest, told it exactly as it was, right from the moment of the Paris bomb. I even talked about the paintings, of how there had been the three downstairs in the room, and now one was missing.

I didn't mention the one in the hotel safe. Well, there wasn't any need, was there? Except if I wanted to hang about in Holland for a couple of years for having come into possession of the bloody thing.

There was a certain amount of coming and going, doors opening and closing, officers talking to each other in the corridors at that maddening pitch where you can't quite make out the words. Not that it would have mattered anyway since they were talking Dutch. But not to me, they weren't.

With me they were talking officialese, and trying to trip me up as well.

Going over the times again and again — was that a.m. or was it p.m?

Getting a description of the man that Tina had met on the day of the Queen's birthday party.

Then talking as though I'd invented him.

Back to being pedantic about the clock: when the shots that had killed Cornelius Carbentus had been fired.

Interesting question that, if you came to think about it: I hadn't heard any shots.

And at the back of my mind there was the question about the three-card trick, the third painting, the one that had been left in Albert's loving hands. When would they get around to asking about that little number? Because surely it wasn't going to be long before the giant, Henk, told them all about it, about how I was whipping out the back way clasping the thing in my little hot hands.

While the murderers had come in the front way.

I finished up getting moved. They led me down the corridor, up a set of stairs, along another corridor — this one had a strip of carpet patterned with Persian motifs to muffle the footfall. I was ushered into a more spacious office. There were long windows, a desk of substantial proportions, and the smoothest looking bastard you could imagine fiddling about with the lid of his fountain pen.

'Mr Holt . . .' Gesturing to the chair on my side of the desk. The officers who'd brought me were waved away. The phone was picked up, a couple of words, a woman entered, set a file on the desk, directly between the gentleman's hands.

Holy cow!

He opened the file, started to play with the top sheet of paper.

I felt as though I was looking down a very long tube.— freedom might have been that tiny dot of light at the end. Or, then again, it might not.

'Mr Holt . . . I trust you are being open with us in this matter, this terrible crime.'

'How many times . . .' The absence of a uniform, the style of the office, they freed my tongue. But he interrupted before I could get going, before I could complain about the number of times I'd gone over the story.

Holding up one hand to stop me: 'This is not an adversary situation — we of the police, and you. Nobody, you must take my word for this, nobody suspects you of a thing.' Reading what was written there again. Marking a spot with the tip of a finger. 'It is established that the shots were fired a little after eight o'clock.'

Eight o'clock! What was the time now? Since I don't wear a watch I asked him. Time, I'd forgotten about it till then. He appeared surprised.

'It is one forty-three.'

I scratched my head. It had been long, the questioning, but where had the time gone to? One forty-three, and clearly, with my interveiwer, you got time right to the minute. Just like your tie had to be straight, your cuffs a certain length.

What did he want?

He wanted the whole fucking story all over again. But this time he wanted to hear more about Haryanto.

And I couldn't help with that. Except to describe the man with the brown hat who could have been anybody.

'Why not a lover?' I asked.

'Why not indeed, Mr Holt?'

Very polite, the police gave me a lift back to where I'd come from. Henk came along too. Albert was there, waiting, he was still holding on to the picture. There was a look about his eyes, challenging me to try to get my van Gogh back.

Even shocked you could see they both felt pretty pleased with that, with scoring the trophy.

'Why didn't you tell the police about it?' I asked.

'There wasn't any reason.'

'You want to make more of a fuck-up?'

'What are you trying to say, Essington?' Albert had got us to first names; I reckon he thought we could do that, now we had deaths in common.

'I'm saying a fuck-up. Albert, Henk, those other guys, did you bother to ask yourself what they might be up to? I mean, did it occur to you to give it more than a passing thought? Did you wonder why, for instance, a man got shot, or a woman had her head smashed in? Try to concentrate, Albert. Did you ever see those people who were watching out the front of that house? Did you catch them talking to another guy, to some small man in a brown hat?'

Albert was the relaxed type. I guess he smoked a fair bit, might have had that one-too-many acid trip. There are a lot of people like that, especially in Amsterdam.

Me, I wasn't relaxed, sitting about in that foreign city trying to work out the next move, just so I didn't end up being dead.

'There might have been a guy,' said Albert.

'He'll live,' Henk said. He was holding on to the phone. Then he restated it, only this time to the wall. 'They say he's going to survive.'

'I'm talking about the painting,' I shouted at the pair of them, 'that's what people are being killed for.'

Henk had been ringing the hospital. For my money there were a lot of times when it was best not to make the recovery. I'd seen Cornelius, I didn't much like the idea of him living.

You can be wrong. Yet, maybe if it had been me under that

163

sheet with some consciousness still, somewhere, enough to make the choice, I expect I'd have had an altogether different perspective, I'd have wanted the medicos to pull out all stops, to have a go at keeping me alive.

'"Might have been a guy" . . . Albert, what are you saying? Concentrate, for Christ's sake!'

'I'm saying I can't be sure.'

'Hell!' I exclaimed. 'You were watching me . . . that means you'd have to see what else was going on.'

'I wasn't watching you, Essington. We were told to keep an eye on . . .'

Henk hung up. He took over the explanation. Neither of them liked to talk about their role as snoops. That was clear enough. Well who would?

'Making sure you didn't remove anything, that was all he asked me to organize. I did it for the sake of family friendship, for the sake of Robert. His memory.'

'I don't give a stuff who you did it for. I'm trying to jog Albert's brain cells into action. There was a constant and changing watch on that house. If they weren't put there by Cornelius, then they were put there by someone else. Nothing difficult to comprehend about that. Let me explain what I'm trying to get across. The guys I could see watching me, Albert must have seen them too. Two of them, taking turns they were. You can't hang about in a street all day and night without being noticed. Nights, the watcher would sit in a car. Today we get Tina bashed to death and Cornelius shot. The two things, the surveillance and the murders, are connected. Somebody else was on to me, therefore on to the picture as well. I saw a man, I saw him twice. The second time I wasn't sure but I would have thought he was talking to one of the watchmen. What I'm asking is for Albert to work at remembering.'

'Albert?' Henk turned to his friend.

Albert shrugged. 'Nothing,' he said.

'You don't even fucking try!'

'We've got this,' Albert said, giving significance to his grip on the painting. 'We've got the van Gogh.'

'More fool you.'

'Why's that?' Albert narrowed his eyes, he was acting wise — the man you couldn't put a thing over.

164

'Henk, you tell him, will you. It could just get his memory going, if he has one.'

But Henk only stared at Albert, and then at the painting. Stared, the mouth hanging open inside all that beard. His arms went up in the air again — that was his gesture, all that the blubber would permit.

Albert was gripping my masterpiece with one hand. The other was clicking — fingernail picking over the top of thumbnail. His cord trousers hung loose about his knees, there was so little of the man, width-wise; I thought he might have caught a disease from the cat. He was wearing a cardigan knitted in brightly coloured, random stripes, which looked like a gift of love from some lost female boarder. It was unravelling in several places.

Henk's gaze seemed to make Albert very nervous indeed.

'We got this . . . what we were after,' he said. Keeping the hand locked on to the painting.

I can say that I was frightened at that time. I had been ever since I'd walked around the corner, since I'd seen the crowd gathered about the door. And then Tina lying there. Holy Jesus! What was I up against? Yet with Albert acting the semi-idiot I got angry. I started to shake. That must have been lack of sleep talking to me. And the shock resurfacing.

'Henk, tell him, for Christ's sake! The last people who were believed to be close to that painting are dead or dying. You can't see that, Albert? Can't you make the connection?'

'He could be right,' said Henk.

'Could be . . . wait a minute! Could be! How can I be wrong? Tell me that.'

Henk walked over to me, put one of the paws on my shoulder, pushed me into a lounge chair, gently, firmly.

'Could be,' he repeated.

What was I doing wasting precious time, sitting talking to such a pair of dummies? Or were they in some sort of shock too? Henk had reacted badly to the death. So had I. Now I was coming out of it and finding the brains of these two totally jammed up.

Why had I gone back there with Henk in the first place? There had been danger in that — well, by my calculations, at least. Yet I was still locked into my game. Still playing with illusion and reality. Pretending that I was interested in the painting they held.

I had a thought: 'Henk . . . Cornelius, what sort of a car's he got?'

'It's a . . . he . . . I've been in the dammed thing.'

'What kind?'

'I'm not much interested in cars. That's the truth. I don't notice them.' Henk shaking his head.

'OK, let's try it this way . . . unless you know, Albert? You know what Cornelius drives?' I was going slow, talking to them like they were children. Maybe that was the way I was going to be talking for the rest of my life, with Karen's foundation.

'Albert, you saw it, didn't you?' Henk prompted.

Albert got into scratching the thin pepper-and-salt hair battling valiantly to make it down to his shoulders. Flakes of dandruff showered on to the cardigan of many colours.

'It was . . . like metallic blue.' He got that out.

'Light blue.' Henk backed up the observation.

'An Audi.' Albert was proud of that, thought it got him off the hook. If he'd been on one.

It hadn't been a blue Audi parked over the road while I was held up by the lightweight heavies. That had been black, a Mercedes. Its blackness emphatic on account of the smoked-glass windows.

'There's someone else who's been after that picture. And,' I continued, 'I have an idea it's going to be us next in the firing line.' Spelling it out. 'So, I'm off. You two . . . I'll leave it for you to work out what to do with the van Gogh. I'd rather be alive. That's my choice. You make yours.'

Henk became Chester Chatterbox as soon as I got to my feet. Spewing out everything he knew just to keep me there, as though I was some magic being who could ward off evil — of course, it was really the other way around: I'd brought the whole lot down upon their heads. That is fact.

'Robert didn't know . . .' Henk started out. 'Cornelius had checked through Germany. He'd been over the records of every van Gogh to surface in that country. He'd paid people to go through the international auction houses, read up on what had been sold since 1945, where it had come from. For several years he'd been at this . . . the records of America, of France, even here in Holland. What he believed . . . believes —' Pulling himself up there, getting the tense right while Cornelius

166

was still ticking '— is that a van Gogh could not remain out of circulation for so long. It would be sold, or loaned to an exhibition someplace, or it would be listed in a book on the artist's work.'

'Not unreasonable.'

'Not at all. Only he found nothing. That's how he came to decide that Robert still had it . . . somewhere, somehow.'

I was edging towards the front door. Going slow however, interested in anything that could help me to look after my skin.

'And,' I added, 'someone else has the same thought.' I was just keeping up with my own mind process. 'Could be they were alerted by Cornelius's search.'

Henk had moved, unconsciously perhaps, to block the passage. He was standing there, filling space. How to get past him? Size is a formidable social weapon. Grossness, it has its uses.

I thought of Tina's family. Of her talk of pressure. Me thinking always of the Carbentus mob, ignoring the other side.

'You don't imagine that he went looking in Indonesia?' I asked.

'Why would that be?'

'You can see the ridges underneath the fresh paint,' said Albert.

'Because that was where Robert's father, the man who owned the painting, finished up, didn't he?'

'Ridges?' asked Henk.

'Look,' said Albert, 'I hold it this way, so the light rakes across, you can see the brush marks underneath.'

They were both into it, eager to get themselves killed.

'See,' Albert went on, 'like a face and a hat or something.'

I was off, take your chance when it's there. I was through the front door and into the street.

Stepping out there was a shock to a shocked system. There was a cold grey light over the city. A wind blowing in from the oil rigs on the North Sea, from whence the wealth came. I'd stepped into their hunting ground, whoever they were. I was the quarry now, had to be. They'd be looking all over the place.

The only chance was if they already believed I'd bolted.

Unless the third card had some life in it still. Unless the

painting in Henk and Albert's hands was passed over to this other interested party. And he was fooled by it.

Fooled for how long?

Fooled till they got it into their heads to widen the search for me, to hunt me down there in France's southern playground.

Some trick I'd set up. I'd tricked myself.

Chapter 15

Room seventy-three was looking neat. You had to hand it to them, they kept it up, even during an extended stay. A new cake of soap big enough to lather a cat. Maybe it was crazy but I felt safe up there. Old ladies move into hotels when they've put enough aside to do so, to feel safe. Not a bad life — nothing much to worry about, no need to step into the street. Only thing to watch is the staff, you have to make sure they stay onside.

A hotel's a world within a world. Sitting about somewhere there are always girls waiting to perform sexual tricks in exchange for money. I suppose some of the bellboys are moonlighting in the same trade. Or you can ring out, get your boy's-toy or your toy-boy sent, gift-wrapped.

Exotic places. I remember the feeling from childhood. The meals might have got you yearning for home cooking, but then they might not. I reckoned I could do without the loving domestic touch in the food. After all, what good is a bread-and-butter pudding if you're dead?

Dead men don't crave the innocence of chops and three veg either.

Dear Karen — I could write it — have moved into a hotel in Amsterdam. Could be here some time, please send shirts and that lightweight jacket I bought in George Street, Sydney, the one with the ticket pocket. Remember, you hated it — out of date, you said.

Oh, and underpants and sox.

Foundation has my blessing, love to Dawn, Rebecca and Renardo.

I didn't send it. I didn't write it either.

Instead I rang for room service and got a meal sent up. Together with a large pot of strong coffee.

That kept me going for a while, eating, drinking the coffee.

And it brought me out of the daze I'd entered. To hell with hanging about in a hotel. Move, Essington, move.

I unmade the bed, wet the towels, generally buggered up the room again, then went to ground level by lift.

I smiled at the woman on the desk. There'd been a man there when I deposited the van Gogh in the safe. When? Oh, so long ago. The painting couldn't have started rotting yet. Not that it mattered. Not any longer, with me that scared.

And there had to be the police, as well. Surely they'd be back on to me sooner or later. Sooner if they found Henk and Albert smashed up, or even if those two cracked, admitted the existence of the painting they were holding.

My problem suddenly seemed to be how to get the real van Gogh into the hands of the people who'd signalled they would do anything to get it. That way I'd buy safety.

Surely.

That was how I was thinking.

I was looking at a display of diamonds in the hotel's entrance. Just loitering, indecisive. There had to be a way to return the painting. But first to make contact.

The stones were mounted and tagged, showing the raw material as they were dug up, still locked in quartz. Then the crude crystal and on through the stages of cutting.

I'd never been able to get that, the money people would spend on a diamond. Spend on a piece of uncoloured stone! Gold, for me that was different, there was something about the yellow of it that got to you. Gold looked fantastic on crudely wrought crowns and things, like those of the Visigoths that I'd seen in museums.

As for the van Gogh; an accumulation of crude and rapid brush strokes on a standard art-shop canvas, that was weirder still.

I was toying with the idea of smashing the glass, of getting caught with one fist clenched tight about the finished article, about the cut diamond, of being carted off and placed under police protection while the staff worked out how to stop the alarm wailing. I was going through it in my mind, how it would work, how I could plea stress, get off. After all, not much harm done and all the wealth that was mine to take into account. The courts are soft on the rich, they adore property. It's nice.

170

It had to be — well, not *the* way, but a way. Except the law had so many other reasons to still be interested in me; the diamond would be the least of it. And even locked up, particularly locked up, a person wasn't safe from outside attack.

Sifting through life's possibilities, that was when I saw him. He was walking in the street outside, looking the man without a care in the world. I was standing just inside the hotel's smart glass doors; that was where the diamonds were displayed, so you could stare at them while waiting for a cab. I caught him first as a reflection; when I turned my head he was strolling on past, digging the ambience.

Except that couldn't have been what he was on about at all.

I went back up, unlocked my room, then returned the key to the desk. That way it looked like I was out. I rang room service, had them deliver a bottle of the good Dutch gin.

I'd decided to go back into my shell, wait for the old brain to set off on some new tack. That was when I'd emerge again. When I got an idea.

I thought about the women locked away upstairs waiting for exercise. But then decided it wasn't worth it. I was in enough trouble as it was, and on all sides. All I needed was to get AIDS positive. That could have been — how do they say it? — 'misfortune never comes single it's plain.'

I was sitting up there in room seventy-three, getting a good look at the surface of the neutral painted walls in the afternoon light. The gin was open and the level going down.

I had the door locked.

At the start of my sit-in I continued working on ways to get the painting off my hands and into those that wanted it badly enough to commit murder. Then my mind got fixed on murder, on the act itself. Particularly on the bashing of Tina. They might have succeeded where she herself had failed, in achieving death, but — Jesus!

Then I was pacing up and down, confused. Getting drunker. Getting indignant. Getting mad.

Probably, well certainly, getting stupid.

What I'd been planning was some easy way out of town. A system whereby I could be out of the situation, all in one piece and clear. Now, with the gin's help, I was getting to where I

171

wanted to go straight through the front door and collect as many of the bastards as I could. They'd had me scared shitless. Maybe I was still scared shitless. But I'd stuffed the nerve ends that carried the message. Or anaesthetized them. One or the other.

I rang down for steak and a bottle of wine. I ordered a hire car for five-thirty. Where would I like it? For how long would I like it?

How long? Why not a week? What difference was it going to make?

I'd like it delivered by courtesy driver right to the front of the hotel, to the bottom step. To where I could open the door, slide in. That was where I'd like it.

My room?

I'd keep it. They had my credit card safely printed, they could write what they liked on that, and I could hold the room — for the rest of my life? Maybe for so short a time. That was the way I put it, 'for the rest of my life'. It pulled me up, the phrase. It'd come out so easily. Too easily.

I ate the steak and drank the wine: it was red, from Burgundy. That was all right.

I was stoked.

Not a good way for me to be. The reflexes dulled, the mind filled with its own weird picture of the possible. There was still time to kill.

There seemed to be a lot of it. It's like that, time, it's got a speed system all of its own. Now you see it, now you don't. As though an off-stage somebody is turning a knob, accelerating it, decelerating it: playing games with us poor mortals.

Between our games and those of the celestial stage crew it makes you wonder how you get to expect anything to turn out as planned. Yet we keep on planning. Or I do. I can speak for me.

Down in the foyer, ten minutes to go. Me standing there with nothing in my hand and not so much in my mind either. Booze coursing through my veins.

I'd rung Henk. They were still *in situ*, the two of them. No, nothing more on Cornelius, he was ticking over as before. Yes, they still had the painting. No, nobody had tried to get in contact. There had been a shaky tone to the voice, no longer the giant's boom. A note of uncertainty.

172

Under that sort of strain for long, they'd both fit into the same pair of overalls. He was melting, I could hear it. ·

Me, I was . . . well, at least I wasn't melting. Not any more.

It was a two-litre, fuel-injected Sierra, what I'd asked for. It was yellow. That was the luck of the draw. A good van Gogh kind of colour. He'd had the *Yellow House*. Me, Essington, I had the yellow car.

It is a fast model, the Sierra with the big motor.

The courtesy driver got out. A big, glowing Dutch girl who looked like I should have kept her with me as a bodyguard. She took the keys up to the front desk. I signed the paper, gave her a cab fare back to the office and skedaddled.

There he was as I came out through the glass doors. Nothing on me but a rolled paper in my hand, something I'd picked up in the foyer but hadn't got around to opening. It would most probably have been in Dutch, anyhow. Still, I carried it, a badge of office: the rolled paper. What it signified I couldn't really say.

He was just along the street, hands behind his back, his back to me. He was talking to a small man who I recognized at a glance.

I recognized him and wished to God that I hadn't jettisoned that handgun with the enormous hole down the barrel.

I didn't let it slow me down. No way. I stepped into the Sierra, took off, burning rubber, round in front of Central Station.

Hey! Essington! Do you know your way out of here?

I hared across in front of a stretch of dock and found myself guided into a tunnel by the stream of traffic. I knew where I was headed then. When Tina and I had taken a tourist boat trip we'd passed over the top of that tunnel, and they'd told us, in four languages, about the breathing tubes that stuck up like towers in the air. So high, as though they were anticipating the ice-caps melting. Holland drowned but tunnel breathing nicely.

Which I wasn't. I was sweating, heat generated from having too much to think about. I didn't want to head north, yet that was where I was going. I wanted to go south, direction Belgium.

I took the first left exit. What was written on it meant nothing to me. I was going to have to drive by the sun. Of which there wasn't a touch. The road leapt the occasional canal, belted past some industrial wilderness and a few big buildings, one of which wore the Shell sign — the big company. Then another left turn, this time on to an autoroute, and a sign saying 'Zuid'. I figured that was worth a go.

I flew down there heading back around the west side of Amsterdam, following signs saying 'Leiden'.

Away, and cooling off. I had the car sitting on around the going average, overtaking trucks; occasionally something would fly past on my left, leaving me feeling stationary.

After Leiden how did it go? The Hague, Rotterdam, then on, passing Breda and into Belgium.

That was where you'd go if they let you. There didn't seem to be anything standing in my way. I sat back, took it easy, even started to put together an idea for getting the van Gogh out of the country. That would make it the final trick to me, if you could look at it that way after so much killing.

I watched the rear vision, and looked ahead, keeping alert for traps. A policeman who smelt my breath would have had me behind bars in a flash. Not that I'd felt it, the alcohol, nothing particular, except the sweat — it might have contributed to that.

Myself in the rear vision, I looked pretty bad: drawn, and red about the eyes. I'd neglected to shave. That was something rare for me. I have an obsession about being neat around the chin, and enjoy the feeling of the blade ploughing through artificial foam, whipping off the stubble. It was a rite of manhood, meaning nothing. Except that it worried me to see that stubble, I got to running my fingertips up against it, to considering the effect, say, on a policeman.

Or I was thinking of nothing at all, just of the car's motion, the displacement of air. And the hiss as it did so. A nice little car: handled well, quick response.

Fiddling about with the mirror, wondering if I could stop somewhere, sharpen myself up. They have those big everything places where you can get a reheated meal and fill up. Places where the truckies get together to chew the fat and pass amphetamines. They have the same atmosphere all over the world, those highway stops. And pretty much the same food as well.

I'd pull in at the next one of those, see if I couldn't buy a packet of razors, straighten myself up in the toilets.

Making the decision, that's when I saw the Mercedes.

The first reaction was to conclude that it wasn't the same car. There had been others, the same model, a couple black, they'd gone past or I'd overtaken them.

Then I thought it funny the way it was settled into my speed.

Crazy thoughts. There wasn't a chance that they could have followed me. Starting from standing in the street. And not with me initially heading north, the wrong way. I reached forward, turned on the radio: 'Don't Cry for Me Argentina'.

Hell!

The car was still there. From what I thought I saw of the driver it could have been anyone. The windscreen was easier to see through than the smoked side and back windows. That was if there were smoked windows. I couldn't see anyone else but the driver. Funny, the way the car stayed there, behind me. I put on a little speed, wound up to a hundred and forty. The car still holding the road like an angel. Nicely balanced.

The Mercedes stuck with me.

Curious. They'll do that, though. It's an unconscious response. You overtake a car, there's a good chance they'll speed up, never thinking you wouldn't be there in the first place if you hadn't come up from somewhere. It's the racing instinct. The same the way people will turn three lanes into a Grand Prix fantasy. I guess it helps to make the miles pass, it's a diversion.

Did I have a Stirling Moss *manqué* on my tail?

Well, if I did, he was sitting low — there was the impression of him observing the road through, rather than over, the steering wheel.

I went up to a hundred and fifty, a little over. The car was happy. So was the Mercedes, still with me. That was taking the unconscious competitive spirit a bit too far. I dived in between two trucks, jammed on the brakes to get with their speed, sat there.

No Mercedes went flying past.

That proved it. How they'd done it I couldn't say. Or could I? There was only one man. He must have been sitting there in the car, waiting. He'd taken off at the same moment that I had. Would have been with me all the way. Keeping me in sight. Could he have one of those car telephones with which to ring back, to call his mates, keep them up to date? Well, why not? You see people everywhere chatting into them. They are

175

the device of the demi-decade, important for status. People reckoned it was smart to hold them to your ear, to be seen; no need to talk, no need for there to be another end.

Get off the road, Essington. Chances were they wouldn't really have any way of talking car to car. The car phones, they're to ring back to your secretary. Or are they?

We'd just crossed an expanse of water south of Rotterdam. It was getting into dusk. Fields on either side of the road, and here and there a brake of trees retained for sentimental value. I saw a notice saying 'Zevenbergen', and an arrow off to the right. There was a distance written underneath, a number of metres. With my foot flat to the floor I passed the truck I'd been sitting snug behind and found myself on the exit. I took it full bore, tyres giving of themselves with a scream. The tail held around the sweeping curve. I just missed a small van as I hit the Zevenbergen road, one car width each way.

Half a kilometre on I took a lane to the right; it was running between cow pastures, Friesians standing around waiting to drop their calves.

Nice, if you have time for it.

I'd figured that I was heading along parallel with the auto-route. I could even have been right.

He was still on my tail. The bastard! There was something in what I'd done — one plus — he couldn't tell anyone where he was getting lost, not clearly enough for them to come out and find us. It was him and me together in the country. Only difference being that he most likely had a gun.

The road did a dogleg. I planted my foot through it. He must have done the same, and was closing the gap. That was a problem. If he wanted to play tag, there was a lot more Mercedes than there was Sierra. More weight, more metal. He was going faster now, as well.

We were approaching a bridge that went high over a canal. It was like a ski jump. The Sierra left terra firma, came down with a bang as the chassis bottomed on the suspension. I hauled on the wheel, hit the brakes, spun the car through a hundred and eighty degrees, swerved to avoid a head-on, slid off the shoulder of the road and the tail slewed down over the grass into deep mud.

I planted my foot. Nothing. Only spinning wheels.

176

I leapt out as the Mercedes went into reverse and headed back at me. No choice but to take off across the grass, in the direction of a copse so small you could see the sky beyond it, between the trunks. Except for where there was a solid rect-angle, something like a barn, either in the copse or on its far side.

The fields were small, there were three fences to climb.

While I was getting over the first fence I heard a shot. Glancing back, I saw my pursuer, braced, taking aim along the barrel of a pistol. It was a long shot, he would have needed luck. It put speed into me though. I was over and off, increasing my lead. Perhaps the shot was just a frightener, something to make me freeze, make me pray.

I threw myself over the next fence, sloshed through a drain-age ditch and bolted on in the direction of the copse, surprising some cows and a pair of ponies that were chomping away at the pasture in the dusk. I looked back when I was among the trees. He was still coming, making slower progress than I'd managed, his short legs kicking out sideways with each stride, like a comic in a film. But totally unfunny.

The trees were growing close together without a scrubby understorey. The building was over the far side, beyond an-other fence which split the copse right down the middle. I dodged between trunks, went over the strung wires and stopped for an instant, looking back again.

Now I couldn't see him. He wouldn't have got to the trees by then but they obscured the view. It was more unnerving to lose sight: suddenly it put him everywhere and anywhere.

It was a barn, big swinging doors opening on to stalls, and a loft up top. On the far side there was an expanse of flat land running to a cluster of houses which just looked too far away. I was gulping air to fill my lungs, and my head throbbed. I pushed myself to do something more than simply drop to the ground and wait. But that was the big temptation, to say bugger it, to give up.

Why would they want to kill me anyway? If I was the one who knew the painting's whereabouts?

There were two doors each leading to a separate half of the building. One was shut, locked in place by a length of sawn timber slid between steel guides set into the cement holding the brick fabric of the structure together. The other hung open. I entered and climbed a ladder leading to the loft.

Only when I was up did I realize what I'd done. I'd cornered myself. Unless I elected to jump from the loft doors at one end. On the assumption that they opened. It was hard to tell, it was pretty dark up there, only slits of the late light getting in through cracks between boards.

I'd climbed up through an open trap-door. I calculated that the wisest thing was to stay close by that entrance. At least I could make it hard for him to get up on to my level. Unless he tried a shot through the flooring. The planks looked thick; the short barrel of a pistol doesn't give a bullet much penetration. And he'd have to be in luck to score a hit, blind.

So that was it.

And remained it for maybe ten minutes. I could hear him down there, walking about — thinking, I guessed. He could probably hear me as well. The two of us. We could have been found like that on the day of judgement. Representing something, some fundamental human obsession; botching our existences and guaranteeing we'd bake in hellfire for eternity. A subject for a painter, an image to use for guiding the young, showing them how not to squander a life.

Too late, too late.

He would have heard me moving about. Heard me go over to investigate the loft doors, rattle them, lift the bar holding them shut. He would have wondered when they swung open, creaking on the hinges. His mind demanding: What the hell is that?

Perhaps he went outside to check it out, what I'd been up to, to make sure the rabbit didn't run. I saw him inside, a small dark shape. Viewed from directly above, a strange shape, something less than human. Not the sort of creature with which you might be inclined to empathize. More like a thing than like a person. The gun, a big ugly object, it was held in one hand at the end of an extended arm, and pointing up at an angle. Someone intent on murder.

I was getting full of nothing. Maybe even a little light-headed. The gin had worn off, all eaten up by the exertion. My mouth was dry; a splitting headache, enough to eliminate most thought processes. I was hardly responding, just seeing, becoming a seeing eye: a kind of biologically formed camera.

My position was neither an advantage nor a disadvantage. That was how things were starting to pan out. I just didn't care all that much. I'd got that far, up into the barn, led there by chance. That felt good, to be arbitrarily guided rather than to stagger on under the illusion that I was making the decisions. I had the insane feeling that I'd hit on some newer, greater truth.

Too late?

That I had a mission: to avenge Tina.

And Cornelius?

I had the Paris images flip up in my mind. The boy on the bicycle, Robert standing there, viewing the world along his nose. And Tina, I was with her again, her crushed skull, the blood —for what? For some fucking stupid notion that had got itself into a warped mind. Into the head of some hoon who was out of sympathy, who could no longer see all those sparks, all those flashes lighting up the universe; who couldn't comprehend the multitude of 'I ams' that we all are. Some crazy mug who took it on himself to put out the lights — for others.

He coughed.

Extinguish us for money!

The thought exploded in me. For money! That was what was down there. Natty too, natty like the man in the brown hat.

I began to tremble. Sugar levels bouncing up and down the scale. Mind feeding itself stimulants to ward off sleep. A splitting ache moving about, stalking the sections of my brain, and finally settling in right behind my eyes, as much a colour as a pain — electric green, the current leaping between points. And that murdering animal down there.

Down there was each and every life-defeating force that had crawled out from beneath nature's rocks as they cooled at the beginning of time.

Crazy, I know, but . . .

I leapt.

The little bastard didn't know what hit him. All of Essington falling out of the ceiling like that. He concertinaed under the weight. The gun rattled as it slid across the barn's cobble floor.

I'd dropped straight through the open trap-door, without a thought in my head; not a calculaton of the moment, nothing. That's why you can't fight a tiger, they don't think, they go straight into it: instant insanity. With a dog, part of that's already trained out of them, just by being handled as a puppy.

But a tiger! Ever watch them prowl a cage, svelte anger in each step? It's an extreme of beauty.

Nothing beautiful in me landing on top of the little gunman, though. Only madness, like drunkenness, insuring against bodily harm.

I trod on his neck as I reached for the gun. He didn't move much, not at first. Didn't have it in him I guess. Then he rolled over, tried to get up on to hands and knees. I kicked him in the face. Then a second kick, that one was for Tina. So was the third.

I got myself out of there before I turned into the Incredible Hulk. I dropped the bar into place, leaving the barn looking neat, both doors closed.

The cars posed a problem. I wasn't driving back along the autoroute in the Mercedes, not with the other lot cruising up and down on the look out for it. But the Sierra was bogged.

Throwing myself at a solution to that one I worked in a kind of frenzy, still not thinking, just acting, and getting it right. Feeling good on it, as well. I'd had that notion before: that I was an animal on which they'd drafted a human consciousness, that the graft hadn't taken all that well. I did better as root stock: hardy, rust resistant.

By working it backwards and forwards against itself I got a loose strand of wire in the nearest fence to break and then managed to pull it through two posts so I had a reasonable length. I did the same trick again at the other end — shades of the station hand — finishing up with thirty feet or so of wire in one piece. Doubled up it served as a towrope, looped around a shackle at the back of the Mercedes and tied to the front of the Sierra whose handbrake I pulled up into a just-on position, to produce sufficient drag to stop it rolling off the other side of the road's camber if I managed it pull it up out of the mud.

The Mercedes had all the weight and the torque to do it, no trouble, a simple case of reversing the cars' circumstances. The Sierra came up on the road and the Mercedes went into the ditch on the other side. I got the Sierra going, eased it forward to take the tension off the wire, uncoupled, then took off. The

180

hope was that they wouldn't have the luck to spot me. I knew that at least one of them had seen the car, they probably had the number.

I was streaking south when the thought struck me that there could still be a way of having me stopped at the border. You'd only have to pass information on to the police to achieve that, to get the car checked out. Maybe officials would hold me up for half an hour, enough time for Brown Hat to bridge whatever gap existed. And who was to say who the police would be working for? There didn't seem to be a country in the world that was still in control of its law enforcement.

I pulled in at the next truck stop, the last in Holland if I got the sense of the notices right. I was mud-splattered, my trousers were torn, I wore a face of stubble. Very much the worse for wear I set about buying a ride south over the border. In the end I got it with a Spaniard who'd carried peaches up to Amsterdam and was back-loaded with drums of some wetting agent, the kind they use with agricultural sprays.

I gave him five hundred guilders and blessed the Lord who'd made me rich.

I sat up there, the hitch-hiker, listening to synthesizer rock; waking back into it each time my head tried to fall off my shoulders. Getting into Brussels was like travelling to the moon. And when I got there, weightless, I bid my taciturn Espagnol *adiós*. I paid cash up front at a hotel where there was a very careful check of my passport, some looking up lists of wanted names, and muted conversations in the back room. Then I passed out on a made bed.

Chapter 16

Morning, Brussels, oh hell!

Grey.

Feeling watched, I made my way through the uninviting streets, looking for a department store. With every step I expected a heavy official hand to drop on to my shoulder with threats of carting me off — the unwanted alien. To be wanted, not to be wanted; it's not just to do with money. You express affluence through your appearance. That's our world, where it's got to. I guess I was saved by the pouring rain. I looked as much a drowned rat as a social undesirable. Any true Christian would have been moved to compassion by the figure I cut, I felt sure of that. Nobody was moved.

I found what I was looking for and went inside, into the warmth, past the heady perfume counters with their painted china-doll ladies, past silken undergarments, up the escalator to brand-name counters; all big labels present, all economically correct. I was in the women's section.

I was forced to ask the way of a man wearing a tag. He kept his distance, in case I was infectious: getting mud-soaked could spread like disease, either by touch or by droplet. Despite the chilly demeanour I was tempted to hug him as reward for his directions.

When God created all and saw that it was good he already had in mind the idea: plastic money. He had conceived the credit card. Amazing! That's the point of his special time–space relationship with the world. As Adam bit the apple the stock market crash of 1987 was also on the cards. It's all always been there. Makes you think, doesn't it? Well, that's the way it was put to me at school. Perhaps I'm theologically out of date.

My piece of plastic — what, four inches by two? — it made a new man of me. They even managed suit trousers the right length. The finishing touch was a brolly.

Back in perfume I had the ladies take turns to dab the precious fluids on their wrists as I sniffed them one by one before settling on what I was told was a safe, traditional fragrance, Chanel No. 5, Coco's gift to civilization.

Walking, searching for a taxi, I ran a hand over smooth-shaved skin — I had been offered toilet facilities once the credit limit was checked. Interesting that God had planned that little touch as well. Almost, one might have thought, unchristian of him . . . or is it her?

I passed a beggar a hundred of the Belgian francs given to me out of the till in men's shoes.

Charming, helpful to a man with a magic card, KLM's desk at the airport popped me into a seat on the two o'clock flight to Amsterdam. I was feeling perky, on the home run. About to pick up a van Gogh for my troubles.

Waiting for the flight I rang the hire firm, told them where to collect the car, explaining that I'd started to fall asleep at the wheel, that I'd had to give up, had caught a bus. What the hell did they care as long as they got the machine or the insurance, and had the imprint of a credit card to charge.

From Schiphol I took a cab straight to the hotel, checked out, picked up my bag and the rolled painting that had been nestling damp and sound in the safe. Then I headed back to the airport.

No calls from there: no need to let the world know my movements. But nor were there flights for Nice. I settled for Paris and we took off at 8 p.m. to arrive an hour later.

I was out of it! The van Gogh spent the night flat, in the chic Sixteenth Arrondissement, drying out. So did I. Euphoric — with nagging doubts.

Of course the sun was shining when we touched down at Nice. Brightly. I never ceased to wonder at the regularity of its presence. Nor at the way that sea shone out its own particular blue. Pollution or no pollution, it was all wonderful, wonderful.

A cab along the Promenade des Anglais, round past the port then up to loop Mt Boron. There it was, Villefranche, its bay, and over the far side, Cap Ferrat. I could see the roof of the Villa Rothschild in the outline of trees along the Cap's profile.

Home. They could snap at me, beat me, surround me with children, berate me with the orthodoxy of Dawn's ideology. I didn't care. They could castrate me, I'd ask for nothing more than a local anaesthetic. I was home. That good feeling. If nothing else there would be Desdemona's warm muzzle resting on my knee for comfort. Giving more than she got.

They were out. Rebecca told me that with a shrug which said: What else would you expect from all these strange people with their customs? The master returns and they are not here to welcome him. In her eyes you could see it writ: It would serve them right if the master vanished over the horizon and never came back.

She just couldn't understand that maybe nobody would turn a hair.

I made a call to my Dutch interrogator in the upstairs office at the police station. He was in, I pictured the hands fiddling with the fountain pen. Surely another perfect necktie today, more immaculate cuffs. He refused to sound particularly interested in the idea that it was me calling. Or that it was long-distance.

'There wasn't any option, not after what I saw had happened to those two in the canal house.'

'Since there is an investigation going on it would have been correct, Mr Holt, to have contacted us before you made a run for it.'

'Well, I'm contacting you now.' How about that?

'Civil of you.' Chilly of him, and facetious as well.

'Fuck you,' I said, then gave him the phone number and the address.

'Those I have already, Mr Holt.'

Good for Mr Smoothie. I hung up. What would happen would happen. There'd be the local constabulary, eager beavers all, to come around and let me know when they wanted me up in Holland.

I'd forgotten to ask about Cornelius.

Vincent van Gogh was laid out nice and flat again, settling himself down to life in a new climate. He'd come up well in spite of the ordeal. There were buckles where the drying had been uneven, and the occasional crack that could have been almost as old as the painting. He looked up at me with a pitiful eye, the dot

184

of a brown-black pupil captured in the middle of crude strokes of orange. There was definitely something about those eyes which anticipated Matisse. That was unexpected in a Paris van Gogh self-portrait. I guessed the sun must have been out that day, breaking through the smog of the late nineteenth century, getting at his pineal gland. That is what they reckon, that there is a gland in your head which responds to sun. Keep it in the dark and you get depressed.

Vincent van Gogh was the exception where that gland was concerned. It was the move south, into sunny Arles, that finally sent him right around the twist. Up till then he'd been what they used to describe as a difficult young man. By the Arles stage he was no longer young, no longer just difficult. He was terrifying the natives with his antics. It was the locals who'd insisted that he be put away. Maybe they thought he was possessed by the devil?

Desdemona and I went off on what was a regular ritual, when I was at home, the afternoon stroll around the pathway leading to the Villefranche beach. We mucked about among the debris carried in by what must have been big seas — piles of weed and, tangled in amongst it, all the rubbish we jettison in this ragtag world of ours. When the dog had done sufficient running to make up for the period of confinement in the garden with nobody paying much attention to her except Charlie, the poodle next door, when she was showing a lot of tongue and standing stiff-legged, belting the breath in and out, I figured it was time for the drink at the Bar Plage. That was the measure of a good day, to sit in the oblique rays of the sun and to drink.

Part of God's plan, as well. A better part.

Me, Essington Holt, I wasn't shifting out of the place again. Life was too short. The radius was going to be a couple of miles. Maybe the occasional trip over Mt Boron into Nice. But only when I was feeling really strong and able to cope with the excitement of the flower market; maybe an occasional visit to the Matisse museum as well.

Desdemona was lapping water out of her ice-cream bowl.

'You didn't throw it away?'

'Monsieur Holt!' Shocked. The waiter was a relative of the good Renardo, who wasn't? The man was like I-don't-know-what, he had strings going out all over the place. I sometimes got the feeling that I was being driven about by the duke of the place.

That he was waiting, like so many other Royals throughout Europe, for this republican madness to pass, for reinstatement to his proper place. So he could get back into rolling heads.

It could have been that the bar's management telephoned out word of my arrival — the timing felt like that. I was picking up my second glass of wine when Molena approached. He had an abashed smile on his face, like someone who was pleased to see a friend but who felt he might be interrupting something.

'Essington?' That tentative as well. As though wondering if we were still on first-name terms?

'Molena!' I don't know, I liked the sound of the word. The face didn't belong to a Claude — well, at least not to an Australian one.

In Australia, if your parents are thoughtless enough to call you 'Claude', you work out some way around it. You start to introduce yourself as 'Smiler' or 'Ginge'. Claude won't even shorten. 'Aude' makes it sound like you were christened Audrey. That would be worse.

'Bob' is good in Australia. Doesn't matter what sort of a little shark you turn out to be, if you're called 'Bob' they'll reckon you're a good bloke.

So it was 'Molena'.

I got up, we shook, I offered him a drink. He said yes, he'd join me. Then asked where I'd been.

I told him: 'Amsterdam.'

'You haven't?' Some alarm.

'That's right?'

'But it's been terrible up there.'

They'd read about it in France, about Tina and Cornelius? That was a surprise, I'd have thought there was enough violent crime in their home territory to fill the ghoulish columns of the papers. Bombs, sure, they went international, everybody got a kick out of a bomb. But a bashing and a shooting, their supply was exceeding news demand.

'What's been terrible?' I asked.

'Chet Baker.'

'Chet Baker what?'

Chet Baker was a blast from the past. A blast from my post-rural city days, listening to jazz, being cool.

'He is dead.' Molena was shaking his head in wonder at the horror of it. 'Dead,' he repeated, as though shattered.

186

Well, that was bad luck to lose a great trumpet player. Not that his style had been so good since a drug dealer smacked him in the mouth and knocked out most of his front teeth.

'How'd it happen?' I was less interested in the trumpeter's death than in the idea that this man, who was becoming the friend I felt I needed at that time, was also an enthusiast for jazz. Nobody listened to jazz except a handful of starry-eyed nutters.

'He fell out of a window.'

'In Amsterdam?'

'The thirteenth.'

'That was a Friday?'

'Perhaps,' thought Molena, 'the date pulled him out.'

'Come on,' I objected, 'you don't go for that shit.'

I neglected to tell him about the other deaths. What was the point?

I said: 'You're turning Socialist again?' There'd been reports that Mitterrand, now he was re-elected, was going to call a general election. Polls indicated that the Socialists would romp it in. That would be France running against what pundits declared was the political tide of the late twentieth century.

Molena must have sensed a probe in the question. He laughed. 'I'm not political, Essington, and I don't go for the bait.'

'Me, trying to catch *you* out? Hardly.'

The sun was getting right down on the western rim. One of the health addicts was swimming the bay, point to point, there and back. When I reckon I need it I go in for that too. I reckon I need it less and less. Maybe, I think, with age creeping up, I should just go along with the physical disintegration.

I ordered two more drinks.

Molena was beating about the bush. I could feel it. At the same time I calculated that the trick was to let *him* broach the subject of the deal. It was his thing. So, it was best that we went along with his timing.

We talked a bit more about Chet Baker, then Molena asked me about Karen, about how she was.

I said we hadn't bumped into each other since I landed back. I reckoned she'd be fine. The silk shop kept her at it over there in Nice.

'Which you don't like.'

'I'd rather it was otherwise.'

187

Cool, the expert, I should have mistrusted the man, he was so practised in his lead up.

I asked about the Maserati. Had he heard from his friend? Was it fixed?

'Indeed, yes. I have it. He has so little room in his workshop that I took it off his hands.'

'It goes?'

'Like the wind.' He slid a hand, el quicko, through the air.

'How much do I owe?' The mean streak. I was worrying about those clothes I'd bought in Brussels showing up on the monthly account as well.

Forgetting I had stolen a van Gogh as collateral, and that I didn't need it anyway.

Molena, hands out: 'He will add it up. The man is an artist, Essington . . . when should he do his accounts?'

I was free to fear that the car work was one of those small favours that sort of lock you into something you want like you want to fall off a building.

Abruptly Molena said: 'Tomorrow we will go and look at my proposal.'

'You mean you've got a child? How the hell did you manage that?'

'Not a child, Essington, but a building.'

'You'd better spell out this idea slowly. Me, Molena, I'm not quick-witted.'

'You are clever enough to play this game?'

'What game?'

'Of being stupid, Essington.'

'I kid you not.'

We'd walked along to the water slide. It wasn't being used. It stood there, grotesque against the deepening African sky. A couple of old codgers were playing *boules* without a great deal of enthusiasm while their wives worked at getting dogs on leads to piss on everything sticking up out of the ground. Desdemona followed them up, checking out the aromas.

Looking back from the water slide we could see over the railway that followed the coastline right across to Genoa and on around to La Spezia. We were viewing a row of concrete boxes stacked on top of each other between the railway line and

188

the main coast road, rather like a child might arrange match-boxes.

Not new to me. I'd been watching them go up, fill space. It seemed inevitable that every inch of ground got filled with some kind of architectural monstrosity. This one looked less monstrous than most. There was a big selling notice poking out on the road side of the construction. There was nothing to read from where we stood, the notice was intended to inform the cars not the trains.

A proprietorial smile spread all over Claude Molena's face. 'There,' he said, 'is the monument to my lack of business acumen.'

'Doesn't look too bad.'

'Too bad! It is excellent, sympathetic, it sits in the landscape, repeats the lines.'

'So do all buildings, Molena, except pyramids.'

'Can you say you don't like my building?'

'I just told you it wasn't too bad.' Keeping the voice flat, not wanting to chalk up anything more on the credit card.

'It is that which they've fought all the way. Every public authority has tried to stop me. You know why, Essington? It is because I am the little man. I am treading on people's toes. On a lot of people's toes. They have slowed me down, forced me to fight in the courts against this order and then against that one. Trying to stop me. They want to come in, to force me to sell the half-completed project at a loss. Then they get the profit. That is the way business is done down here.'

'I understood you were the native, Molena. That you had the contacts.'

'Not for something like this. And not a native either. I am an import, Italian. But, mind you, this is truly Italian soil. My family come from across there.' A vague gesture to the south-east. 'Even there we don't control the big business. We are the peasants. Here, on the Côte d'Azur, we're displaced by the French since they took us over in the last century.

'The banks, the big companies, they are all controlled from the north.'

'Well, that's bad luck.' I could feel the next move, sense the sentences forming in Molena's mind. Maybe I should have sprinted off into the twilight.

189

'This is why I've suggested an arrangement, Essington. You have said that you have a friend who has trouble adopting a baby. If that friend was to want to put money into my building I am certain that an adoption would be no trouble.'

'That sounds like a very questionable deal.'

'Not at all, nothing questionable about it.'

'Desdemona!' I called the dog. 'Then I'm still not sure I want to hear about it.'

'I asked you before, Essington, don't you trust me?'

'I trust you, Molena, sure. But I happen to know that there isn't any other way to get a baby unless you become caught up in some racket.'

Caught up in some racket! I'd just stolen how many million dollars' worth of painting?

'A racket! Essington, I am offended.'

'You were offended last time I said something to that effect. Molena, if we're going to discuss this thing you're going to have to be a hell of a lot less sensitive. Come on,' I said, 'let's have a coffee.'

The Bar Plage was closed by then, and they were cleaning up, so we wandered further along to a terrace café tucked into the bottom of the cliff which, in its less steep moments, becomes Villefranche-sur-Mer. An American, caught in a time warp, was strumming away on a guitar and singing 'Starry, Starry Night' — very Vincent van Gogh.

Even if the lyrics, to my mind at least, were not really Vincent's cup of tea.

Chapter 17

A cold welcome. That would be putting it mildly. Bloody freezing.

'When did you get back?'

I shrugged. There wasn't anything to be done about that tone of voice.

'Well?'

What could I say?

Sitting there, Lord and Lady Muck, picking at poached fish. Me being abstemious; needing to be, psychologically. I'd returned after being too long away at the wrong time, bridges burnt. Karen didn't see that I was lucky to be back at all; she couldn't anyway, I hadn't told her.

'What's that upstairs?'

'What's what?'

'The painting, lying there?'

'Do you really want to know?'

It's difficult being like that, both of us holding out. Karen didn't want it, I knew that. It wasn't written into her character.

She shrugged, forked a bit of fish off her plate, held it just outside her mouth. She was considering. 'Is it what I think?'

'Depends on what you think.'

She devoured the morsel, spoke through it. 'Stuff it then.'

'Karen . . .'

'Yes . . .'

'The foundation idea. That's fine with me. It really is. I've been going over it in my mind. It would be great, something for me to do, as well. I need something.'

'That's not how it looks to me. You just piss off, don't you, Ess? Anything goes wrong about the place and you vanish in a puff of smoke.'

'Is that fair?'

'Of course it is. I put up the foundation idea, you don't like it,

191

so, whoosh . . . no more you. What the hell am I supposed to do, sit here and twiddle my thumbs?'

'It was only that I thought we weren't going to see eye to eye on it. What I'm saying is that I've changed my mind.'

'It's a van Gogh, isn't it?'

I nodded.

She drained her glass.

We ate in silence for several minutes. A minute's a long time — well, it can be.

'A van Gogh,' she repeated.

'That's what it is.'

'You don't want to do anything about children. It would be tokenism, the troubles of the world are too great and there are too many of them. So why lift a finger? It was just some kind of middle-class self-indulgence. That was what you said, Ess. Tell me . . . what's a van Gogh then?'

'Not *middle-class* indulgence.' My try at getting us to see the funny side.

It didn't raise a smile.

'I'll grant you that,' Karen kept on, 'nothing average about a painting worth . . . what? Would I be going over the top if I suggested five million?'

'I wouldn't have a clue. It's just a sketch. Perhaps five million — US dollars though.'

'Or more?'

'Could be a lot more.'

'It could be, couldn't it?'

I said nothing, mopped a piece of bread over the plate. Rebecca made sauces. They didn't serve them like that anywhere else in the world. Not even in the Tour d'Argent. Not that I'd tried there, your father has to book the table for you at birth.

Karen put down the eating implements. She folded her hands on her lap. Her mouth was set as a line, lips turned in. There were things that might erupt as tears making her eyes swell.

Oh my God. I felt . . . This wasn't the real Karen. All the stuffing was knocked out of her.

'Do you know what Dawn said when I told her about your objections, Essington?'

'You told Dawn.'

'Of course, who else has there been to talk to?'

'Karen . . .'

'Do you know what she said?'

'I can imagine.'

'You can?'

'At least I think so, only I'd lack the skills, I couldn't give it real bite. Tell me verbatim . . . I can take it.'

'You know what Dawn is . . .' A stifled sob.

'I know . . . it isn't that which worries me, Karen. She likes to hump girls, that's fine. There are a lot of people who want to do that. It's the puritan ideology she's taken on board along with the erotic drive that I sometimes find hard to take. The combination. I'm sorry, she's your chum.'

'Don't tell me that, Essington. You two, you get along all right. I've seen it. There's a friendly banter. You couldn't live without it, picking at each other. But, what it boils down to . . . you're both the same kind of beast.'

'Karen!' I was surprised. What was going on? 'What did she say?'

'What you said.'

'What do you mean?'

'The same argument, as though the pair of you had gone through it together, rehearsed the lines. Essington, I don't think you undsrstand how I feel though. Dawn doesn't understand either. When I lost that baby, Ess . . . Oh, Ess . . .'

She chucked the empty glass at the wall.

When Rebecca opened the door I was holding Karen, attempting to comfort her. I could feel the misery of each sob, they went right through me as well.

Rebecca shut the door.

'I've changed my mind, Blue, now I agree with you. We start a foundation.'

'A van Gogh, Ess. Do you know how many people could live off a van Gogh?'

I knew how many could die as well.

I said: 'Dawn's wrong. The same as I was wrong. We were repeating things that are current. That's the easy way to think, parrot-mouth wise. Us, we need our solution. The personal one. Bugger the ideologues. We want to do it so we go ahead.'

'No we don't.'

'We don't?'

'That's what really got to me, Ess. You're right, both of you . . .
I know it. Totally right. I can know it but not accept that it's true.
You understand what I mean?

'Do we have a cigarette?'

I hunted up the packet. Rebecca always returned it to the same
drawer. A place for everything, everything in its place. Karen
blinked as I brought the flame up. She drew in hard. And again,
then stubbed it out into her plate.

She walked over to the glass doors opening on to the lower
terrace. 'Essington, that's what got to me. That the desire could be
so strong. That even the idea of being able to think — I mean to
think straight — it's . . . it's nothing is it?

'What are we? Fed all this garbage about every damn thing and
we can't even control how we react. None of us can, not when it
really matters. You're right, you're both right. I know it. I should
sit down and take it. Invent some new game to get me through life:
start more shops, print more silk. Go and piss in the pockets of the
swines — they are swines, you know that? — the people who run
the fashion industry up there in Paris. The ultimate bunch of
phonies. You wouldn't use them for anything, they don't even
look good.'

Off on a tangent.

She stopped. Turned around. She went slack, stared at me, her
arms hanging down by her sides. 'Essington, it is nature talking
through me. It won't shut up.'

'Then we try the foundation.'

'No we don't.'

'What then?'

'I wish I knew, I really do.'

I rang Molena before we went to bed. I told him I wanted to get
into the scheme, pronto.

The morning, we agreed, we'd meet first thing. I wanted
something watertight before I played around with Karen's
emotions.

I put the van Gogh away in a drawer, locked it, then we slept,
woke, talked, slept, talked our way through the hours of darkness.

With a brave face and a bit more make-up than usual, at ten
o'clock Karen headed off for the silk world. Renardo drove her in

194

the Bentley Continental. I'd suggested that. I also wanted him to pick up a stretcher for the van Gogh. It was still a standard size, no problem about that.

Waiting for Molena to turn up I tried a call to Amsterdam. Henk picked up the phone. I asked him how he'd got on with the painting.

It wasn't a van Gogh. He tried to make it sound as though he'd picked that straightaway. To sound as though it was Albert who'd let himself get carried away.

'That might be why you don't have a bullet in you by now.'

Silence at the far end.

'Cornelius?' I asked.

'He is dead,' said Henk. 'They said he had recovered a little, that he was strong, should make progress. And then he died.'

'That's tough,' I said.

I hung up.

It must have taken the other lot much less time to figure out that the Loos forgery they'd snatched wasn't the real McCoy either. They'd been on to it right away.

Those were the two decoy cards used up. I still held the third, and it was safe upstairs. And it was the genuine article. What was I to do with it? Firstly I was to tack it on to a stretcher. After that I'd have to consider the problem. Was it a moral question? Or an ethical one?

And there was the complication that I didn't know any of the people who might have a claim to it.

Clever little me to sniff the painting out, to get it safely home. Maybe it was meant to be my reward.

That was how I was feeling. I was feeling fairly good, feeling quite clever. Cornelius . . . I'd never know the man. He'd died. So had Chet Baker. So had a lot of people. So would we all. The trick was the things we did before we died.

I was looking forward now to making life work at home. We had the ingredients so it had to be no more than a mind problem. There was the sun, shining. And Desdemona down on the fence discussing philosophy with the poodle.

No, I was on the up.

Molena honked at the grill gate that kept us sealed off from the wild world. I pressed the button, it slid open and he eased the Maserati up the gravel surface of the drive. Hell, he'd even had the man respray the bodywork — no more crazed and oxidized paint.

The whole thing was concrete. There were the boxes I'd seen from the waterslide, with their concrete slab floors and the walls that looked as though they'd been cast somewhere else and fitted into place like with a children's building set. Yet the feel wasn't too bad. There was a Post-Modern touch: predictable, absolutely kitsch Greek columns placed here and there, supporting nothing, simply referring to the Roman history of the coast.

The thing Molena kept on telling me about was the fact that every apartment had a view of the Mediterranean. That was clever. And he'd had an inspiration with the planting of twenty-foot palms. They helped to locate the building in the landscape.

'What do you think?'

'It's fine, looks good.'

'You really think so?'

He was like a kid, or some artist, seeking appreciation.

'I like it.'

'So, what do you say?'

'It's not just me, you realize that, Molena, it's Karen.' We'd dropped the pretence. We were now talking about us, about the Holts — we were the ones with the adoption problem. As though that was news to Molena. 'If there's anything fishy or that's liable to come unstuck, I'd want to know it now.'

'I give you my word.'

Who but me would take the word of a type like Molena?

Answer, nobody.

'As I've told you, Essington, it simply is not true that there is a shortage of children for adoption. In China there are thousands of unwanted female children, people get rid of them so that they can have another attempt to create a son. The rule of one family, one child — that is what it leads to. There is a market in South American babies, as well. It is only fanatics, religious or political, who are stopping the whole thing. They claim the infants are reared to become servants, or perhaps that they will learn to worship non-kosher gods.'

'I understand all that, it's the paperwork that I want to be dead sure of. It has to last a lifetime.'

'It will, I promise.'

196

What Molena had put together was a package. Something unthinkable to any other than such an anarchist mind. He didn't give a stuff for the law, for the regulations. Adoption, building, it was all the same. All he was after was saving his neck. And maybe sustaining a certain style. I got the feeling that that was all he'd ever been after. Did it make him less reliable than the holier-than-thous who devoted their only mortal trip to creating regulations?

He wanted money.

I buy four of the apartments as is, for well below their final market value, and that supplies him with a bank. He finishes the lot, using my purchase money, then we sell. It looked all right to me. The price he quoted sounded good. There would be documents drawn up and, providing my lawyer didn't pick holes in it, I was in. If the market dropped, then the worst I could expect was to be stuck with four white elephants for a few years. They could always be rented to provide some sort of a return. Molena was in that bind as well, it was something we'd have to share.

Part two of the deal couldn't be committed to paper. That was where the trust really came in. In exchange for me being the bank for the apartments he would produce a baby. He'd looked into it after our first conversation. They were available. The worst I'd be doing was saving a child from some southern Italian orphanage. He spoke about those institutions with feeling.

Naples — we were to be blessed with a tiny Neapolitan. As far as paper was concerned, there would be a birth certificate coming up, with us as the legitimate parents; names, ages, the lot, all in the right order and in the right place.

My qualms had been about the mother.

No need. One hundred per cent untraceability. That was the feather in Molena's cap.

Some deal. Yet I was getting to feel an equivalent of the tug of nature that Karen had described. Nothing logical in what I was getting us into. It was a response to the voice inside, to something primitive. In my case I was turning us into a family. Anything less and as sure as eggs get to be little chickens we'd fall apart. The past month had made that clear. It was all right to be back together, even to be talking pleasantly for a while. The problem was still there — a beast waiting to emerge again.

197

'I'll talk to her.'

'Talk to her, are you mad?'

'Molena!'

'You can't talk about this sort of thing, Essington. Think about it, the ifs, the buts. We are dealing with something that can't be discussed. It is too hot. Too many side-issues. What if the mother this? What if the mother that? What if in thirty years? These are questions without answers. But they stop you, Essington. They can make you incapable of doing a thing. A deal like I'm proposing, you embrace it. These little girls, they don't want children . . . not till the idea is put in their sweet heads by an earnest nun or, worse, a social worker of some kind. Thank heaven there aren't too many social workers in our beautiful Napoli. If the idea is fed to them they like it. But it could be any idea. They would still like it.

'Essington, that is the essential element of politics, the feeding of ideas. Look what Mussolini was able to feed as an idea? Swallowed by most of Europe! Believe me, Essington, the mothers don't want the children. We are talking about girls, fourteen years of age, less, some on the way to being addicted to heroin. Mauled by drooling bankers, retired generals. OK, they will weep some evenings, remembering. Remembering which child? For how long will they weep? Will they even know that they weep? Really, I ask you, will they know why? No. It is just the tears of the damned.'

'Fine, Molena, you've made your point. Perhaps I could get a tape recording of that, play it to Karen.'

'You don't need a tape recording. She will know. If she knows anything about the history of humanity, she will understand.'

It was agreed. He'd bring the papers around in the next couple of days.

'Hey! that's quick.'

'I've been putting this together for a while.'

'You were that confident?'

'I had a feeling. When you get them you just have to follow.'

That was my argument now too, and Karen's I guessed.

Chapter 18

A big morning in the silk business. Karen had gone off an hour earlier than usual, taking the Citroën. There was a presentation to be finalized for Dawn to cart off to the United States on the evening plane. Their business aggression seemed boundless: there was a shop set up in Paris, significant sales being made to Japanese designers and now this move to pick up outlets in the States. Both Dawn and Karen were keen to get out of the retail end of marketing and to concentrate more on creating the fabrics. That was where the satisfaction was.

I watched the car vanish and the grill gate slide shut — the magic of electricity. Then I poured another coffee and topped up with hot milk from a second gleaming white jug.

Not too bad.

There was a United States warship sliding across on my side of the horizon, trying to keep the likes of me feeling secure. Its masters not seeing that their toy could have had the reverse effect.

What did I have to worry about?

Some time I'd need to straighten things up with Grantley. He'd be thinking kinder thoughts about me by now, but there was still the problem of him helping to nick the painting. There had to be something in it for him. Yet how to pay that something without causing offence? There'd be an answer, it would come.

And there was nothing surer than that I'd be making a return appearance in Holland, most probably several, helping the police prove their point, whatever that might turn out to be. But those trips would take place on some unspecified tomorrow. Till that time I could forget about it.

Rebecca called me to the phone just as Renardo brought the Bentley, in all its yellow splendour, to the front of the house. That was his first and usually his only move for the day, the slow

199

drive around from the garage, then a quick rub-over of the paintwork with a chamois.

Not a bad life if you can get it.

'Mr Essington Holt?' Not English. Maybe the inflection of the Netherlands.'

'Who's speaking?'

'Is that Mr Holt?'

'Can I tell him who's calling?'

Rebecca kept on doing that. She couldn't get used to the idea of me being wary of the phone. That attitude was so very different from my deceased aunt's: she'd liked nothing better than to send samples of her biting wit along the wires. Me, I had my mail delivered to the silk shop in Nice; that was also the address on the plastic credit cards, on all things like that. Villa du Phare was a refuge. Minimum communications. Just the trees and out beyond them the lighthouse doing all the signalling anyone could use.

Yet, when someone did get the number, Rebecca, who just refused to understand, rushed to the nearest handpiece with a manic joy. Maybe their phone never rang either. Not that I could believe it; the Pincis were involved in a lot of local activity, or seemed to be.

'I am speaking with him, I think,' said the voice.

Insistent bastard. 'What can I do for you?'

'My name is Haryanto Carbentus, Mr Holt. I believe you have had contact with my family.' Very correct the way he spoke. Stiff, but getting it clear.

'Is that so?'

'With my relative, Robert Carbentus.' Shivers running up my spine.

'I knew him in Australia . . . let me see . . . would it be thirty years ago?'

'Surely more recently than that, Mr Holt?'

'Mr Carbentus, can I ask you what you want? I've got a lot . . .'

'I'm sure you have, Mr Holt.'

'Then?'

'First, Mr Holt, I explain myself. I belong to a Javanese side of the Carbentus family.'

'And . . .?'

'I will be blunt with you. I have come here, to Europe, to recover some property.' Cool as all get out.

'Is that so?'

'My half-sister — I believe you met her, Mr Holt — she was . . .'

'Was?' Me trying to sound uninformed.

'I would have thought you knew . . . She is dead, Mr Holt.'

And, by the sound of things, he couldn't give a damn.

'Get to the point, Mr Carbentus.' Was this really a Mr Carbentus?

'It is a painting, Mr Holt. I believe you have stolen this painting.'

'You're right, Mr Carbentus, I did steal a painting, one by the artist, Pieter Loos.'

'That is not what I'm talking about.'

'Try what I'm talking about then, just for a change. I'm talking about a man in a brown hat who was leaning on Tina Carbentus right up to when she was killed. A man, Mr Carbentus, who had been putting pressure on her for some time, some years, Mr Carbentus. Because she was sleeping with her half-brother, that was one reason. The main reason being because she should have been finding out where he'd hidden Daddy's Vincent van Gogh. Does that add up for you, Mr Carbentus?'

It had fallen into place in my mind. It felt right. This was the man I'd seen talking with Tina on the far side of the canal. He'd been Indonesian like his half-sister. The result of old man Carbentus putting it about. With his dick hanging out it seems he hadn't been able to keep his big mouth shut either. Spinning yarns about the painting, about the wealth it represented. They'll do that, your visitor from across the waters: they'll tell fantastic tales of breeding, of property, of lost fortunes waiting to be reclaimed. They've been telling that story since the first keel was laid.

'Mr Carbentus, before I hang up on you, can I ask you one thing? Who killed Tina? Did you? Or was it one of those amateurs you hire?'

'You will see me, Mr Holt.'

I put the phone down. I was shaking. Shaking angry. Then I was just shaking. That was when I'd fully grasped the essence of his message. And its meaning.

201

I would see him.

I put the cap on a bad start to the day by telling Rebecca that if she answered the phone like that again I'd have the fucking lines ripped up. A man has a right to resist telecommunications.

I removed the van Gogh from the drawer, took it into the room I'd adapted as a studio once when optimistically envisaging myself whiling away the days up there, making pictures. There was a canvas on the easel, it had been in place for four or five months, nothing more than colour notes inside a jumble of loose, brushed lines. A landscape — imagined, with rolling hills and paddocks marked out as warped rectangles. In the middle distance I had a horse with its head raised, alert. Right up the front, staring out at the viewer, the head of a boy. I'd put too much into inventing the thing. There was something wrong, I could feel it, but couldn't put my finger on what it was.

So, it had sat like that, in limbo.

I laid the van Gogh out on a drawing table and examined the fold-overs. There were signs of wear. I'd need to stick paper in there, glued against the surface of the canvas as reinforcement, just like Grantley had suggested.

I went through what I had and found a couple of sheets of Japanese mulberry paper which is exceptionally strong because of its long fibres, and it is soft — it would sit close to the canvas without causing distortion when stretched.

Rebecca interrupted with a stiff face and the message that Mr Molena had rung. Could I return the call? She rebuffed my attempt to get the relationship back on a normal footing after the dressing-down I'd given her following Haryanto's communication. I'd thought about that while I'd been gluing the paper to the canvas. Rebecca, who had been my friend, who had made things easy for me in all sorts of ways, and I'd snapped her head off, as though I thought I had the right.

Wealth can do that, it can distort your perspectives.

How could I tell her that the burst of temper was because the call had been from a murderer?

It would have been worse to pass on that information. It would have made her protective; I'd experienced that before, as well.

'Molena.'

'Essington, could I visit you tonight?'

'How's it going?'

'It's done.'

'Already . . . Do you have them coming off conveyer belts?'

'As I said, I had made preliminary arrangements.'

'Are you sure you don't trade in these things?'

'We are to trust each other, Essington, that was agreed.'

'You mean you bring the baby tonight? We aren't prepared, Molena, we just don't have the stuff.'

'The papers, for you to sign. The baby will come later.'

'That's better, what time?'

'After sunset sometime, around eight o'clock, eight-thirty.'

'See you then.'

In our bedroom the small package, perfume, still gift-wrapped from the Brussels department store. It was sitting on top of a ridiculously ancient chest of drawers with mother-of-pearl inlaid into every front panel. That was where I'd kept the van Gogh since getting home. In the bottom drawer.

Karen hadn't paid the package any attention. Originally it had been intended as a present, something I'd brought back — the traveller returned. That was what we men did — a length of silk from faraway China, rubies from India. But once in the house it had seemed inappropriate, like evidence of some thinking that was totally out of touch; that was after I'd come face to face with the reality of Karen's sadness. Nor did it fit in all that well as a gesture to someone who was trotting the world herself half the time, dealing in bolts of silk. She should have been bringing one of those men's underarm deodorants to her beautiful layabout boy.

Except I'm not so beautiful.

The perfume might have been a way of placating Rebecca. I thought about that, entertained the idea, then dropped the package into the bottom drawer. Something else I'd got arse about. They had me confused, Dawn and Karen, now Rebecca. I was losing hold of my role in life.

I looked through the window and across the grass. There was Desdemona, she wasn't confused. She was sitting between her legs, staring out to sea like a retired captain. That was also her springing position. Seeing her like that made people uneasy.

I rang Karen. How was it going? How about a drive when she'd got through the business with whoever they were?

That would be fine.

We worked out that I'd pick her up at the shop in the rue de France, mid-afternoon.

'I've someone coming, around eight.'

'Who's that?'

'I thought a drive, maybe a drink up in the hills. The sun sets later up there.'

'"The sun sets later up there" . . . you and your schoolboy geography. Who're we expecting tonight?'

'I'll tell you about it when I see you. It's a business deal.'

'Oh no!'

'Oh yes, I'm afraid.'

'About three,' she suggested.

'Fine.'

Rebecca caught me in the corridor. 'There was another call this morning, I think it was the man who called first.'

'What did you tell him?'

'I asked to take a message.'

'And?'

'He hung up.'

'Rebecca, I'm sorry about this morning. It's that man . . . he's . . .'

What was I explaining for?

'That's all right.' She shrugged. They live in the real world. People snap each other's heads off all the time. Me, I'd never grown into that. Living with my mother, the two of us pussyfooting around all the long day.

'We stick to that then, Rebecca . . . I don't take calls direct.'

'If you like.'

I finished off stretching the van Gogh, propped it up against the wall, examined the thing. Well, not a masterpiece, not by any means, but historically important as a document. Not that they made such distinctions out there in the marketplace: you get an authentication for the thing and they'd be ripping one another to pieces for it.

After all, hadn't people been doing just that already?

If I was going to hang on to it — and I hadn't got my mind clear about that, not yet — the thing would be to keep it out of the way. Out of everybody's way, allowing time to befuddle the human memory a little bit. Even me, with at least half the bones in my body being dishonest ones, would feel awkward about hanging it straight up on the wall.

So it went back into the mother-of-pearl inlay chest of drawers' bottom drawer, but not with the bottle of perfume by its side. This time it went into the bottom bottom drawer which you got at by removing a front panel. That had been one of my aunt's little joys, secret hiding places; after her death it had taken months to get into them, despite the clear instructions, even scribbly diagrams, in her will.

Then Desdemona and I went off for our constitutional, and playing about by the sea.

Renardo hated the Maserati being there. He glowered at the thing when I eased it around the front of the house. He was raking, making patterns in the gravel, striations radiating out from the Bentley's wheels. Me having the Maserati was his own blasted fault, him being so possessive about the great yellow tank. As though it was some extension of my dead aunt, some part of her that was remaining with us here on earth. What was I supposed to do? Get stuck at home or go about everywhere with a chauffeur? As though it was the Twenties!

Me taking the Bentley off on my own was quite simply not on, not with Renardo. So, an impasse.

And the Maserati was scab labour, that was the way he saw it.

I mentioned the weather, we ummed and ahed. Then I told him that there was a madman around who'd been ringing up.

That perked him up. Renardo . . . well, to tell the truth, I had a fantasy of him being the local Godfather. Of it simply suiting him to be connected to my house. It was a good address and he really didn't have to do anything more than he would in his own place.

I told him to take care. Being fair, I explained a bit about what had happened in Amsterdam. Just so he'd know what we were up against. If we were up against anything more than threats.

You can't tell. There was no way of knowing what Haryanto Carbentus would do to get his hands on the prize. He'd come a long way already.

Renardo stood, the expression somewhere between funeral director and the dead. He was thinking. An old man who'd seen a lot of life. He certainly wasn't running about with arms flapping. Just thinking, nothing more.

'I could get some of my people . . .'

'Renardo, it isn't like that, I don't think. I simply thought it was better for you to know. The place is secure enough as it is.'

Aunt had transformed the Villa du Phare into a fortress. There was the remote-controlled gate; the rest of the perimeter was a fence, chain wire with barbs running along the top. All an expression of how much she'd feared for her art collection. And well she might have done.

I'd added Desdemona — well, the fact is that the dog had sort of added herself. Formidable.

Karen already looked interested when she emerged from the shop, you could see that she couldn't wait to hear what sort of a disaster I was planning next. I was double parked and already the good Niçoise drivers were leaning on their horns. That always tempted me to pocket the key and simply walk away.

'Where to?' I asked.

The Citroën could rest up in the parking station for the night, get its molecules together. We took off in my flash tank.

I repeated: 'Where to?'

'It's your idea.'

That's the thing about the hills in behind the coast. They are an idea. You go up into them and there is . . . well, just hills. Maybe I lack the right romantic response. They burst into flames in the summer and take a few lives when they do. So you travel through the occasional stretch of death landscape while getting to where you may not really want to finish up. The people who manage to get the conflagration going each year were already gathering strength in the streets. June hadn't come around yet but the premature summer crowd was there in force: all those people who arrive early to miss the crowds. If that movement goes far enough the place will finish up empty in July. Which isn't likely.

It was slow going in the traffic. Unbelievably slow. Heading for the middle road, the Moyenne Corniche; not much sense of destination. That meant easing across to the east of town then coming around the back of Mt Alban. I was working at it.

'You brought the dog!'

'She likes it.'

'One day, Essington, you may be asked to choose . . . Desdemona or me.'

'I like the harem as it is.'

'Pig.'

'So I can take it that things went well this morning?'

'Better than well.'

'And Dawn, beating their heads together in New York?'

'It's full on, Ess. I tell you, they can't get enough of the stuff. Don't ask me why.'

'Fresh ideas, I suppose.'

'It has to be something. The trade off the street is going to seem like petty cash. The problem now is to get the set-up, to be able to guarantee delivery. For that we need . . .'

'More staff.'

'Not so much that, Ess, we need to get a good system. Get it ultra-efficient. People talk about recessions, about crashes, about the house falling down. There isn't a sign of that in the marketplace. There is money out there and the rag trade's after all it can get.'

'The right business at the right time.'

'Where are you taking me, lover boy?'

'Karen, we're headed up into them there hills and we is going to have a time of it.'

'Hands on or hands off?'

'You write out the rules.'

Us playing at happy. Us pretending that there wasn't any problem, that you could close your mind off in any direction you wanted, be selective.

'Essington . . .' Total mood change.

The dog had her head out the window, tongue out, shoulder leaning on my shoulder.

'Yes?' Apprehensive.

'Can we draw a line across that page?'

'What you want . . . only it may not be necessary.'

'May not be necessary! What are you saying?'

There was Eze coming up. Perched high above the sea. A standard outing: you went to Eze when the weather wasn't right for swimming. One of those quaint villages dating right back, perched up on rocks so the inhabitants, when they weren't at their worship in the Chapel of the White Penitents, could pour molten lead over the heads of their screaming neighbours.

We were in a stream of traffic. 'How about Eze?' I suggested.

The car made the decision for us. It spluttered, then it stopped.

'Eze it is.' Karen ironic. She'd never approved of the Maserati buy. 'Male fantasy' was what she'd called it.

What do any of us have but dreams?

'Your friend, Molena.'

We were walking along, feeling vulnerable on the edge of the road, cars belting past. I was keeping a good grip on Desdemona's short leash.

We had maybe five hundred metres to where a narrow road branched off and led to the clump of houses within the fortifications. They are mostly taken over by artisans and artists of various descriptions eking out a living ripping off the endless stream of visitors. I suggested that we walk down to the sea. But first I'd have to ring to get the car collected. That meant going to the bar.

We settled at a table. I went off and made the call. When I returned Karen had ordered coffee.

Clean living, no booze.

'Karen . . .'

'Essington . . .'

Both speaking at once.

'You,' she said, giving me vocal right of way.

'I worked out that we can adopt a baby, Karen. I've found a way.'

Not a doubt, not the shadow of a doubt showed on her face. 'Essington Holt!' She pounced on me, startling Desdemona who went into her crouch. A chair fell backwards. 'You haven't!'

'Blue, tonight we get the papers.'

'How . . .? You didn't tell me!' Suddenly indignation, yet tempered with the joy.

'I didn't know.'

'How, Ess, how've you done it?'

'This is the bit you're not going to like.'

'There's a catch?'

So I told her what I'd settled with Molena. Explaining it while the car he'd conned me into buying sat up there on the road making Mr Maserati's face red.

Karen and I went over the transaction in detail, going through the objections I'd already raised, me filling in with Molena's responses.

It didn't trouble her one bit. Nothing did.

I recounted the stuff about the child prostitutes of Naples, all of it. We wrestled in there for a while, asking each other about how the mother felt, would feel, should feel.

No answers to that now — would there ever have been?

'Ess, we should risk it anyway.'

I couldn't believe it, Karen agreeing just like that.

She said: 'At the worst it wouldn't be so very different to the whole foundation thing. They'd just be borrowed. This child, Essington, the odds are against the mother surviving other than as some empty shell. It's awful, I know that, awful. But hell, it's real . . . like Moses being found in the bullrushes.'

'It may not be Moses, Blue, it could be a girl.'

Nietzsche, a notice tells us, used to walk up to Eze or down from Eze or both. That was where he wrote *Thus Spake Zarathustra*. I know about Nietzsche because when I was young and wild there used to be this joke: 'Let's go to the Botanical Gardens and do some Nietzsche study.' That, it must be admitted, is all I know about the mad old philosopher.

He couldn't have been completely off the planet if he'd elected to walk up and down the track they've named after him. It was beautiful. We were going downhill, that was easy. The sea in front of us all the way, late-afternoon light shining on it through thin streaky cloud. The water's surface looked like a sheet of aluminium foil rolled out. We passed between neglected olive trees interspersed with the local pines. It felt sort of nineteenth century, walking along like that. No cars. They were both above and below us, roaring along in their endless procession, but not with us.

'Essington, I forgot, there was a man came in looking for you. Said he was doing business with you in Amsterdam.'

'What did he look like?'

'Small, Vietnamese he might have been, or Thai.'

'Or Javanese?'

'Dreadful, isn't it, not being able to tell the difference?'

I was making that little effort you need to make if you want to stop your heart jumping out of your chest. Haryanto was being thorough.

'He had a very smart summer suit, the latest style, a fraction baggy. And a hat, kind of old-fashioned with a soft brim.'

'And brown.'

'You do know him?'

'Why? What did you say?'

'I said there wasn't any Essington Holt that I knew of.'

'Karen, that man is dangerous. It could be he's mad as well.'

'As well?'

'He went off his rocker, smashed a woman's head to a pulp.'

'In Amsterdam?'

'I should have told you about it, Blue. We haven't had the chance though, have we?'

'I'm sorry, Essington.'

'Nothing to be sorry about, Karen. Only, you know it's half your fault getting stuck with me.'

'More like entirely, Ess. And it's great.'

We'd made it to the lower road where it runs just above sea level at Eze-Bord-de-Mer. I'd told most of the story by then. Our immediate need was a way to get home. We walked along watching for a vacant cab. No such luck. There were about six kilometres to travel and it wasn't so pleasant with no footpath and the dog getting spooked by passing cars. Before we got past the cluster of buildings just along from where the Nietzsche track headed for the cliff tops, I swallowed my pride and went into a bar to ring for Renardo to come and fetch us. Like a pair of runaway children who'd gone as far as they could go, we were to wait patiently by the roadside for rescue to turn up in the form of a yellow Bentley.

The phone didn't answer.

I tried again. Same result. That was strange. There was never a time when the phone wasn't attended. Rebecca seldom left the house. Only for shopping trips, and then she was careful to manage it so she went off when either Karen or I was at home. I don't think the house had been vacant since my aunt bought it in the 1950s.

I rang service difficulties while a middle-aged woman acted out her displeasure at having access to the phone denied by someone who obviously wasn't getting anywhere. An operator tried the number. It was fine, it was ringing. She told me, with considerable annoyance, that there must be nobody at home.

I rang for a cab. We stood outside and waited for it to turn up while people passed stories about us around the bar, having overheard my raised voice as I'd tried to get some sense out of the plastic and the wires; and having noticed the lion with the mane shaved off.

The cab took twenty minutes to turn up. It was going on for seven o'clock. After a brief argument about Desdemona, which I settled with money, I told the driver to hurry. Karen hadn't said anything for a while. I guessed that she was thinking, thinking of Amsterdam. Thinking of the man who'd come to shop.

I had the driver stop at St Jean-Cap-Ferrat — once a fishing village but now given over to real-estate agents and piss-elegant restaurants. At one of the latter I tried the number again. Me, right up by the front door, gripping the phone like a lifeline; the *maître d'* watching over a wasteland of white tablecloths and polished glasses, wanting me to go and for customers to arrive. Still no answer.

Very odd.

Karen didn't want to get left behind in the town. That was when things really started to fall apart. We argued about it. I said I'd be able to handle something on my own. That way I wouldn't be worrying about her.

She told me that there wouldn't be a problem in front of us if I didn't go round stirring things up. What did I need to pinch a van Gogh for anyway?

'I didn't steal the fucking thing,' I lied.

'You brought a maniac down on us. Worse, down on Renardo and Rebecca — old people, Ess. What chance have they got?'

The driver wanted to know what to do. As though the meter wasn't ticking over nicely enough. Stupid bastard.

The grill gate was closed. The Bentley was parked outside the front door, on the gravel. The house, standing there at the top of the drive, it had a curiously untended look. No lights. The stucco 'villa' façade suddenly uninviting, its warm ochre gone the colour of old bones in that half-light. The garden trees and shrubs cast no shadow.

The Bentley? That was fine, Renardo often didn't put it away till eight or nine o'clock. Except somehow then, suddenly it was wrong. Was it pulled up a fraction short of the mark?

I discovered that my remote control device for the gate was back at the Maserati. So I paid the cab off out on the street while Karen searched for hers in a seemingly bottomless shoulder bag. Eureka! It was in her hand. She pointed it, pressed the button. Abracadabra, the grill slid open.

Maybe that was fine. Well, Karen and I walked towards the house. Unaware of tension, Desdemona headed off to say hello to her wee friend, the poodle, who was barking shrilly through the boundary fence.

Shoes crunching on the gravel, I couldn't hear another sound — only our shoes, my gravel. On the house side of the Bentley I found its door hanging open. Now nothing felt right. Everything felt wrong, totally wrong.

I whispered to Karen, told her to head off, to get help. Amazingly, she obeyed. She was making for the gate when a voice instructed her to stop. There was a gun pointing directly at my chest. The man who must have been Haryanto was standing a couple of steps outside the front door. The gun was black, biggish; he held it in both hands, braced.

Funny that, in the dying light, I could see the gun in detail. Not so much the man but his weapon.

Karen came walking up. Her shoes on the gravel the loudest sound next to the throbbing at my temple.

'Come inside, Mr Holt. I have an exchange to propose.'

Karen drew level.

'Do be careful, both of you. I think you understand why, Mr Holt. I am not playing games.'

'Renardo, Rebecca?' Karen asked, a note of terror in her voice.

'The driver of this car —' Indicating the Bentley '— and the woman, they are quite safe.' Long pause. 'At this moment, at least.'

He let us pass before him through the door, then motioned us into the front reception room. It was empty.

'Where are they?'

'Safe, Mr Holt. Safely locked away, I promise you.' His voice had no nerves in it. The effect was chilling. No nerves, at all; no anxiety, nothing. A bizarre, matter-of-fact quality.

'What do you want?'

'My inheritance, Mr Holt.'

'What are you talking about?'

'Mrs Holt, sit down. No, not over there. Your husband over there, standing if you please. You sit here, thank you, sit by me.'

We did as we were told. Karen frozen, bolt upright, perched on a chair by Haryanto's side. He pressed the barrel of the gun in among the strands of her pale apricot-coloured air, and against her head.

'I don't have it,' I said.

'You have one minute, Mr Holt.'

'I don't have the fucking thing!'

'That is what Tina has said. Her language was better, of course. However, it is an answer that I do not find acceptable.'

'Why did you kill her?'

Sudden hysterics, he shrieked: 'She was a slut and a thief. Filth!'

Then apparently calm again.

So I started talking, getting at him: 'That's the hold you had over her, how you got her to go with you in that car. You forced her to cooperate, to help you search.'

'You have a minute, I have warned you.'

'But she couldn't do it, not in the end. She stuck with the Dutch connection.'

'I warn you. For your curiosity I will tell you this. She had no money, she had been sleeping with her brother. No family would have tolerated her. She should not have lived.'

'Essington . . . for Christ's sake! Give him what he wants.'

I was going to keep on talking. That was until I saw his thumb move, taking off the safety catch.

'It's upstairs.' I said.

Karen had squeezed her eyes shut.

'Then take me.'

'OK.'

We were side by side, Karen and I, taking care not to put a foot wrong. He came behind. We went out the door of the room and into the entrance foyer. The stairs led up from there, grand style, in a sweeping curve.

The front door was swung open. Turning away from it towards the staircase I thought I caught sight of something: an animal silhouette against the pale evening sky. I hesitated. Haryanto slashed the gun barrel down the side of my head, the front sight ripping across my ear.

Karen screamed, then Desdemona charged.

The report of a shot resounded in the foyer as I was hurled forward by Haryanto's body against mine. I was underneath him; I could hear the dog's snarling and the human voice now passed through a scream into another language. And then that voice being smothered, extinguished.

Dazed, back on my feet, I found Karen gazing in horror, fingers of half-clenched hands thrust between her lips.

Desdemona was ripping at the small man's throat. Then her jaws locked around what seemed to be the whole neck and she tore it apart.

I picked up the gun.

Not that there was going to be any use for it, not any longer.

Chapter 19

Karen had come up well. Me, I was the mess. Renardo was a mess too. He'd needed a doctor for where he'd been bashed over the skull with the butt of the gun. Luckily not a full-on blow; but stitches, and a headache. We'd discovered them both, Rebecca and Renardo, locked in a linen cupboard — him semi-conscious by then, slumped as close to horizontal as the space had allowed.

Rebecca had been too occupied nursing him to let her imagination go out of control. She'd managed to rip up sheets in the dark, making bandages to stem the flow of blood from his head wound.

The least concerned of the lot of us was Desdemona. She was behaving as though the day had been like any other, as if the one to come would bring with it a repetition of what had past. That's the thing about dogs, they don't let the world get on top of them. Instead they deal with what's served up to them as seems appropriate at the time.

The police weren't so sure about Desdemona: a Great Dane that had killed a man. There was a strong feeling that she should be put down. Real human justice that! And as far as I was concerned there was no way that it was going to be carried out.

Even before they'd arrived I'd put her on a chain at the back of the house, round by the garages. That showed that I was taking the problem of a killer dog seriously, didn't it?

'A male dog,' the police inspector pointed out, 'it could be castrated. A female . . . there is nothing for it but to be put down.'

If Dawn could have heard that! 'You do the same with police officers, when they kill?'

No answer. But a look saying he'd do the same with me, given half a chance.

It wasn't in my interests at that time to be cheeky to the police. If they were concerned about the dog, then they were even more

215

so about me. There had been contact already with their opposite numbers in Holland, pretty soon after I'd bolted out of Amsterdam. So it was with a certain smugness that the French law confronted me at the villa.

Then they were using my phone, putting calls through, all over, international. I could imagine the conversations . . . them fishing about in each other's minds for some way to explain my involvement in the deaths, those at the canal house and this one, *chez* Holt, on Cap Ferrat. That's what police are trained to fossick out — coincidence.

I'm never so sure about coincidence, about things seeming to be connected. Take Robert Carbentus's death, for instance. And then take the subsequent chain of events. You'd think that there would have had to have been some link there, but no, there wasn't. Robert's death had been to do with the French elections, he was killed because he was standing on a street, representing everyman: the international innocent victim.

Under questioning I placed a lot of emphasis on that one, on the bomb. I kept on asking if they were going to charge me for those deaths as well. I'll do that, get hot under the collar and then try anything, go to any lengths not to cooperate, particularly when confronting a uniform.

Charge? The police protested, nobody was going to charge me with anything. Well, not yet, at least. But it would be appreciated if I would change my attitude, help them with their investigations.

Which meant filling them in on Haryanto. So I did what I could, which wasn't all that much; there would be others up in Holland better informed on the subject.

I gave them a spiel on coincidence, trying to explain that the whole lot of what had happened was due to chance: if I hadn't met Robert Carbentus in the Australian outback a million years ago. Me, I was the coincidence, the link.

Somebody once observed that you can hide more by talking than by staying quiet. I guess that was what I was doing then. The thing that I wasn't going to tell them was about the third card, the one that came home under my arm, the van Gogh. That had been the trigger for everything, hadn't it? Even the fatal reason for Robert standing in a Paris street at that particular time.

216

I'd firmed up on my trophy. It was my reward. It was wages. If van Gogh was the reason that Robert had wanted to see me in the first place — to get advice on revealing it, on executing a sale — then I reckoned that there was justice in it finishing up in my possession. That's the higher justice, I suppose you might call it, the more subjective one that others often fail to understand when we try to explain.

Well, that's been my experience, at any rate.

Without the van Gogh, what the police had trouble with was why there'd been the attack in Amsterdam.

I had that question fired at me in French.

I'd already fielded it in English with my smart Dutch mate in the upstairs office, where us rich foreign suspects get the kid-glove treatment. I'd fielded it with half-truths. Sure, there was a story of a van Gogh. I had to say that, didn't I? After all, there were Henk and Albert who would have told their tales, no doubt with face-saving embellishments. And probably with the attacks on Pieter Loos's art career thrown in for good measure.

So, sure, there was the van Gogh story.

'Do you mind if we look through your house, Mr Holt? All we need to do is to verify that there is no such painting here. After all, you have quite a collection yourself, it is your interest, is it not? And you have a history of involvement in such things, some of it bizarre enough, if you do not object to this assessment.'

'Some bizarre enough,' I concurred.

We were heading up the stairs when Chevet arrived. Thank God for Chevet. He was my lawyer, recommended by Renardo several years ago. But lawyer was not the word, he was more a magic man. Chevet with his mane of white hair, the ferocious cast of his features, was a considerable figure in the region, having recently locked horns with a young investigating magistrate in a case that turned into a television news sensation.

I invited him: 'Join the tour of the house.'

'I will orchestrate it,' he growled, for me alone to hear.

And after that moment, despite the fact that I was in the centre of the labyrinth of justice, I knew that we would get to the outside. Claude Chevet would be my guide. And it would only cost an arm and a leg. Well, I was lucky to have them still attached.

217

And I was lucky to have the van Gogh concealed in the inlaid chest of drawers because, argue as Chevet could, even squabble over points of legal procedure, things would have been more complex had there been a portrait of Vincent gazing at us from any of my walls, and not appearing on the insurance list.

Renardo and Rebecca — it wasn't till half-way through the following day that I was let off the police leash and introduced to the details of their meeting with Haryanto.

The story was that Renardo had been out in the Bentley, down to Villefrance. It seems that he'd left it in the parking area beside the Gare Maritime, where people coming ashore off the pleasure ships were checked before being let loose on French soil. Then he'd wandered about the town, met up with some friends, taken a walk along the wharf, just for the feel of it.

Before heading for home he'd climbed the steps beside the church, making for the butcher on the Place Poullan. This was to pick up Rebecca's order and the kilos of meat that Desdemona consumed over a couple of days.

The butcher was a relative of the Pinci family, so there had been some conversation out in the Place on the marble seats beside the fountain. When Renardo took leave of his cousin and had finally descended to the car with a laden plastic bag in each hand, the thing farthest from his mind had been to be jumped the instant he got the motor going. Since he'd loaded the meat on to the front passenger seat both front doors were unlocked. It wasn't till he'd depressed the clutch and was on the point of moving the shift into reverse that the door was wrenched open and Haryanto leapt in, thrusting a pistol smack into Renardo's stomach.

'I drove home at gunpoint. A Browning 9mm with ambidextrous safety catch.' Renardo knew about these things. They were one of his specialities. 'The man spoke no French, but I could follow sufficient of his English to understand that he knew where we should go.

'He had been watching, you see, watching the house. He was familiar with the car. He knew the Maserati as well, I think.'

Of course, Haryanto had seen the Maserati in Amsterdam. It wouldn't have taken long in the streets of the Côte d'Azur to pick up both of them — everyone always circling, passing, repassing. That is the problem with outlandish cars — apart from being boring — they give you away. Just like low number plates. People pay fortunes to be given away, so the world knows where they're parked and when.

If that isn't stupid!

'I had no chance.' Renardo, sorry for himself. Embarrassed not to have carried off some fantastic commando feat. 'He forced me to come in through the gate. That was how he got in. And then, unfortunately, the dog wasn't here. Nobody was here, only my Rebecca.'

I think, with him, the psychological damage was worse than the physical. His complexion had turned a nasty yellow-white, his hand was trembling. That, I had never seen before.

And he was ashamed, no amount of reassurance could get him over that. It would, I thought, take months. As it was, it was weeks, but difficult ones, heart-wrenching, to see a proud man go under like that.

Molena was in his own form of shock. The phone call that night had caught him as he was on the point of heading off in our direction, the eight o'clock appointment. I'd said nothing other than that there'd be some trouble.

He'd spent more than twenty-four hours deciding that I'd reneged on the deal. I could hear the relief when I called up in the morning of the second day and suggested that we meet at Le Poisson Rouge on the wharf at Villefranche. Rebecca had enough on her hands with Renardo; she'd have done lunch but it would have been a cruelty to ask.

'Not a comment,' I commanded when he raised his eyebrows at the dressing on my ear where I'd been slashed by the gun sight.

'How the hell?'

'You know Karen?'

Molena, standing, looking his most elegant. Even the touch of grey at the sides, you'd have thought the bugger dusted it in for effect. He took her hand, pecked it, eyes smiling.

'Do I wash it?'

'Please, Mrs Holt, never.'

Suddenly all concern: 'Essington, what have you done?' That face twisted as though he would share the agony if he could. As though he must empathize — it was impossible not to do so.

'I was thumped.'

'And that is why . . . when you rang not to come . . .' The chink in his armour — he let on for an instant that he'd spent the hours watching his apartments go down the tube.

'Sit down, Molena, please.'

'What would you like to drink?'

'It's my lunch.'

'Mrs Holt?' he asked, the two of us vying for the role of host. 'You see, Essington, it's my country.' He called a waiter.

'Please spare me the performance. Mr Molena, before we go further, could you tell me if it's on, is it real?'

'Mrs Holt, everything that I have arranged with your husband is watertight.' He tapped his pocket with an open hand. 'I've brought the papers along with me.'

'One thing bothers me . . .' Karen suddenly looking very serious.

Molena was doing a theatre of going to water. He was already distraught, even before she'd put the problem. How could I but like him? Such an obvious character. At times even the clown. That was nice.

Karen ploughed on: 'You say you can arrange for this child to be adopted by us in some . . . let's say quasi-legal fashion.'

'Not quasi,' he objected. 'Totally illegal. We have to accept that. Totally illegal. These documents I have here, but which must have more details added, they are all false, totally false. They purport that it is yourself, Mrs Holt, who has given birth to the child.'

'If it's black . . .?'

'It will not be black.'

'Returning to my problem, Mr Molena.'

'Claude, please.' Would tears flow from those distressed eyes?

'What worries me, Claude, is the heroin. That's a problem. I've read that children of addicts tend to be born with the addiction.'

'Is that true?' He looked to me, to my ignorance, for guidance.

'I believe it is true, Claude.' Karen held out her hands, fingers spread . . . a very French gesture. Her father's blood showing through.

Molena considering: 'These mothers, I am told, are very young. They are still children themselves. I think the addiction is not so developed with them. These are girls of thirteen, fourteen, fifteen. It is a terrible situation . . . today, Naples! It is run by criminals, like Sicily . . . these are Mafia controlled. Drugs is the power source. They drive the economy of these places. Prostitution, that has always been part of Naples. Only today it is worse.'

Molena, hunting about for something more to say.

'I see,' said Karen.

Silence.

We ordered fish of the day all around. Who was interested in fancy dishes designed for the people bused in, or those off the pleasure boats? You ate there, not for the food, but for the water across the pavement, for the small, brightly painted boats with the nets bundled up on their bows.

I wasn't drinking, I asked for water. Karen and Molena decided to share a bottle of Pouilly Fuissé.

You could see the worry, his eyes travelling, charting thoughts, ideas. Trying to find a way around the obstacles. To keep things going he asked for more details of why I had a pad bandaged to my ear.

'I don't want any comments . . . no van Gogh jokes either. I've had those already from Karen.'

'The gallant Essington here, he as good as invited an un-invited guest to blow my brains out,' Karen said. But you could see from her expression that she was thinking of this child, of its chances; and of her own in gaining its confidence, its love.

'It's what happened,' I confirmed. Karen had been sure about that — me trying to talk Haryanto around while the gun was pressed against her skull. She'd said that it would have been a different story if it had been my head in the way.

Molena didn't want a domestic squabble blowing up on top of everything else: 'Then we forget this other business. This is terrible. You should have said. You must be . . .'

'Don't worry,' Karen reassured him, 'we are. We're wrecks, shocked. Renardo — you know Renardo, I believe? — he was clubbed. He's laid up.'

'Renardo . . . my friend! This attacker, he's got away.'

Karen's head was shaking from side to side as though at the wonder of it all. 'He didn't,' she said.

'Then, the police . . .'

'He's dead.'

221

That might have been Molena's first genuine reaction, when he repeated: 'Dead!' Maybe up till then he'd thought we were exaggerating.

People at the adjoining table looked across at us.

'Dead,' I said.

'You killed him? Essington, you've done this?'

'The dog,' Karen finished up, offering the hint of a tired smile, as though that was such a weird thing to have to say.

'My God.'

'You know, Molena,' I said, ' "God", that's 'dog' backwards in English.' We weren't talking English. And I always found that a fraction tiring, never fully believing in the French sounds I was making.

Karen got back on to the heroin. She'd thought about it, I could tell. Must have been going over the problem since I first mentioned the deal. She said that it was hard to consider a problem like that. Having a baby, that was risky too. There were genetic problems, things could go wrong mechanically. How should you look at something like this addiction problem? It was more like a soliloquy that she was delivering: thinking out aloud. Molena and I picked away at the fish, dodging the bones, piling them up on the side of our plates.

Molena refilled the glasses. I touched up my water with a drop of wine for the taste. The old Essington head wasn't feeling a hundred per cent. I was nursing it, and would be for a couple more days at least.

Karen asked: 'Can you tell me how you are so certain about getting the child?'

'I cannot. That is the problem. I must not. Someone says something . . . then it passes on like that. What is the point in saying that a thing is a secret if you go and tell it to the world? I can only say this. Maybe it is a help if I tell you that I have a relative working in Naples. She is assisting in some way. We are not talking about a racket. What I can arrange is illegal but it is not . . . it is not criminal. How should I say? The morality is sound.'

Karen shook her head, as though to get it clear. She stared out to sea.

'Do you have a cigarette, Claude?'

'I don't smoke . . . but . . .' He was on his feet, straight to the nearest waiter, explaining the need for cigarettes, gesturing in our direction.

Karen reached across, grasped my hand tight. She said, smiling: 'Getting out of bed's a risk, isn't it?'